THE TEST

The bedroom was bathed in the same warm light as the living room, the floor area dominated by a large brass bed. Rachel had lost count of the number of times she had lain spreadeagled on that bed, gagged, bound or otherwise, while Michael pleasured her in ways she had never imagined possible.

But what she saw now made her gasp with surprise.

Another woman was lying face down on the bed. She was naked, her arms and legs stretched far apart, her hands and feet fastened to the four tall corners of the brass frame. As Rachel peered closer, she realised that the woman had not been secured at the lowest point. Her arms and legs were fastened midway down, so that she hung over the bed, suspended several inches above the red satin sheets.

THE TEST

Nadine Somers

This book is a work of fiction.
In real life, make sure you practise safe sex.

First published in 1999 by
Nexus
Thames Wharf Studios
Rainville Road
London W6 9HT

Copyright © Nadine Somers 1999

The right of Nadine Somers to be identified as the Author
of this Work has been asserted by her in accordance with
the Copyright, Designs and Patents Act 1988.

Typeset by TW Typesetting, Plymouth, Devon

Printed and bound by
Cox & Wyman Ltd, Reading, Berks

ISBN 0 352 33320 0

*All characters in this publication are fictitious and any
resemblance to real persons, living or dead, is purely
coincidental.*

This book is sold subject to the condition that it shall not,
by way of trade or otherwise, be lent, resold, hired out or
otherwise circulated without the publisher's prior written
consent in any form of binding or cover other than that in
which it is published and without a similar condition
including this condition being imposed on the subsequent
purchaser.

One

The lift rose smoothly and swiftly to the penthouse suite. Rachel let her coat fall open, admiring her reflection in the gilt mirror that filled one side of the large, spacious compartment. Long auburn hair tumbled about her shoulders, a few loose strands curling across her face. Pushing them away with her fingers, she leant forward, gazing into wide, hazel-green eyes, checking that she hadn't overdone her mascara. She had made a special effort today. She hoped Michael would be pleased. She moistened the corners of her mouth with the tip of her tongue, her lips more full than usual, and burnished lavishly with red. Stepping back, she looked herself up and down. Her black halter neck plunged provocatively low and her large, pear-shaped breasts strained against the thin fabric of her dress. The skirt was slit over one hip, the hem cut indecently short, and ending hardly lower than where her panties would have curved into the plumpness of her pussy, were she wearing any. She turned to one side, parting her long, stockinged legs, her skirt opening briefly to reveal a tantalising glimpse of tanned thigh and lacy suspenders. Black stilettos elevated her ankles, emphasising the smooth curve of her calves. The thought of what Michael might do to her – no, what he *would* do to her – made her stomach shiver with anticipation. Their affair had lasted only a year, and today it would end. But it had been a year she would never forget and this, she happily concluded, was how she wanted him to remember her.

It was strange, but for the first time in their relationship she felt nervous and ill at ease. Perhaps that was because it was almost over. Michael had resigned his Cabinet post and was moving to Brussels to take up his new position as Commissioner for Trade. He had asked her if she wanted to go, too, but she had declined. He was married, of course. In her experience all the best men were. He had never spoken about his wife – other than to claim that he and she lived separate lives – and Rachel had never asked. She had known from the beginning that there was no future to their relationship, and certainly no point in uprooting to another country merely to continue a liaison which they both knew had reached its natural end. But it had been good, and today would be the best of all. It would be something to remember each other by during those cold, wet, Belgian nights. It would be something special.

The lift eased to a halt, its twin gold-leafed doors parting effortlessly like soft steel curtains. The door to Michael's apartment lay directly opposite. The corridor between the lift and his suite was like a sea of thick red Persian pile. Turning her key in the lock, Rachel glanced back as the door opened. Twelve months on and she had still not lost the habit of looking over her shoulder to check that she was alone; that she had not been followed by one of those tabloid reporters who were so keen to expose ministers like Michael who strayed from the straight and narrow. It was silly, of course, because there was only one apartment on this floor, and that was Michael's. There were no nooks, crannies or other hiding places and yet, try as she might, she still worried.

Inside, the flat was warm and inviting, its curtains closed against the late afternoon sun, a scattering of low table lamps dimmed to honey gold. A bottle of champagne lay cooling on a table by the sofa, alongside a tray bearing two glasses and a small bowl of exotic, brightly coloured fruits. Rachel let her coat slip from her shoulders, catching it carelessly in her hand a moment before it hit the carpet.

The bedroom door opened and Michael emerged. His thick brown hair tumbled across his forehead and his shirt was unbuttoned to the waist. Rachel heard the sharp intake of breath as his eyes feasted on her outfit. He smiled as she swayed towards him, trailing her coat with one hand, the other reaching up to meet the firmness of his exposed chest.

'Rachel, you look fantastic,' he murmured, in the brief moment before their arms closed around each other and their mouths locked in a fury of animal longing. Rachel let the coat fall, her arms sweeping wide about Michael's shoulders, her hands pressed to the back of his neck. One of Michael's hands now held her fast around one shoulder, while the other clawed at her buttocks. His fingers scooped at the hem of her dress, uncovering her bottom, before plunging into the warmth of her crack. She squirmed with pleasure as she felt Michael's penis straining inside his trousers, pressing against her exposed pubic ridge. His strength had always both surprised and aroused her. When he held her in his arms she felt curiously safe and vulnerable at the same time. If he chose to, he could crush her in those large, powerful hands, and at the back of her mind was the knowledge that it was that very thought that excited her more than anything else.

Suddenly he broke away. Rachel could feel her heart thumping at her ribcage and her breath was reduced to short, sharp swallows of air. She wanted him now, at this very moment, on the floor, across the sofa, anywhere, she didn't care. But Michael had something more in mind. Michael always had something more in mind. She felt so damp she wondered if she'd wet herself. His eyes burned with excitement; the river between her legs became a flood and her knees wobbled girlishly. It was crazy, but he always made her feel this way, so wanton, so abandoned that it was hard for her to think straight. She wanted to tear his clothes from his body and ravish him where he stood. His hands were at his waist, fingers pulling at a growing loop of leather, drawing it through the bright gold buckle of his belt. He unzipped himself and let his trousers fall to the floor. Rachel dropped to her knees, her fingers tugging at his pants, drawing them down over his straight, muscular hips. His penis surged into view, long and hard. His thick shaft was smooth and unmarked, and the large, plum-shaped head was warm and wet with a thin film of pre-come. She fell on him like a starving woman, her mouth circling his glans, her lips anchored to his flesh. She felt him bend slightly at the waist, his fingers ploughing through her thick red hair. He pushed his hips forward so that his rough, hairy thighs framed the softness of her face.

Rachel sucked greedily at the hardness filling her mouth, hollowing her cheeks, and drawing Michael deep into the back of her throat. Supporting his shaft with the top of her tongue, she held him tight between her lips, enjoying the silent throb of his penis. She wanted to swallow him whole, to empty him, to feel him kick within her mouth and splash against the back of her throat. And at that moment she would pull back, swiftly and smoothly, and he would reach down, his powerful hands hooked around her upper arms, lifting her to his chest. Her legs would circle his waist, her labia covering his still-pumping shaft, and she would engulf him. They would come together, as they always did, and she would kick and scream and sink her teeth into his neck, and he would hold her tight against him and hammer the last of his seed deep into her. And that would be only the beginning.

But not today. Today was different. Today, his hands

were soft against the back of her head, caressing and stroking. His hips swayed gently left and right, his penis probing, enjoying the suction of her lips as he bided his time in the delicious haven of her mouth. Rachel felt the gentle pressure of his fingers, moving her face backwards, and allowed his penis to slither wetly from between her lips. She raised her head upwards, meeting the longing in his eyes. But when he bent to take her in his arms, it was to pull her upright, holding her fast as his lips closed over hers for a second time, his hardness tight against her belly.

Suddenly releasing his hold, he took her by the hand, kicking his pants to one side and half-turning towards the bedroom door. She was confused and disappointed. This was not the way they usually began.

'I have something I want to show you,' he said. 'Something I hope you'll like.'

Something I hope you'll like. The edge to Michael's voice was palpable. Rachel experienced a sudden rush of adrenaline; fear laced with excitement. Opening the door to the bedroom, Michael paused.

'More depends on this than you can begin to imagine.'

Rachel's curiosity went into overdrive. Her heart was beating twenty to the dozen. Michael had often surprised her during their year-long affair. Now there was something in his manner that was shouting at her that this was to be the biggest surprise yet.

The bedroom was bathed in the same warm light as the living room, the floor area dominated by a large brass bed. Rachel had lost count of the number of times she had lain spreadeagled on that bed, gagged, bound or otherwise, while Michael pleasured her in ways she had never imagined possible.

But what she saw now made her gasp with surprise.

Another woman was lying face down on the bed. She was naked, her arms and legs stretched far apart, her hands and feet fastened to the four tall corners of the brass frame. As Rachel peered closer, she realised that the woman had not been secured at the lowest point. Her arms and legs were fastened midway down, so that she hung over the bed, suspended several inches above the red, satin sheets. She lay so perfectly still that Rachel wondered if she was even aware of their presence.

She circled the site of the woman's captivity, examining her with a detachment she might have reserved for a caged animal in a zoo. A skintight PVC hood covered the woman's face, a crimson letter 'M' seared across the forehead. There were holes for her nose and mouth, but not for her eyes. Rachel became increasingly aware of the woman's powerful physique. Her body was perfectly feminine: her waist narrow, her hips smoothly flared. Her breasts were large and heavy and her long, pointed nipples almost touched the satin sheets. Yet the muscles in her arms and legs were highly developed and, from the way she maintained her quiet stillness, she clearly possessed considerable strength.

'So what do you think?' Michael's voice cut sharply into Rachel's thoughts. Her heart was beating faster than ever and she was suddenly aware of how dry her mouth had become. *Something I hope you'll like,* that's what Michael had said. Rachel realised, looking at the woman, that she should not like it at all, that it was wrong to like it. But she realised, too, that she did like it, and that something in the spectacle of this chained, silent fellow female was arousing her in a way she couldn't explain. A warm feeling grew in her stomach, leaking downwards and outwards until she could feel her juices dribbling sweetly across her thighs. Michael was suddenly standing behind her, his penis hard between her buttocks. His hands circled her waist, while his fingers pulled at the thin gossamer of her dress, sinking into the softness of her damp sex. She felt giddy with excitement, twisting the back of her head against his chest, responding to his touch and to the woman's prone, suspended body in the only way she could. What was happening to her?

Rachel reached down with both hands, her arms crossed, and gathered the hem of her dress within her clenched fingers. Michael pressed one hand into the small of her back, bending her forward slightly, his fingers riding high, pushing the material across her shoulders. Rachel tugged the dress over her head and flung it carelessly to the floor. She unclipped her bra at the front and let it slip away from her breasts. Michael's other hand slid upwards, across the sensitive curve of her tummy, cupping her left breast, twisting the nipple between his thumb and forefinger. Rachel squirmed against him, hollowing the small of her back, angling her bottom into his hard, muscular abdomen. The hand at her shoulder swooped low, covering her mons a second time. Michael pushed two fingers into her vagina, the edge of his thumb pressing hard against the nub of her clitoris. His penis dipped, sliding the length of her crack. His hips swivelled as he nudged his penis towards her opening. Rachel tossed her head from side to side, shivering with delight. She choked back her relief as he found the target, cleaving into her, driving deep into her sex.

'Bastard!' she yelled. 'Dirty, filthy bastard!' She wriggled furiously, grinding her backside over Michael's groin, her eyes clamped shut, the vision of the suspended woman emblazoned in the darkness like a whitened silhouette on a huge black screen. Her cunt was on fire, unquenched by the wetness leaking across her thighs. Her orgasm struck suddenly and with a vengeance, like a thunderstorm breaking between her legs. Her knees sagged and she would have fallen to the floor had Michael not pulled her hard against him, thrusting in what seemed perfect rhythm to the contractions in her womb.

And then it was over. Michael's fingers pulled away. He withdrew his penis, with clinical swiftness. Rachel's head lolled forward and she whimpered like a child. It was always the same. She had never known a man so capable of delaying his own release. She had known him give her a dozen orgasms before emptying himself inside her. This was only the beginning, she reminded herself, only the beginning.

Michael bent down, one arm around her shoulders, the other curling beneath her thighs, lifting her up in one smooth, unhurried movement. Rachel buried her face in his chest, snuggling like a child as the last eddies of excitement swirled from her vulva. There was a double thud as her shoes hit the floor. She looked down and saw that Michael had carried her to the far side of the bed. Carefully, he lowered her to the mattress. She gazed into his eyes, her face a picture of confusion. He smiled back reassuringly.

'Trust me,' he urged, taking hold of her left arm and stretching it above her head. She tilted her face backwards in time to see Michael clamp a small, golden handcuff around her wrist. Glancing first right, then down, then back again, she realised for the first time that a second set of restraints hung from the upright stanchions of the bed. Michael took hold of her left leg and eased it gently towards one corner, snapping a foot cuff around her ankle. The thin golden chains holding her to the bed were slack enough – but only just – to allow for further, limited movement. While Rachel was taking this in, Michael crossed to the far side of the bed and reached over, one arm around her shoulder, the other around her waist. Suddenly the post-orgasmic fog lifted and her muscles tensed. Michael stopped at once. Rachel had belatedly realised that she was being secured to the bed – directly beneath the naked Amazon.

'We can stop now, it won't matter,' said Michael quietly. The concern in his voice was genuine. Rachel knew that if she asked him to release her he would. But she was aware, too, that if she turned away now, the something else he had promised would be lost to her for ever. That this was not it, she was certain. This was a prelude, but a prelude to what?

She smiled back. 'I want it,' she answered, stretching her right arm towards the far corner of the bed. Michael smiled, tugging gently, easing her beneath the other woman. As Rachel passed under her, their breasts met, nipples briefly rubbing one against the other, their rounded flesh melding. Their thighs pressed against each other and the woman's belly shimmered against Rachel's with a lightness that tickled.

Astonishingly, the woman had still not roused herself in any way. Only the occasional flexing of her muscles as she actively worked to maintain her motionless state revealed that she was not just some lifelike human doll, suspended over the bed.

Warm air fanned Rachel's cheeks and she noted the steady, rhythmic pulse of breath. She caught a brief glimpse of the woman's lips. They were full and red, like her own, gently parted, but otherwise as motionless as the rest of her. Michael snapped the final cuff around Rachel's right ankle and secured her in place beneath the silent, faceless Amazon. She pressed lightly against Rachel's body, like a sensual mirror image; the warmth of her skin transmitting itself to the woman below. Rachel found the smell of her warm, delicately perfumed flesh surprisingly heady and invasive.

Rachel and Michael had shared some unusual experiences over the past twelve months, but nothing had prepared her for this. She realised, to her surprise, that she was becoming aroused once more. She had noticed the woman's mons for the first time as she slid beneath her. It was soft and shaven. Now it nudged against the thickness of Rachel's own red pubic hair, their clitorises so close that all she had to do was raise her hips a fraction and they would touch. She had never been this intimately close to another woman. She had always imagined that it would appal her, and now found herself wondering why it did not.

Rachel looked to her immediate right, her cheek brushing the Amazon's hood as she turned. Michael had removed his shirt and was now absolutely naked. His penis was fully erect, bobbing against his tummy as he moved to the foot of the bed. He was holding something dark and familiar in his right hand. With a rush of excitement, Rachel saw that it was a black leather tawse. A flood of memories crowded in on her. Michael had never used force without her permission. Was he about to break their golden rule?

Above her, for the first time, the woman stirred. As Rachel turned back, the hooded head dipped suddenly low and a pair of rich red lips covered hers. Caught completely unawares, Rachel's first reaction was to twist her face away, to evade the dramatic, unasked-for intrusion. But as she moved to her right, the woman moved with her. Rachel's lips parted instinctively, her half-formed protest allowing the woman's tongue to enter her mouth, lapping against the inside of her cheek, driving towards the back of her throat. To her complete surprise, this time Rachel did not shy away. Instead she responded in kind, her own tongue twisting around the invader, pushing past her lips, driving into *her* mouth.

Something moved between her legs – or rather, between their legs – and she felt the mattress shift beneath her bottom. Michael was kneeling at the foot of the bed, his knees brushing the inside of Rachel's upper thighs. Her pussy seemed to be moving of its own accord, pushing upwards – or was it the unknown woman's pushing down? She twisted her hips, as best she could in her tightly confined state, rubbing her hairy labia against the Amazon's baby-soft mons. Something hard pushed between their bodies, driving them apart.

Rachel realised with delight that it was Michael's penis, wriggling through their plump conjoined tunnel of flesh. A loud thwack rent the air. Rachel heard the familiar sound of stinging skin as Michael applied the tawse with cruel and immediate effect. The Amazon let out a short, muted cry, her tongue hardened and a blast of warm air beat against the back of Rachel's throat. The whip clearly pleased the woman, and her plumpness bore down on Michael's shaft, squirming, crushing its underside to Rachel's weeping vulva. Her head was spinning; a cluster of nerves tightened between her legs and a familiar warm tickle of sensation was stirring in the hardened flesh of her clitoris. Rachel's tongue pushed deep into the Amazon's mouth and her hips swivelled from side to side. A second thwack stung the air, and then a third. The woman jiggled madly overhead, her breasts rubbing left and right, her nipples like hard warm pebbles, denting Rachel's softer flesh. Michael's erection jerked against her pussy, driving her towards the point of no return. She wanted to come, she had to come, she must come!

Suddenly it was over. Michael's penis was plucked away and the Amazon's body seemed to float upwards. Rachel drove her buttocks high, desperate for the one brief touch that would take her over the edge. Her mouth broke free and her eyes glared past the tangle of their flesh. Michael's hands were wrapped around the Amazon's hips, hoisting her lower half into the air, denying both women the contact that would complete their pleasure. His penis nudged between the other woman's thighs, his hips flexed, his thighs angled towards her body. Frustration clawed at Rachel's belly.

'Michael, you bastard!' she yelled. 'Don't do this to me! Please!'

He ignored her pleadings, pushing forward, his penis pressing between the Amazon's open legs, nudging at the entrance to her sex. Rachel twisted her head furiously, whimpering like an angry, frustrated child. Between her legs, Michael grunted sharply, his hips thrusting forwards, the mattress shuddering beneath Rachel's bottom. Above her, the Amazon swayed and shook and sobbed with undisguised delight, her head thrust back, her blacked-out eyes turned sightlessly towards the ceiling. Rachel wriggled and swore. It wasn't fair! After a moment or two, the woman lowered her head. This time, Rachel needed no encouragement. She raised her mouth the fraction necessary and anchored her lips to those of her Amazonian bedmate. Their tongues flashed past each other, twisting and turning in the warm dampness of their mouths. Rachel wanted to taste the woman's excitement, to feel Michael within her and savour the other's pleasure if that was all she were allowed.

The Amazon was at the edge of orgasm: her muscles tight, the heat of her breath filling Rachel's stretched, devouring mouth. Then, somewhere in the darkness, beyond Rachel's tightly closed eyes, came another thwack, and then another still. The Amazon's body shook with pain and the last drops of frustrated pleasure soaked across Rachel's tongue as she groaned miserably into the latter's mouth. Michael's penis was at the entrance to Rachel's sex now and she could feel his slippery shaft sliding into her. She could hardly believe it, after all the frustration and all the longing. She wanted to weep with happiness. She rubbed herself against him and ground her hard pubic bone into the underside of his groin, twisting her hips happily left and right. Above her, the woman's mouth softened against her own, grown suddenly and unexpectedly tender. It was a new and surprisingly pleasurable sensation. Their tongues lapped gently around each other, like thoughtful, dancing lovers, no longer insistent and hard, but teasing and inquiring. A warm glow spread from the centre of Rachel's belly, flooding her groin, sending what felt like a tidal wave of juices weeping from her swollen, flesh-filled sex.

Michael moved slowly inside her. The gentle probing of his penis matching itself to the rhythm of the Amazon's tongue. It was as if the two were moving in perfect, practised unison, an intense twin pleasuring that was unlike anything Rachel had ever known. When the woman thrust deep, so did Michael. When she withdrew, slowly and teasingly, he seemed to mirror her, move for move. Rachel wanted to clench herself around Michael's manhood, to hold his penis tight within her, denying him his careless escape, using his hardness to drag herself over the brink. But she was so wet that Michael was able to enter and withdraw as he pleased, using her slipperiness against her, to excite and frustrate, to tease and deny. It was unbearably cruel, and in spite of herself she knew that it was a torture she both wanted to end and prolong.

Slowly, and with deliberate care, Michael lowered the Amazon on to Rachel's body, the woman's flesh once more pressing against her hips and thighs. Another thwack rent the air and the Amazon gurgled weakly into Rachel's mouth. Rachel suddenly wanted to reach out and hold her close, to soften the pain, to let her unknown partner know that she was not alone. And yet, confusingly, part of her wanted the woman to suffer more; for the blows to increase in number and intensity. That the Amazon was a willing victim was all too clear. She had raised no protest, transmitting complete acceptance of her fate with every sensual wave of her body. Her fleshy breasts were squashed tight to Rachel's own and her hips were swaying from side to side. Their thighs rolled back and forth, one against the other, as Michael bore down with all his weight, wriggling his penis deep inside Rachel. The women's vulvas were locked tight, their clitorises touching, their bodies joined together in the same delicious rush towards ecstasy.

Suddenly, with cruel deliberation, Michael pulled himself free. Rachel moaned into the Amazon's mouth, a muffled yelp hitting the back of her throat as Michael thrust himself into the latter's vagina. Her pleasure lasted an instant before Michael withdrew. Rachel squirmed with selfish delight as his penis found its renewed target between her legs. Then she too bellowed in angry despair as Michael's hips pulled back, his cock bobbing for a moment in the tightness of her sticky crack, before re-entering the Amazon, cleaving deep. His fingers dug into her buttocks, scraping her tender, tawse-blemished skin. Muffled distress broke over Rachel's tongue; pain laced with pleasure as Michael drove himself in and out, plundering the other woman's pussy. Then, pulling free once more, he returned to ravish Rachel, her body writhing greedily beneath that of the Amazon. And so it continued. First one woman, then the other, harder and harder, faster and faster. Rachel's head was spinning. Her breathing grew more rapid and her head was giddy with frustration. Above her, Michael drove himself on with manic abandon. His breath escaped in short, sharp blasts, his legs beating against the Amazon's buttocks and the soft underside of Rachel's splayed thighs. Rachel was on a carousel, a gigantic surreal wheel of madness and delight. Suddenly, above her, the Amazon's body tightened and stilled. Rachel's breath caught in the back of her throat as the Amazon's tongue snaked impossibly deep inside her mouth. A ball of nerves unrolled across her tummy, down towards her groin. The Amazon grunted into Rachel's mouth, gave one last helpless shudder and came, her smooth vagina pressed to Rachel's hairy mons, their juices mixing freely as Rachel climaxed too. Michael withdrew for the last time, thrusting himself between them, burying his hardness in the hot, slippery tunnel of flesh formed by their joined vulvas. Their mutual release broke over his manhood as he emptied himself across their linked and trembling bellies.

Rachel was still recovering as Michael unlocked the cuffs that held her arms and legs apart, pulling her gently free, across the bed. She felt his hand in the small of her back, raising her into a sitting position, her head lolling forward, burying itself in the warmth of Michael's chest. She pressed her mouth to his skin, smearing her lips with his salty taste, filling her lungs with the smell of his maleness. His fingers stroked the nape of her neck and eased through the dampness of her hair. He was cuddling her like a baby. She was exhausted and happy to rest, for a moment or two, in the sanctuary of Michael's arms. Laying her down, he turned his attention to the Amazon and released her from her more serious restraints permitting her, too, to rest at last.

Through half-closed eyes, Rachel watched as the hooded woman pulled herself upright, swung her legs over the edge of the bed and stood up. She stretched her arms towards the ceiling and swayed her long, athletic body from side to side. She turned her head and pressed her fingers to her face, as if rubbing her eyes. When she turned back, she was no longer sightless, and she leant forward, placing two small black patches on the bedside table.

Michael raised Rachel a second time. She opened her eyes wide and shook her head, awareness gradually returning. He dabbed at her tummy with a soft handkerchief and quickly wiped her dry, before placing a red silk dressing gown around her shoulders. It felt smooth and warm against her skin. He pressed a small card into her left hand, curling her fingers into a fist and squeezing gently.

'You have to go now,' he said.

His words brought her up short, blowing away the last vestiges of fatigue.

'What do you mean?' she asked stupidly.

'You have to go,' he repeated, bending down and

pressing her crumpled dress into her hand. To her right, the Amazon had turned towards them and appeared to be waiting impatiently for Michael and Rachel to conclude their business.

'I don't understand,' murmured Rachel, struggling to find her voice.

Michael smiled. 'Trust me,' he said.

Rachel was confused. She wondered if she had fallen asleep. Perhaps she was dreaming? None of this was real. None of it could be real, surely? She turned the card over in her hands. It looked like a small business card, embossed with gold lettering. The words were blurred as her eyes suddenly grew wet with tears.

'Trust me,' repeated Michael, guiding her towards the door. 'It's all in the card. The next step.'

'But it can't end like this,' protested Rachel.

'If you take the next step then this isn't the end. It's just the beginning.'

They were at the door and Michael's arm was behind her. He was turning the handle.

'Read the card, follow the instructions. Then you'll understand everything.'

He leant towards her, his lips soft against the side of her face. She raised herself on tiptoe, pressing herself close, not wanting to let him go. Behind them, the Amazon stirred impatiently. Rachel saw that she was holding something in her hand. It was the tawse.

'Enough!' she cried.

Her interruption caught Rachel by surprise. It was the first indication the Amazon had given that she was not a mute. Michael turned to face her. Rachel expected him to voice some objection, but instead he crossed quickly to the bed.

'Go!' said the Amazon – a woman, it seemed, of startling vigour, but few words.

Michael moved silently and smoothly, like an automaton. He lay on his back and spread his arms and legs. The Amazon took hold of his left wrist and snapped it into the lower cuff, then did likewise with both his ankles before moving to the far side of the mattress.

Rachel watched in silent confusion as the Amazon snapped the last restraint around Michael's right wrist, then lifted her left leg towards the bed. Before Rachel had time to second-guess her next move, she had swung one powerful thigh over Michael's head and was kneeling astride his chest, facing his feet.

'Michael is mine now,' declared the Amazon. 'If you wish to know more, do as he asked and follow the instructions on the card. Then, who knows? You may meet again. If there's anything left of him by the time I've finished.'

Behind her mask, Rachel felt the woman's face break into a cruel smile.

'Now go. I won't ask you again.'

An icy finger stroked the length of Rachel's spine. There was a cold and dangerous edge to the woman's voice. Authority laced with threat. Rachel suddenly realised that Michael had not spoken since the Amazon had first broken her own silence, just as she had not spoken earlier, when he had ruled supreme. Roles had been reversed, clearly and unequivocally. When the Amazon had said, 'Michael is mine now', she had meant precisely that. Whatever game they were playing, its rules were unquestionably clear.

Rachel backed towards the door. She was moving in a daze. This was not how it was supposed to end. This was not how she had imagined it would end. But, then, what had she imagined? Michael had been unlike any other lover she had ever known. Perhaps she should not be so surprised that it was ending like this. The card felt cold and heavy in her hand. She twisted it blindly between her fingers.

The next step.

Michael's words reverberated through her brain as her fingers closed around the door handle. The brass felt warm and clammy, turning slowly, slipping against her palm.

The Amazon threw her right arm forward, towards Michael's midriff. The tawse flashed black across the tanned brown of his stomach, a blur of leather licking at his groin. His penis jerked upright, his narrow hips twisting in response to the pain whipping through his reddened glans. A muffled groan broke from somewhere behind the woman's large hips. The angle of her body had altered. Rachel stiffened, and a muted cry caught in the back of her throat. The Amazon had shifted backward and was now sitting on Michael's head, her bottom pressed over his face.

'It is the price he must pay for his pleasure,' said the Amazon calmly, flicking the tawse forward a second time, lashing the upper side of Michael's penis. His legs bent sharply at the knees and his muscles were tight as his buttocks bounced twice in quick succession. The Amazon wriggled her powerful hips from side to side, stifling Michael's tortured response.

Rachel bent down to retrieve her shoes. She moved three steps back, turned and slammed the door behind her. For several moments she stood there, motionless, her back pressed into the warm oak, clutching her shoes and dress between sticky, trembling fingers. Her heart pounded like a blacksmith's hammer, her breasts rising and falling as if driven by powerful, unseen pistons. On the other side of the door, she heard the same, familiar sounds, over and over again: the swish of the tawse; the crack of leather breaking over a man's skin; Michael whimpering. His cries were muffled by the sheer weight of the Amazon's broad, unshiftable backside. Whatever his punishment was to be and however long it was to last, Michael had accepted it willingly. This was what she found so difficult to understand. The Amazon, too, had been prepared to suffer at Michael's hands, in return for her moment of triumph. What hold did each have over the other, for them to willingly submit, in turn, like this?

Another blistering crack rent the air, followed by a louder moan yet. Rachel covered her ears for a moment, unable to take any more. Then, with shaking hands, she tugged her dress over her shoulders, slipped her feet into her shoes and bent down to retrieve her discarded coat. Dropping the small gold-embossed card into her pocket, she took one last look around the apartment. A hundred memories crowded in on her. How could it end like this?

And then she turned and ran . . .

An hour later, Rachel found herself standing on the steps of a large, detached house in the centre of Belgravia. She turned the card over and over in her hand, no longer needing to read the now familiar gold-embossed inscription: *Six o'clock. 38 Lightwater Square, Belgravia. FDLV.* Taking a deep breath, Rachel reached forward and pressed a small white concave bell marked, LADY FRANCES DE LA VIE.

Two

The door was opened by a tall, large-busted woman, in her late twenties. She wore a smart blue business suit, with the jacket buttoned over a starched white blouse, stretched tight over an ample bosom. Her skirt was cut short, ending just above the knees, and her legs were encased in black stockings or tights, set off by shiny, black stiletto heels. Her long blonde hair was tied back in a severe bun, drawing attention to her arched eyebrows, piercing blue eyes and high cheekbones. It was an arresting image: an unspoken assertion of power and authority behind a sheen of female allure.

The woman stood to one side, silent and expressionless. But her silence answered Rachel's single, unspoken question: she was expected. She stepped over the threshold, her eyes lowered, feeling oddly ill at ease, as if she were back at school, walking into the Headmistress's office. The door closed behind her with a muted click: there was no going back.

'This way,' indicated the woman, crossing the wide expanse of well-lit hallway. She paused outside a large, oak-beamed door. Turning the handle sharply down, she stood to one side and ushered Rachel forward. Rachel wanted to ask a question. She felt the need for words. All this silence was very disconcerting. But there was something in the woman's manner – a striking if veiled authority – that held her back.

Rachel had taken barely three steps into the room

when she heard the door shut loudly behind her. Before she could react, a key turned in the lock. She flung herself forward, twisting and turning the handle. The door was locked. She hammered her fist on the thick, dark wood, but it was useless, she was trapped. She turned back, her eyes scouring her new surroundings, her brain racing. Don't panic, she urged herself, don't panic. Not yet at any rate. She was here because of Michael, and she was certain he would never knowingly place her in any danger.

She was in what appeared to be a large, well-furnished drawing room. Her attention was immediately engaged by the dazzling variety of paintings that covered the walls. The owner was evidently a person of wealth and discernment. To the middle right, a broad mahogany escritoire dominated a wide expanse of bare, parquet floor, while to her immediate left, a large chaise-longue and two leather armchairs hugged a tall marble fireplace. A large mirror hung over the ornate hearth. There was one large double window in the room, directly opposite, draped with rich, red velvet curtains. An idea struck her and she hurried towards them. The room looked down on to a private, tree-lined courtyard. She considered hammering on the window, but there seemed little point. A moment's inspection revealed the glass to be triple-glazed, and besides, she reflected, who was she going to call to for help?

Rachel crossed over to the desk. It was sparsely covered: a telephone, desk diary, two or three pens and a large, pink, leather-edged blotter. Behind it stood a high-backed leather chair. Rachel started. She suddenly noticed that there were curtains behind the desk, a wide expanse of rich purple drapery. No one covered a wall in curtains, she told herself, rapidly circling the side of the desk.

Reaching out, she raised the edge of one heavy swathe of velvet, exposing a small, darkened alcove, and beyond that further still, another door. She stepped into the recess, her fingers closing around a warm brass knob. The handle turned and the door opened.

Several banks of low wall-lights dimly illuminated the room beyond. It took some moments for Rachel's eyes to adjust. But when they did, what she saw made her catch her breath. It was, she reflected, a day for surprises. In the centre of the otherwise empty room stood a dais, and on either side of the raised platform, barely discernible in the shadows, hung two unmistakably human figures.

Recovering herself, Rachel took two or three steps forward, unable to believe the evidence of her own eyes. The bodies were those of two young, well-developed men. Their arms were stretched high above their heads, their wrists cuffed into leather hoops fitted to the end of long chains set into the ceiling. With two striking exceptions, the men were naked. Their faces were hidden behind skintight black masks, almost identical, Rachel realised, to the one worn by the Amazon in Michael's flat. Like hers, a letter was emblazoned on to the forehead, but this time it was not the letter 'M' but the letter 'S'. And there was something else, too. Something very different, something she had never seen before. She stepped closer, allowing her eyes to adjust to the gloom. Each man's groin was encased in what appeared to be some sort of leather jockstrap. A thin black cord ran around each man's waist, its function, apparently, to support the rest of the device. To the front, a black sheath encased each man's strikingly erect penis. To the rear, a small wad of plastic protruded from each man's rectum. As in the flat, when she had first seen the naked Amazon suspended across Michael's bed, Rachel discovered that, far from horror or disgust, what she felt was overwhelming curiosity and an unexpected rush of excitement.

As she leant closer, Rachel felt certain that she could hear a gentle whirring. Without warning, one of the men jerked sideways. Rachel jumped back as a distressing moan escaped from somewhere in the darkness behind the man's hood. His legs kicked savagely against the dais, but did not rest upon it. Rachel realised that all he had to do was lift his feet a few inches, rest them on the low stand, and his agony would end at once. Why he did not – in fact, why either of them did not – seemed a complete mystery. She dismissed as ludicrous the possibility that each had no idea how close he was to relief. No one could hang suspended like this for long and not try their hardest to ease their plight.

Both bodies glistened with sweat. The men's muscles were large and well defined, tight with effort, hard and gently trembling. Rachel wondered how long they had been in this state. The man who had lost temporary control seemed to have recovered his former composure. Almost immediately, however, a strangled cry broke from the depths of the second man's throat. He threw his head sharply back and his body jiggled in mid-air as if he were choking. As he swung himself left and right, droplets of his sweat splashed across Rachel's face. She pressed her palm to her cheek, drawing her fingers down towards her mouth. She tasted his salt as it touched the tip of her tongue. Exerting enormous strength, the man drew his hands down several inches, raising his body towards the ceiling. Rachel watched him with growing desire. There was something about his utter helplessness that excited her imagination. She found herself suddenly wondering what it would be like to lower herself on to his thick, twisting member, to feel his powerful arms around her waist. She imagined her wet lips pressed against his granite-like chest, her teeth gnawing at his nipples as he drove his manhood into her vagina. It took all her self-control not to reach out for his shackled penis, and squeeze it between her fingers. It seemed for one brief moment that he was about to take his rest at last. But instead he held his new position for several seconds, moaning fitfully, before allowing his body to drop once more, a muted grunt escaping his masked lips.

'Yes,' came a female voice from somewhere behind her. 'It is a fascinating spectacle, is it not?'

Rachel spun around. The speaker was standing a few yards away. She stepped out of the shadows and Rachel realised, belatedly, that she had been there all along. She was tall, slim and elegantly dressed in a flowing black gown that reached almost to the floor. One side was slit from the waist down and, as she moved forward, Rachel caught a fleeting glimpse of a long, shapely, stockinged leg. The woman's hair hung low, like a dark wreath about her shoulders. She was very attractive, in her mid-thirties, possibly, but with a firmness that belied her age.

'Who are you? What is this place?' Rachel heard herself speaking for the first time since she had entered the house; indeed, for the first time since she had left Michael, if she ignored a few cursory words with a taxi driver.

'My name is Lady Frances De La Vie,' replied the woman. 'And all your questions will be answered,' she continued, walking past Rachel and towards the two suspended men. 'In time.'

Lady Frances circled the two bodies, smiling, evidently satisfied with what she saw. 'Excellent,' she remarked. 'They really are two of the finest slaves to have graced my dungeon.'

'Your dungeon?' repeated Rachel. The word made her feel distinctly uneasy.

Lady Frances reached forward and took hold of the nearest man's scrotum, cradling his sheathed balls in the palm of her hand. He moaned pitifully and swivelled his hips. She reached out with her other hand and took hold of the second man's balls. He threw his head back and wept like a child.

'This device is my own invention,' explained Lady

Frances. 'I call it a duplex.' She released the two men simultaneously. They jerked like perfect mirror images of one another. 'The duplex has two parts: a penile sheath which, as you would expect, covers the penis. The rear consists of an anal insert, a small plug that fits into the rectum – here.' As if to emphasise her point, she pressed a hand between each pair of male buttocks. The two men twisted and turned, moaning in transparent distress. She withdrew her hands almost at once. The men continued to wriggle and weep, like fish on an angler's hook. It was impossible to tell whether they were in pain or ecstasy. Rachel wondered whether it might not be a little of each.

'There are electronic sensors inside the duplex which stimulate the flow of blood into the penis. This takes a man close to orgasm. However, another sensor detects when he is about to come and shuts down the circuit. This way he can be kept on edge indefinitely.'

Rachel felt her blood run cold. There was something both incredibly thrilling and unbearably obscene about the whole idea. These men were clearly – and willingly – undergoing the torments of the sexually damned. But why?

'The butt-plug vibrates inside the rectum, stimulating the prostate gland, which as you know can trigger orgasm. However, it too is shut down an instant before release. A most exquisite torture, don't you think?'

'I think it's cruel,' declared Rachel, suddenly finding her voice.

'Of course it's cruel,' replied Lady Frances. 'But the rewards justify a little suffering now and then. These two certainly think so.'

'But why do they let themselves hang there?' asked Rachel. 'Why don't they rest on the dais?'

'Because that would be the end of their ordeal,' replied Lady Frances. 'And they don't wish to end it. Not yet . . .'

'I don't understand,' said Rachel.

'The dais contains the key sensor,' explained Lady Frances. 'If a man rests his weight on it, it completes a circuit. The restraining sensors in the penile and anal sections of the duplex are shut down. The victim experiences immediate orgasm, triggered simultaneously in both the penis and the rectum. The pleasure is quite indescribable. And I should know – I've tried a modified version.'

'But if it's so wonderful, why don't they give in straight away? Why do they fight it?'

'Because delightful though the reward for failure may be, the rewards for success are greater still.'

'They must be,' said Rachel. 'So what are they, then?'

'Ah,' smiled Lady Frances. 'Now that would be telling.' She stepped back. 'I think you've seen enough. We can conclude this conversation in my study.' She glanced at her watch. 'I have a pressing appointment within the hour, so time is short.'

Lady Frances turned and walked towards the alcove entrance. Rachel followed with some reluctance. As she passed through into the outer room, she gave a final backward glance at the two young men. Though she was almost embarrassed to admit it to herself, the sight of their helpless, pleasure-racked bodies had excited her to the point where her still panty-free pussy was wet and tingling.

Back in her study, Lady Frances sat in the dark leather chair, motioning to Rachel to sit opposite. 'Michael thinks very highly of you,' she began.

Michael! Rachel's heart jumped. In her excitement she had almost forgotten why she was here in the first place. A vision flashed in front of her: of Michael tied to the bed, the Amazon straddling his face, lashing him with her whip.

'Michael –' began Rachel, only to be stayed by Lady Frances.

'Michael is perfectly safe,' she replied. 'He and his

"visitor" are – how shall I put this? – old sparring partners. It is your future we have to discuss.'

'My future?' repeated Rachel.

'Why are you here?' asked Lady Frances.

'I don't know,' replied Rachel truthfully.

'You're here because you are curious. And because Michael thinks you could become one of us. With a little time and training.'

'One of us?' said Rachel.

'Do you always repeat everything that's said to you?' asked Lady Frances. Rachel fell silent. She was confused. Perhaps, she decided, the less she said the sooner she would find out what was really going on.

'What do you want out of life?'

The question was unexpected. It took Rachel by surprise. 'I don't know,' she replied honestly. 'I haven't given it much thought. To be happy I suppose. And successful.'

'Well then, do you consider yourself happy and successful?'

'Things aren't that bad. They could be better. I hope they will be.'

'Does sex make you happy?'

If the first question had been unexpected, this next was even more so.

'I don't see what my sex life has to do with you,' retorted Rachel, her hackles rising.

'On the contrary,' replied Lady Frances. 'It has everything to do with me. It has had since you began seeing Michael so regularly.'

A terrible thought struck her. 'You're not his wife?'

'Good lord, no. His wife is another story altogether. Michael chose you because he saw your potential. I trust his judgment.'

'Potential for what?' asked Rachel.

'There exists an organisation, in which I have the honour to hold a – shall we say – not inferior position.

The members of this organisation are people who have chosen to push back the frontiers of their own lives, to step over certain boundaries. To them – or should I say "us" – life is an adventure. We wish to experience it to the full, in ways most people would never dream of.'

'And Michael is a member of this organisation?'

'Yes. Though when I speak of an organisation, I am not being entirely accurate. There are three organisations, the Sisterhood, the Brotherhood and our controlling body, the Fellowship.'

'The Sisterhood?' intoned Rachel. 'You mean you're a bunch of feminists!'

Lady Frances smiled and shook her head. 'Nothing quite so dull. To give us our full title, we are the Sisterhood of Pleasure. Our boundaries are sexual. We wish to explore lust in all its incomparable variety.'

'You mean you're hookers!' This time Rachel surrendered to an urge to be completely blunt. She was tiring of her Ladyship's overbearing manner.

'Again, you are way off the mark,' replied Lady Frances. 'As you will discover when you join us.'

Rachel leant back in the chair and said, 'What makes you think I want to join you?'

'Because Michael is never wrong – and neither am I. If I hadn't believed you were Sisterhood material, I would never have invited you here.'

'You don't know anything about me.'

'Oh but I do,' countered Lady Frances. 'I've seen you in action over the past few months. And very stimulating it has been, too.'

'Seen me?' Rachel heard alarm bells ringing.

'There is a very large and ornate mirror in Michael's bedroom. I know it's a terrible cliché, but I'm afraid it's a two-way device.'

'I don't believe it!' declared Rachel. 'Michael would never do such a thing.'

'Of course he would,' retorted Lady Frances.

Rachel fell silent. Lady Frances was right. Of course he would. With Michael, anything was possible. Hadn't that been part of his appeal?

'I don't believe in wasting time,' declared Lady Frances, pushing a sheet of paper across the desk. 'If you join us, this amount will be paid into a private account once a month for the rest of your life.'

Rachel did an immediate double take. The last time she had seen so many noughts together, they had been on an Italian banknote.

'If you decide to leave the Sisterhood, or if we decide to terminate your membership for any reason, an identical sum will be paid into your account once a month for the following ten years.'

'You've got to be joking,' said Rachel.

'I never joke about money,' replied Lady Frances. 'Or sex.'

'And if I decide to leave now?'

'You will receive this amount within seven days, and never hear from any of us again.' Lady Frances pushed a second sheet across the table. The amount was for five times the figure written on the first sheet.

'Now I know you're having me on,' responded Rachel.

'I'm being perfectly serious,' said Lady Frances. 'The money is yours to keep whether you join us or not.'

'You're giving me this – whatever I do?'

'Yes.'

'I don't know what to say.'

'I think you do.'

'But I still don't know what it is you're offering me.'

'I am offering you life,' said Lady Frances. 'An opportunity to dare to be different. That's all.'

'When you put it like that it seems hard to say no.'

'It's easy to say no,' replied Lady Frances. 'Saying yes will prove the more arduous option. But by far the more fulfilling.'

'I'm not sure.'

'Yes you are. I've watched you. You're different. And "different" is what we in the Sisterhood seek.'

'I need to know more before I decide.'

'There is very little to tell. To become a Sister you must undergo a rigorous training.'

'Where?'

'At a place we call The Hall. And before you ask, its location must remain a secret. If you were to walk away, which I very much doubt, we need you to know as little as possible.'

'And this training. What does it involve?'

'It will test you to your limits, both physically and intellectually. You will learn much. And the most important will be obedience to the Sisterhood.'

'Obedience?'

'The Sisterhood is not a democracy – though you are free to leave whenever you choose. There is a hierarchy. The Madams and Masters will oversee much of your training. They in turn report to the Mistresses. They in turn to the High Mistresses, of whom there are fewer still.'

'And you? Who do you report to?' asked Rachel.

'That would be telling,' replied Lady Frances enigmatically. She glanced at her watch. 'I must ask you for your answer.'

'Now?'

'Yes. If you need to think it over, you are not the woman we seek. It's really that simple.'

Rachel's eyes scanned the sheet of paper several times without blinking. The amount of money on offer was staggering, but it was not the money that called to her. It was the mystery, the excitement. Already she felt a wetness of anticipation between her thighs. She knew what her answer would be. She had known it all along.

'All right,' she said. 'I'll do it. I'll join you.'

Lady Frances reached to one side of the desk and pressed a small button. Almost immediately, the door opened and the silent, business-suited woman came in.

She was carrying a small silver tray in her hands, on which sat a tumbler of clear liquid and a tiny silver box. She placed the tray on the table.

'Thank you, Madam Karen,' said Lady Frances. Rachel's ears pricked up at the use of the word 'Madam'.

Lady Frances took the tiny silver box and released its catch. From inside she extracted a small pill, which she dropped into the tumbler. It immediately frothed and dissolved. She picked up the glass and placed it in front of Rachel.

'You want me to drink this?'

'Obedience to the Sisterhood,' responded Lady Frances.

'What is it?'

'A mild tranquilliser. It's very fast acting. You will sleep for approximately twelve hours. Long enough for us to convey you to The Hall where you will begin your training.'

'But I can't just up and leave like that,' protested Rachel. 'I've got my job to sort out. There are bills, the bank, my flat.'

'Everything will be taken care of. The Sisterhood is now in control.'

Rachel stared at the glass tumbler. 'I'm not sure,' she murmured.

'You're worried. It's perfectly understandable. Here am I, a perfect stranger, asking you to take what I claim to be a sleeping pill. For all you know I could be a homicidal maniac. Is that it?'

Rachel felt silly, but it couldn't be helped. 'Yes,' she replied. 'Something like that.'

'Perhaps a small demonstration is needed,' suggested Lady Frances. She turned to Madam Karen and nodded curtly. Before Rachel could react, her arms were pinned against her back and her head forced flat against the hard, oak desk.

'Stop it!' was all she was able to blurt out before being suddenly hoisted upright. One of Madam Karen's hands pressed over her face, clamping her mouth shut. The fingers of her other hand held Rachel's wrists fast, her grip unbelievably strong. Rachel struggled fiercely, but could hardly move. She was frightened, but there was something else, too. She was aroused. She shouldn't have been, but she was. Her lubrication was running down the inside of her thighs: first the Amazon, then the men in the dungeon, now this. Her world was being turned upside down – and she was enjoying every minute of it.

Madam Karen's knee pressed between her legs, scissoring her thighs apart, forcing her unknickered pussy hard against the edge of the desk. The nerves in her vulva were jangling. Lady Frances reached down and opened a drawer. Rachel choked back sobs of pleasure, grunting fitfully into the palm across her mouth. She couldn't help herself. She was rubbing her pussy into the wood, grinding her clitoris against the serrated edge of the desk. Lady Frances was holding something in her hand. It was a black rubber dildo. Rachel's eyes widened like saucers. The dildo was huge, at least ten inches long and two inches thick. The crown was exquisitely shaped, like a real swollen glans, complete with a perfectly reproduced urethral slit. Lady Frances stroked her fingers along the shaft, squeezing and kneading. As Rachel watched, the impossible happened. The fake penis began to foam; thick wads of cream spurting from the eye of the glans. It was the final straw. Rachel drove her clit hard against the desk top and the dam burst between her legs. She had never felt so abandoned. Lady Frances pushed the still-foaming dildo towards her open mouth. Rachel stretched her lips wide, covering the huge black head of the artificial manhood and sucking hard. Something warm and wet hit the back of her throat, sweet and sticky with the consistency of cream. Great gobbets of liquid streamed across her tongue, out of her mouth and down her chin.

Suddenly the dildo was plucked away. Rachel

collapsed over the desk, completely spent. Madam Karen released her vice-like grip, stepped back and resumed her position at Lady Frances' side. Rachel fell back into her chair, utterly exhausted, her face hot and flushed. She felt suddenly embarrassed by her wanton display and wiped the goo from her chin, unable to think of any excuse to justify her behaviour.

Lady Frances threw the used dildo to one side. 'Another little toy of mine,' she explained. 'It's just sweetened cream, by the way, pumped through the centre of the dildo. Useful when the real thing isn't immediately to hand.'

Rachel rubbed her wrists. 'What was all that about?' she asked angrily, beginning to recover her composure.

'It was cream but it could have been poison. Yet you drank it willingly. And if Madam Karen were not a convinced pacifist, she could have broken you in two.'

Or even in four, thought Rachel, looking into Madam Karen's cruel blue eyes. Anyone less inclined to pacifism was hard to imagine at that moment.

'If I wanted to hurt you, I could do so very easily. The choice is yours. The Sisterhood is a dictatorship. But it is one we all freely enter into.'

Rachel's eyes wandered from Lady Frances to Madam Karen and then back to Lady Frances. What on earth was she getting herself into?

'The Sisterhood demands total obedience,' said Lady Frances. 'That obedience begins now. Your faith must be unquestioning. It is all we ever demand of you.'

Rachel took a deep breath. She stretched out her right hand and her fingers closed around the glass. It was her choice. To walk away now would be easy, and probably very sensible. But Lady Frances was right. She didn't want to walk away. She wanted to know more, to experience more, to begin a new adventure. A great adventure, perhaps. What the hell! She picked up the glass, pressed it to her lips and swallowed.

Three

Rachel awoke with a start. She was naked and lying in bed. The mattress was firm and comfortable with pink silky sheets. The room was clean and well lit. Having taken in her new surroundings, the very next thing she gave her attention to was the fact that she was not alone.

Beside her, another woman stirred. She was young and small-boned, with short blonde hair, cut in a youthful pageboy style. Like Rachel, she was naked, and lying on her back. The sheet had slipped to below her waist, revealing a pair of small, lemon-shaped breasts with tiny pink nipples. The woman's eyes opened and she sat upright, her face a picture of sleepy confusion.

'Who are you?' she asked abruptly, pulling the sheet up around her breasts.

'My name's Rachel. And don't you think it's a little late for false modesty?'

The other woman's face broke into a broad grin. 'I suppose you're right,' she replied, letting the sheet slip away. 'Just instinct, really. My name's Sally.' She stretched out her arm. Her hand was small and warm, but she had a surprisingly strong grip.

'I'm a dancer,' she explained. 'Modern ballet, classical, that sort of thing.'

'Really?' replied Rachel. 'Me, too. Well, that is to say, I've done some dancing. I spent three years at drama school. I did a bit of everything. Apart from finding any work when I left. I've been moonlighting as an MP's research assistant for the past twelve months.'

'So how many ministers have you fucked? Pardon my French,' asked Sally.

'Only three,' replied Rachel. 'Two of them were one-night stands. But the third . . .' She paused. Michael had been special, no – was still special. She wasn't sure she wanted to talk about him yet, at least not as a mere notch on her bedpost.

Sally jumped out of bed and walked around the room, hands on her hips, looking for all the world like a mischievous schoolgirl. She was short, a little over five feet tall, with small breasts, a tiny waist, and a bottom perfectly flared yet hardly larger than a boy's. Rachel wondered how old she was. Probably in her early twenties. Twenty-two? Twenty-three? Yet dress her in a gymslip and boater and she could have passed for a virginal sixth-former.

Rachel stood up and stretched her limbs, examining their sparsely furnished surroundings. The room had a distinctly functional air about it. There was a small wooden dressing table, a chair, the bed, and two doors, one presumably to the outside world, the other possibly opening into another room. The walls were painted pale cream, and a salmon-pink carpet warmed her bare feet. A large, rectangular mirror disturbed the monotony of one side of the room, and a small clock the other. It was 6.32. She assumed it was in the evening as fading sunshine streamed through the single small window that afforded restricted views across a wide landscaped garden, a nearby wooded area and hills beyond. Out of the corner of her eye, Rachel saw Sally's head turn, and was aware of her new friend looking her up and down. To her surprise, Rachel found that far from being embarrassed at the intrusion, she positively welcomed it. She possessed no false modesty. She knew she had a good figure. Her long legs were firm and strong, her waist was narrow, her tummy washboard flat. Her hips were wide and her bottom marginally larger than she might have wished. Still, she reflected, no one was perfect. Her breasts were big and heavy, and she considered them her finest asset. She loved to hold a man's face between them and hear him mew with almost childish pleasure the tighter she hugged him. Men, she had long since discovered, were funny like that.

Without warning, one of the two doors opened. Rachel felt the breath catch in the back of her throat as a third woman entered the room and crossed rapidly to the bed. The air of authority surrounding her was unmistakable. Both Rachel and Sally knew at once that she was a Madam. She wore a black PVC basque, laced tightly at the front, a mesh of thin cross-straps hugging her flesh from her belly to her bosom. The outfit was cupless, her breasts large and rounded, nipples long and erect, like thick pink thimbles at the centre of each wide, dimpled areola. The basque was suspendered, the woman's long, shapely legs encased in black fishnets and platform-heeled, calf-length boots. A thick, studded choker adorned her neck, two broad, similarly fashioned bracelets circling her upper arms. She wore a shiny black thong, fastened either side of her wide hips by small bows. A leather tawse hung from a sheath attached to a cord-like belt that girdled her waist. Black, elbow-length gloves completed her dark, dominating ensemble.

The woman threw something black and shiny on to the bed. 'Get dressed, and come with me,' she ordered.

If they were to dress, reflected Rachel, it was presumably not for dinner. Two pairs of short black boots lay on the bed. Apart from that, the remainder of their wardrobe appeared to consist of little more than a collection of leather straps, of various lengths and widths. The entire outfit – if you could call it that – was held together by a series of small metal links. She wasn't even sure she knew how to put it on!

'Hurry up,' shouted the woman. 'I haven't got all day.'

Rachel picked up the nearest outfit and held it in the air. It was clearly a harness of some sort, with adjustable straps. Quickly locating the bra end, she slipped into the outfit and began to tighten the various links. While she and Sally dressed, the woman circled them slowly, like a zookeeper inspecting her latest exhibits.

'My name is Madam Janet,' she explained, matter-of-factly. 'During your time at The Hall you will be under my command. Others will oversee your training, but I will oversee you. Is that clear?'

Rachel and Sally nodded together as if they were joined at the neck.

'The rules are simple. There are at present twelve Initiates undergoing training. You are grouped into pairs, each pair being under the command of an individual Madam. At all times you will obey the commands of Madams without question. Still clear?'

'Yes,' answered Rachel, tightening the last of the adjustable straps. There was a sudden blur of black, followed by a harsh crack. Rachel yelped instinctively as Madam Janet flashed the tawse against the foot of the bed, missing her by an inch.

'You will also speak to a Madam only when she has given her permission. Is that understood?'

The two girls nodded sharply – and silently. They would have to be careful, thought Rachel. Madam Janet clearly had a taste for the whip.

Rachel was aware of Madam Janet looking them up and down. She seemed pleased with what she saw. The harnesses criss-crossed the two girls' bodies, hiding little from view. Thin straps ran down from their shoulders, linking to a bra-like device that lifted and separated their busts. The triangles of leather that held each breast in place were linked at the centre, from which point two further straps ran down to a thick leather waistband, joined to the latter by an even larger chrome loop. Two further straps ran between the girls' legs. Rachel looked down and saw that the effect was to push her labia forward, drawing attention to her hairy, plumped-up vagina. She found her attention wandering to Sally's small breasts and tiny waist. Her skin was white and her hips so appealingly boyish. Her little vulva seemed almost lost between the straps and her light, fluffy pubic hair was hardly visible. Madam Janet's voice cut into her thoughts.

'When outside your room, you will wear your harnesses at all times. Is that understood?'

The two girls nodded silently. They had learnt their lesson. They weren't going to give Madam Janet any excuse to use the tawse if they could help it.

'There is one further rule. No Initiate is permitted to orgasm without the permission of her Madam.'

Rachel could hardly believe her ears. She smiled instinctively. Madam Janet's hand tightened around the handle of her tawse.

'I see that amuses you.'

Rachel lowered her eyes at once, remembering in the nick of time not to reply.

'The Madams are sensitive to your bodily needs and permission will not be denied without good reason. However, unauthorised orgasms will be severely punished. And I mean *severely*.' She paused. 'You may ask questions if you wish.'

Rachel raised her eyes. 'When you say we're allowed to orgasm, do you mean we can masturbate?'

'Provided you ask my permission in advance, yes. You are also free to enjoy each other, or alternatively one of your instructors should both parties be willing.'

'You mean we can do it with women?' asked Rachel, a little perplexed.

'A Sister's prime objective is the search for ultimate pleasure. The means, as you will discover, are infinite.'

'But will we have access to men, too?' asked Sally.

'My, my,' remarked Madam Janet. 'We *are* eager to couple, aren't we?'

Sally's face flushed a deep red. She hadn't intended to make it that obvious.

'Men will be made available from time to time. It all depends on your progress,' replied Madam Janet. She glanced up at the clock. 'We must hurry now. The introductory briefing is about to begin. You'll learn more about your time here and get to meet your Sister Initiates.'

Madam Janet moved to the rear of the two women. Though she had returned the tawse to her waistband, she was still holding something in her other hand, a curious mixture of metal and leather. The women remained motionless as Madam Janet proceeded to fasten studded collars around their necks. The collars, in turn, were linked to each other by a chain, about two feet long. There was a small hoop at the rear of each choker, into which Madam Janet now threaded individual lengths of leather. As she pulled hard on the reins, Rachel and Sally were forced to move their feet quickly, to avoid being pulled over. It took only a moment's reflection to realise that they were now not only linked together, but also under the immediate physical control of Madam Janet.

'Excellent,' said Madam Janet. 'Now, I think it's time we began.'

She moved to the front of the two women, lifting the reins over their heads. Then she led them from the room as if she were escorting prime beef to the cattle market.

They were gathered together in a small, oak-panelled room. There were twelve Initiates in all, as Madam Janet had indicated, grouped into pairs. All the women were dressed in identical leather harnesses, joined together at the neck and under the immediate control of their individual Madams. The Initiates were seated on chairs arranged in a semicircle around a raised stage area: six either side of an aisle, with their Madams standing directly behind them. There were another dozen chairs set out on the stage, so it was obvious that they were awaiting more arrivals. Like Madam Janet, each overseer wore a cupless basque and calf-length boots and carried a small whip at her waist. Glancing quickly either side of her, Rachel realised that she had never seen so much seductively attired flesh on show at any one time. A seventh Madam stood guard at the main door, legs apart, her tawse held firmly in both hands. Suddenly the door opened and a tall, raven-haired woman entered the room. She was as scantily dressed as all the other females, though her uniform, if you could call it that, reflected Rachel, was very different to those worn by the Madams. The newcomer wore a stunning black PVC G-string playsuit that barely covered the top half of her body. Fastened by a high neck collar, it plunged past wide, bare shoulders towards her ample bosom, before narrowing sharply until all but vanishing in a tiny V that barely covered her vulva. A fishnet front panel emphasised the large swell of her breasts, the dark areolae surrounding her unseen nipples partially visible as she moved. She was followed by about a dozen men and women. The women were dressed in the uniform of the Madams. The men were bare-chested, and wearing tight leather trousers and shiny calf-length boots. Rachel had never been very good at guessing ages, but she doubted there was anyone under twenty or over forty. They were indisputably good-looking and well built in their obviously different ways.

The arrivals followed the woman on to the stage. She turned to speak briefly to one of the men. As she did so,

Rachel saw that the reverse of her outfit consisted of little more than three spaghetti-thin strings, a bra strap across the middle of her back, a tiny waistband and, finally, and most eye-catching of all, a shoelace-thin cord that plunged down between her big, rounded buttocks. Her long legs were encased in thigh-length leather boots. Like the Madams, she wore a whip at her waist. Rachel couldn't help noticing that it was longer than the ones carried by the Madams and had a gold phallus-shaped hilt. As everyone else sat down, she turned to face her captive audience. Her face was firm and angular, her eyes wide and heavily lashed. She had high, pronounced cheekbones and full, blood-red lips.

'Welcome to The Hall,' she began. 'My name is Mistress Katrina. I am in charge of your training during your time with us.'

Mistress Katrina walked up and down as she spoke, gazing intently at the row of Initiates, looking each woman in the eye. Though her legs were almost completely hidden by her leather boots, the powerful nature of her body was obvious. Her thighs, in particular, were hard and meaty. Rachel could think of several men she knew who would have jumped at the chance to put their head between those thighs and dare Mistress Katrina to do her worst. It would be a foolhardy request, reflected Rachel. Mistress Katrina's thighs looked as if they could crush cannonballs.

'As you are already aware, you report first and foremost to your individual Madams. If you have any problems, you should attempt to resolve them with your Madam first. If this proves impossible, you may make an appointment to see me. I do not usually involve myself in day-to-day events. Generally, should our paths cross, it will not be good news for one of us.'

Rachel lowered her eyes instinctively when the Mistress's gaze alighted on her. Mistress Katrina smiled enigmatically and moved on.

'Your Madams will have explained most of the rules to you. What they will not have explained is the regime that is in force here. The Hall is much like a university. Sixteen weeks from now, some of you I hope, though not all, will graduate as full Sisters. In the meantime, however, though your official status is that of a Sister Initiate, you will be addressed as "Sister", if for no other reason,' she smiled, 'than the fact that "Sister Initiate" is such a mouthful.'

Rachel felt herself relax a little. However difficult the regime might prove to be, Mistress Katrina, at least, appeared to have a sense of humour.

At that moment, Mistress Katrina's gaze alighted on one of the Initiates, a small, freckled girl with wide hips and large breasts. Her short, wavy red hair was in stark contrast to the luxuriant thatch that spilled from the V of her harness. Mistress Katrina eyed the girl's hairy vulva and smiled. The girl smiled back and Mistress Katrina promptly frowned. The girl lowered her eyes in suitably chastened embarrassment.

'Your every action at The Hall will be monitored,' explained Mistress Katrina. 'You will be awarded credits for success and you will lose credits for failure. Your overall score will remain confidential. Not even you will know how well – or how badly – you are doing. If your marks drop below an acceptable level, however, you will be asked to leave The Hall.'

Mistress Katrina paused for a moment to allow the Initiates to digest this last piece of information. Rachel frowned. If they weren't told what their credit levels were, it meant they would need to be on their toes at all times. Perhaps, she reflected, that was the point of the exercise.

'To your training, then,' continued Mistress Katrina. 'You will be taught by a mixture of Madams and Masters.' She raised her left hand and gestured to the men and women sitting behind her. 'The course is varied and arduous. It will be physical as well as academic. By the time you leave us, you will, among other things, be fully conversant with the musical merits of Handel's oratorios, the weaknesses inherent in Spinoza's ontological arguments and the place of synthetic Cubism in post-Impressionist art history. You will also – to use a crude colloquialism – be capable of administering a blow job that would wake a dead man.'

A barely suppressed flood of giggles broke out along the entire row of Initiates.

'Apart from that,' concluded Mistress Katrina, 'it only remains for me to wish you all a happy, and I hope successful, time with us.'

The Madams tugged sharply on the girls' reins, indicating that they should stand up. The audience was clearly at an end. Quickly and quietly, Mistress Katrina left the stage, followed by her entourage of Madams and Masters. As soon as the main door had closed behind them, the Initiates were led towards a smaller side-exit. Once through it, they found themselves in a long passageway. At the far end, another door opened into a large, white-walled area that appeared to be some sort of classroom.

Two or three minutes passed in complete silence. Then a door to the right-hand side of the room opened and a man entered. From his bare chest and tight leather trousers, it was obvious at once that he was a Master. He crossed to a small table, and threw down a clipboard, some paper and a pen. Rachel hadn't registered any particular details of the Madams and Masters who had stood on the stage, but this man was well over six-feet tall, with blond hair cropped to the scalp. She hazarded a guess that he was probably in his mid-thirties. Though she couldn't exactly say why, she felt there was something inherently foreign about his angular features. His chest muscles were firm and well pronounced, his skin smooth and lightly tanned. Rachel wondered if she were the only woman there who found her eyes riveted to the noticeable bulge between his legs. Somehow, she very much doubted it.

'My name is Master Stéfan,' he began, introducing himself. 'I am your acting instructor.'

Rachel smiled. She had been right, then. The accent was slight, difficult to pin down, but distinctly East-European – Hungarian perhaps or Polish.

'I fulfil two roles at The Hall,' he continued, adding mysteriously, 'and for your sakes, I hope you will only come to know me in one capacity.' He allowed his gaze to wander over the assembly, before continuing. 'There are many times in our lives when we are called upon to play a part. When that time comes, no one will ever doubt your sincerity. I guarantee it. Because if I can, then you will not be admitted to the Sisterhood.'

Rachel felt herself relax. She had spent three years at drama school. Hopefully this would get her off to a good start.

'We will begin,' continued Master Stéfan, 'with the noble art of seduction. Your task is simple and, for me, a very pleasurable one. You must convince me that you wish to fellate me desperately. You will cajole, you will beg and reluctantly I will submit.'

If he could convince any of the women in the room that he would submit reluctantly to being fellated, decided Rachel, he was a better actor than any of them would ever be.

Master Stéfan's hands were at his waist. Twelve pairs of eyes were riveted to his groin as he unzipped himself, delved inside and pulled out his penis. Even in its limp state it was unusually large. Rachel wondered what it must look like when it was fully erect. Out of the corner of her eye she saw one or two of the other women stretching their mouths and licking their lips in anticipation. She could almost smell the female hormones in the air.

Master Stéfan stood with his feet apart, astonishingly relaxed, reflected Rachel, for a man displaying his penis to a roomful of sexually aroused young women. She wondered how many times he had done this before.

'Is there anyone here who is not prepared to act out this fantasy?'

He cast his eyes about the room. No one responded.

'Excellent,' he continued. 'A second question. As there are so many of you, I will of necessity be forced to restrain myself from reaching orgasm. However, should I choose otherwise, is there anyone here who is not prepared to allow me to come in her mouth?'

After a moment's pause, a solitary hand went up. It belonged to a tall, dark-skinned girl in one of the other groups.

'I quite understand,' said Master Stéfan. 'Unfortunately, this means you can take no further part in our training. Madam Susan will escort you to your room where you will dress and leave The Hall at once.'

The girl looked shocked. 'I didn't realise,' she protested. 'All right. I don't mind. You can come in my mouth if you want.'

'It is not a case of me wanting,' replied Master Stéfan. 'It is a case of you being willing. You were not. That is an end to the matter.'

The Madam who had been standing guard at the door came forward. She unclipped the girl from her partner, took the rein in her hands and pulled the reluctant Initiate away.

'No, please!' she screamed. 'I'll do anything! You can have me! You can do anything you want with me! I don't care! Anything! Please! Please!'

How any man could resist such an offer was beyond Rachel. But Master Stéfan made no reply as the struggling girl was dragged away, still pleading, by Madam Susan. On the other hand, reflected Rachel, as she cast her eyes around the room, he was really rather spoilt for choice. As the weeping girl departed, Rachel realised for the first time just how strictly the rules were going to be applied. It seemed there were to be no second chances. It was a daunting prospect.

'Now,' resumed Master Stéfan. 'Let us begin.'

At the far end of the line, the first woman, a tall, wide-hipped brunette, was unclipped. She seemed a little unsure of herself. Rachel felt sorry for her. Going first was never easy.

Master Stéfan reached down and fondled himself lightly with both hands. His penis began to uncurl and visibly thicken. 'Well?' he asked.

Whether it was the ever-so slight edge to his voice, or simply the thought of engaging with his manhood, the girl suddenly sprang into life. She threw herself to her knees and began to crawl towards him.

'Please, Master Stéfan,' she cried. 'Will you let me suck you? Please! I want to suck you.'

'No,' he replied. 'I don't want to be sucked, thank you.'

And so it began: the girl pleading, Master Stéfan refusing, until at last he allowed her the honour of being the first to take his penis into her mouth.

If the first girl's acting left room for improvement, thought Rachel, her fellatio was apparently spot-on. Indeed, if Master Stéfan's reaction was anything to go by, she would prove a hard act to follow.

'Excellent,' he murmured, running his long fingers through her hair, pulling her closer to his crotch. In his erect state, mused Rachel, he must have been very large indeed, for the girl's lips appeared to be stretched to their limit around his hidden shaft.

'Now for your second lesson,' he whispered, and Rachel couldn't help but wonder if the lowering of his voice was deliberate or a genuine reflection of his growing excitement. 'You will fellate me to the point of orgasm. Do you understand?'

Between his thighs, gagging on his erect member, the girl managed a quick nod and a grunt.

'But you must withdraw at the last instant. You must judge the moment to perfection. Neither a second too soon nor a second too late.'

Her face buried in his groin, the girl mumbled her understanding of the rules.

Master Stéfan began to jiggle his hips, driving his penis into the back of the girl's throat. Rachel felt her heart beat faster and a familiar warm glow spread across her lower tummy. If the pair of them kept this up much longer she was going to have to struggle to contain her excitement. She wondered how many other women were feeling the same way.

Suddenly, Master Stéfan's body tightened and he thrust his hips forward two or three times in quick succession. 'Yes!' he screamed. 'Yes! Yes! Yes!'

Immediately the girl withdrew, throwing her head back, awaiting the jets of male cream that would spatter her face at such close quarters.

Master Stéfan stepped back and smiled triumphantly, his fully erect penis exposed for the first time as it fell from the girl's mouth. It was even larger than Rachel had imagined, very straight, with a thick girth that would clearly take some accommodating wherever he saw fit to place it.

'Too soon,' declared Master Stéfan. 'I was only pretending. You can never trust a man when his cock is in your mouth, I'm afraid. Whatever he tells you.'

The girl got up from her knees. She looked despondent. Master Stéfan picked up his clipboard from the nearby table and made a few notes as the woman returned to her Madam. He was some actor, reflected Rachel. She would have to try and remember that when her time came.

The women now followed in quick succession. Some were good, some were very good and some were so bad they could have walked into any prime-time TV soap opera. One girl threw herself at Master Stéfan with such reckless abandon that it seemed for one moment she was going to gnaw his penis off. He scowled darkly while scribbling his assessment. Rachel could imagine what he was writing. Something like: *Enthusiastic, but must have all her teeth removed before being let loose on me again!*

Every woman withdrew before Master Stéfan climaxed. It soon became obvious that he was playing a game with them. Despite his initial suggestion that he might ejaculate in someone's mouth, he clearly had little or no intention of doing so. His control was supreme. Rachel found herself reminded of Michael, a thought which, in her present state of arousal, did her no favours at all.

Rachel was last but one to advance on her instructor. By now he had been inside the mouths of no less than nine women. None had lasted more than a couple of minutes before pulling out, certain that he was on the point of orgasm. When her turn finally came, Rachel approached her task with mixed feelings. She wanted to make him come. She wanted to be the one to take him over the edge. But, she asked herself, if she did, would that count against her? It was a moot point. But it was a challenge, too. One that she knew she would find difficult to resist.

Rachel walked right up to him, aware, as she approached, of his eyes locked to her advancing bosom. Well, she reflected, so even Master Stéfan had his Achilles heel. Stopping short, she held his gaze for several moments. Then, quickly and quietly, she pressed herself close, raising herself on tiptoe, rubbing her harnessed flesh against his bare chest. She pressed her nipples flush against his. She leant past him, her right cheek touching his, one hand grazing the length of his bare back, the other moving softly over his left hip. She remained motionless for several moments, allowing the smell of her body to wash over him, to do its work in reminding him that she was not just another pupil. She was a woman, a warm woman, a slightly wet woman, a woman with large, friendly breasts if that was, as she guessed, his particular turn-on. Being seduced was all in a day's work for Master Stéfan. He was like a chocoholic in a sweet factory, gorged and sated by all the goodies on offer. Somehow she had to be different. Somehow she had to bring him to life in a way the others hadn't been able to.

She nibbled his lobe, then extended her tongue and flicked wetly at the inside of his ear.

'I want you,' she whispered. 'I want you in a way no one has ever wanted you before.' She drew her hand away from his hip and brushed her fingertips downwards, across the top of his penis. 'I want your willy,' she murmured and immediately felt him stiffen in her hand. It was a trick she had learnt some years ago. Breast men were very often mummy's boys at heart. Reverting to childhood terms for the penis invariably made them go weak at the knees.

Rachel immediately fell to hers, deliberately brushing her breasts against his shaft on her way down. Sitting back on her haunches, she looked up at him plaintively, with tears welling in her eyes. It was one acting skill she had learnt well. The words seemed forced from the back of her throat.

'Please ...' she whispered softly, leaning forward, flicking the tip of one finger against the roll of his foreskin. 'I want to kiss your willy. Your big, beautiful willy ...'

His body tightened perceptibly and his penis, which had softened and fallen, began to fatten again and rise. She returned both hands to his hips and squeezed hard. Hollowing her tongue, Rachel wrapped her wetness around the underside of Master Stéfan's bulbous glans, pushing upwards, raising his penis inch by inch. Her hands climbed slowly across his thighs until they rested either side of his groin, her fingers spread to their fullest extent. Then, deliberately slowly, she lowered her head. Widening her lips around the top of his now fully restored member, Rachel paused with feigned reluctance for one exquisite moment before finally taking him into her mouth. She drew him deep into the back of her throat and held him there, his entire length lodged as far as it would go. Then, pulling back, she began to suck him, first drawing him in, then expelling him, then licking, then tickling with the tip of her twisting tongue. And all the while she kept her breasts pressed up against his thighs, aware of the excitement it clearly afforded him.

Master Stéfan began to sway languorously. He threw his head back and moaned. He moved his hips from side to side, his hands trawling through Rachel's long auburn tresses. She felt his body tighten and his balls roll awkwardly against her chin. His breath was coming in short, sharp bursts and she wondered if another part of him was about to follow suit. His movements were becoming more urgent, the swivelling of his hips more frantic. Had he been any other man – with the possible exception of Michael – she would have been certain that he was on the point of spending himself deliriously in the back of her throat. But he was a consummate actor. And what if she did make him come? Would it be held against her? He must know what she was up to, know that she was attempting to drag him screaming over the cliff edge. It had gone beyond a game. She was raping him with her mouth. He knew it and she knew it. This time he couldn't win, this time he couldn't hold out. This was revenge for all the women he had defied. She would show him there was one woman he could not defy. She was the Master now. She would make him come whether he liked it or not. Her only concern, as she twisted her hips from side to side, was that she might reach her own forbidden orgasm first.

A primeval grunt broke from the back of his throat. The base of his shaft pulsed and his penis jerked inside her mouth, once, twice. Almost too late, she pulled back, wrenching her lips free, falling on to her heels. Saliva ran down her chin, and her hair was damp with sweat. Master Stéfan's penis danced madly in front of her eyes, his face contorted, his entire body swaying on the brink of collapse. He bared his teeth like a wild animal, grunting with exertion. And then suddenly it was over. He drew himself up to his full height, his penis still proudly erect, dripping with Rachel's saliva. But he had not come. It was impossible, Rachel told herself. How could he have held back? How could any man have held back?

Master Stéfan looked down at her. His eyes shone with triumph. He was still the Master, in spite of all her efforts. But she knew and he knew that he had been taken perilously close. He reached for his clipboard. As she walked back to rejoin her Madam, Rachel hazarded a guess at what he was writing. It was either something brilliant – or something she was not going to like at all.

Now only Sally remained. She tiptoed forward, fell to her knees, hands joined, and pleaded like a little girl. It was a role that came naturally to her, reflected Rachel, her thoughts turning instinctively to gymslips, white socks and boaters.

Master Stéfan put up little show of resistance. It had been a long day and perhaps even he was feeling the strain, particularly after his encounter with Rachel. For the first time all afternoon, he seemed suddenly lethargic. Sally was sucking on him, like a baby at the teat. Her movements were blissfully gentle, unhurried and soft. Rachel felt the tingling between her legs grow ever more urgent. She imagined Sally's little head bobbing up and down between her own thighs, licking and kissing and caressing. It was all she could do to remain upright. She tried to banish the thought from her mind, but it wasn't easy.

Between Master Stéfan's legs, meanwhile, little seemed to be stirring. Sally continued her gentle ministrations and her instructor swayed mechanically from side to side. She looked up for a moment and caught his eye.

'Don't worry,' he said, 'I'm a long way from coming yet.'

Turning away, his eyes momentarily met Rachel's. Something came over her, an unexpected spirit of rebellion rising in union with the sap between her thighs. Defiantly, she splayed her legs, thrust her hands on to her hips and pushed her breasts forward to their fullest extent.

Suddenly, Master Stéfan's hands gripped the back of Sally's head, his long fingers twisting through her blonde locks, holding her fast. He grunted loudly between clenched teeth, pumping his hips with joyful abandon. He was coming! This time he really was coming! He emptied himself into the back of Sally's throat, his spunk overflowing from her mouth, spilling across her lips, and running down her chin. She tried to pull away but he held on to her, twisting this way and that as if dragged by his penis; a penis now thrusting haphazardly out of control, excited to final fruition by thoughts even he dare not admit to.

When he had finished, he pushed Sally away. She looked up at him, his warm seed dribbling down her face, unsure as to whether it was yet permissible for her to rise.

'Let that be a lesson to you,' remarked Master Stéfan coldly. 'Never trust a man when he says he won't come in your mouth.'

He reached down and wiped her face with his hand, gathering what remained of his ejaculate on the pads of his fingers. He pressed them to Sally's lips.

'You may lick them clean,' he instructed. She opened her mouth and drew his fingers inside, lapping gently, swallowing two or three times until his hand was spotless.

Master Stéfan glanced the length of the room and his eyes met Rachel's. Had he always intended to climax in the last girl's mouth, she wondered, or was it something else? Was it her? Had she been responsible? If she had, she wondered what effect it would have on the rest of her stay at The Hall. Had she made a friend – or an enemy?

Four

Rachel might have spent longer pondering her predicament but for the fact that she suddenly realised how hungry she was. The Initiates had been taken from the acting class along two adjoining corridors and into a large dining area. A single, long table dominated the room, with six seats either side. Food was already set out: large plates of steak, jostling alongside tureens of buttered vegetables and bowls of mixed salad. The girls were given permission to chat as they ate. Apart from brief introductions all round, however, no one seemed eager to talk. There were too many names to remember, though Rachel registered the tall, wide-hipped girl as Rowena, and the generously proportioned redhead as Maria. There was a Candie and a Kimberley, and she thought a Shirley, but by the time they had finished eating Rachel had already forgotten who was who. Like everyone else, she was beginning to tire after the excitement of the last few hours.

After the meal, the girls were escorted back to their rooms. The first thing Rachel and Sally noticed as they entered was that a brightly coloured chart had been pinned to the wall.

'This is your timetable for the first week,' explained Madam Janet. She unclipped the rein that attached her to the two women, but not the chain that held them together at the neck.

'Unless it is deemed necessary, you will remain linked

together at all times,' she explained. 'There is only one bathroom, so I hope neither of you suffers from false modesty.'

Without waiting for a response, she crossed to the door. 'Although it's not been a long day, I imagine you're both ready for a good night's sleep. It may be the first time either of you has slept with another woman. What you get up to is your own business, but remember, no orgasms or you're in trouble.'

Rachel wondered if Madam Janet got some sort of thrill from speaking like this. Well, if she did, reflected Rachel, that was her problem.

Madam Janet paused at the door. 'An alarm will sound each morning at exactly 6.20 a.m. You will have ten minutes to freshen up and then your day begins.'

After she had gone, Rachel and Sally studied the chart on the wall. There was a wide variety of classes, both physical and academic. Philosophy, art, music, French and history jostled alongside politics, etiquette and business management. On the physical side there was circuit training, weightlifting, running and, a little incongruously thought Rachel, ballroom dancing. It was a wide repertoire. There were some sessions simply labelled sex classes. Rachel and Sally quickly found that the second door led into a small bathroom, with toilet and shower. They tried to see if the chain was long enough for one of them to be in the bathroom and the other outside, but it wasn't and they quickly abandoned any attempt at privacy.

It was an odd experience climbing into bed together. Politely, and with a little embarrassment, they wished each other a good night. Sally turned over and, to Rachel's surprise, seemed to fall asleep almost at once. The bed wasn't large enough to keep her distance and Rachel soon found herself snuggling up to her new friend. She felt Sally's little bottom press into her tummy and enjoyed the feel of her soft warm flesh.

Instinctively, she slipped one arm around her bedmate's shoulder. Sally wriggled gently in her sleep. It had been a long day, thought Rachel, full of new, and surprising, experiences. That was her last thought before drifting into a heavy, untroubled sleep.

The Initiates were huddled together on the grass quadrangle at the front of The Hall. It was a little after 6.30 in the morning. Rachel and Sally had been woken, given their regulation ten minutes to wash, then Madam Janet had arrived and had led them outside. Dressed only in their harnesses, the cold air chilled their flesh after the warmth of The Hall.

Mistress Katrina walked up and down the line, inspecting each girl in turn, like a company sergeant-major. She seemed wide awake and alert, in stark contrast to most of the Initiates.

'I imagine the fact that there is life before nine in the morning has come as a shock to some of you,' she observed. 'The bad news is that you will follow this routine for the next four weeks.' She paused. 'Permission to groan inwardly,' she added as Madam Janet stepped forward.

'It's time to test your fitness levels,' explained Madam Janet. 'These are probably not very high, so we'll have to change that.' She raised her right hand and gestured into the distance. 'You will run around the inner quadrant three times. The circuit is a little over one and a quarter miles, which makes about four miles in all.'

Four miles! Rachel's heart sank. She hadn't run that far since she was sixteen and in the school netball team. Even then she had hidden behind a tree, pulled down her shorts, fantasised about her best friend's father and masturbated herself silly for an hour while the other girls jogged round the school grounds. She didn't fancy her chances of getting away with that sort of ruse on this occasion.

'Those who cannot run may walk,' continued Madam Janet, 'but this will be noted and credits will be deducted. Anyone who attempts to cheat in any way will be severely dealt with.'

Madam Janet's eyes swept up and down the line of shivering women. 'You must all be getting cold,' she said, 'so the sooner you start the sooner you'll finish. There will be extra credits for the first team home. Minus credits for the last team.'

The girls were beginning to hop up and down, running on the spot to keep themselves warm.

'With your permission, Mistress,' said Madam Janet, bowing her head deferentially in the direction of her superior.

Mistress Katrina nodded, and Madam Janet turned back towards the gathered Initiates. 'You may begin,' she said.

For a moment or two, it seemed that no one wanted to make the first move. The girls exchanged a variety of uncertain looks before the tall brunette suddenly grabbed her partner's arm and began to stride out across the grass quadrangle.

'Faster than that!' yelled Madam Janet, as they all followed suit, 'or you won't be back till tomorrow!'

It was awkward running in pairs because each girl had to adjust to her partner's pace. One group had become a threesome since the dismissal of the girl from Master Stéfan's acting class, and they seemed to be finding it harder than the others to coordinate their actions. Though Sally was small, her fitness as a dancer was obvious. Rachel, who had imagined herself fit, soon realised that she was anything but. For the first circuit, there was little to choose between any of the groups. As fatigue set in, however, gaps gradually started to appear. By the time they began the third circuit, the Initiates were well spread out. The brunette and her partner, who had begun first, were well ahead. Two tall blondes were in second place, Rachel and Sally were in third, though some way behind the first two pairs, and the unfortunate threesome and another pair were lagging so far behind they were out of sight.

Running down a now-familiar steep grass verge for the third time, Rachel suddenly drew up short, grabbed Sally by the arm and flung herself to the ground, pulling her startled friend on top of her. Sally caught her elbow awkwardly on a fallen branch and squealed.

'What is it?' she asked abruptly, sitting up and rubbing her bruised arm. 'Have you hurt yourself?'

Rachel ignored her. 'Keep down!' she whispered urgently, pushing Sally's head below the level of the verge.

Pressing a finger to her lips, Rachel scrambled sideways, skirting the edge of a clump of beech trees. Sally, still totally bemused, wriggled behind on her bottom. Again, Rachel put one finger to her lips, raising her other hand and pointing uphill.

'Look over there,' she whispered, 'just beyond the bushes. Can you see?'

Sally followed the line of Rachel's outstretched arm. At first she saw nothing. Then something sparkled in the undergrowth. It was the unmistakable glint of sunshine on glass.

'Those are binoculars!' she squealed. 'Someone's spying on us!'

'Exactly,' confirmed Rachel, 'and I'd like to know who.'

'It could be one of the Madams,' cautioned Sally. 'We probably shouldn't interfere. Besides, we're far enough behind as it is.'

'I know,' agreed Rachel. 'But to be honest I'm exhausted. I need a rest. Anyway, aren't you the teeniest bit curious?'

'I suppose I am,' answered Sally truthfully.

'Right then,' declared Rachel. 'Come on, let's find out

who's spying on a group of naked women running around the grounds of – well, wherever it is we're running around the grounds of.'

Quietly, the two girls edged their way towards the clump of bushes from where the reflection had come. Sally was about to say something when Rachel put a hand over her mouth to silence her.

'Look!' she whispered.

Half hidden in the bushes was a young man, kneeling upright, and holding a pair of binoculars to his eyes with one hand. His other hand was between his legs, stroking his fully erect penis. What really took their breath away, however, was how he was dressed, or, to be more accurate, how he was not dressed. He was almost naked, apart from a leather harness virtually identical to the ones that Rachel and Sally were wearing.

'Who is he?' asked Sally quietly, now that Rachel had removed her hand.

'I've no idea,' replied Rachel, 'but we're going to find out. Come on.'

They were on him before he knew they were there, covering the last few yards at a run, flinging themselves at his back and wrestling him to the ground. Sally held on to his legs, while Rachel rolled him over and sat firmly on his chest. The binoculars went flying. Rachel expected the young man to struggle, to attempt to shift her in some way, but instead, to her surprise, he surrendered without a fight and lay quite still.

'All right,' said Rachel. 'What's your game? Who are you?'

The young man's face tightened into a frown. 'You weren't supposed to find me,' he said. 'I'll lose credits now.'

Rachel's ears pricked up. 'What do you mean you'll lose credits?'

'I'm an Initiate, like you – a Brother Initiate,' he admitted. 'My name is Adam.'

Rachel fell silent for an instant, trying to make sense of this unexpected revelation.

'I didn't know there were Brothers at The Hall,' she responded. The idea suddenly crossed her mind that this was some sort of a trick.

'There aren't,' he replied, shifting awkwardly beneath her.

'Then I don't understand,' said Rachel. 'I mean, what are you doing here?'

'I'm from Brotherhood Manor. It's – well, I can't tell you where it is, but it's where we do our training. This is a sort of day out if you like, only it's part of our training, as well.'

'In what way?' asked Rachel.

'Well,' he explained, 'we were supposed to see how close we could get to you without anyone spotting us.'

'You didn't do very well, did you?'

His face turned crimson. 'No,' he admitted quietly, 'I suppose I didn't.'

'We?' repeated Sally.

'Sorry?' he said, twisting his head sideways. He was unable to see Sally because she was out of sight behind Rachel.

'You said, "we",' continued Sally. She let go of the young man's feet and wriggled into view. He wasn't struggling. Rachel decided that there was probably no need for her to continue sitting on his chest either. But she was enjoying herself. Brother Adam was very handsome, and though his penis was out of sight behind her, she knew he was still erect because of the lovely tickling sensation in the small of her back each time the top of his glans brushed against her.

'There are five of us,' he confided. 'We're supposed to spy on you and report back on everything we've seen.'

Rachel felt suddenly sorry for him. 'Well who's to know you have been caught?' she said. 'We don't have to tell, do we?'

'I'm afraid you do,' he replied. 'When you get back you'll be asked if anything happened. If you lie and they find out, you'll be in serious trouble. Besides, it's not playing by the rules, is it?'

'No, I suppose it isn't,' admitted Rachel.

'There is one other thing,' said Brother Adam.

'What's that?' asked Rachel.

'Well, it's a bit embarrassing actually.'

'Let's hear it,' said Rachel, adjusting her position slightly. She realised that she was growing more excited, her pussy in danger of lubricating over the young man's chest. At this rate, he might not be the only one to feel embarrassed.

'If I get caught,' he continued, 'I lose twenty-five credits. But if I can get you to have voluntary sex with me I get fifteen credits restored.'

Rachel smiled. 'Well, I think we can help you there, can't we Sally?'

'Definitely,' she confirmed, her face breaking into a broad grin. She cast a lustful glance at Brother Adam's erection. Far from subsiding, it seemed to have grown larger while Rachel had been sitting on him.

'Sally and I are not allowed unauthorised orgasms,' admitted Rachel.

'I know,' responded Brother Adam. 'If you have a climax I'll have to report it.'

'You really do play by the rules, don't you?' said Rachel.

'I'm sorry,' he said, glancing up at her. 'You've got beautiful breasts by the way.'

'Would you like me to smother you with them,' she asked, 'while Sally fucks you every which way?'

Rachel felt the top of Brother Adam's penis dig into the small of her back. What was it with men? The dirtier you talked, the more excited they all became.

'That would be lovely,' he said.

'Well, bad luck,' replied Rachel. 'It's strictly

pussy-fucking on this occasion.' She slid forward, towards the young man's face. She felt the chain linking her to Sally tighten around her neck for a moment.

'I'd let you lick me,' said Rachel, smiling down at him, 'but I don't think I could stop myself coming.'

Brother Adam's face broke into a broad grin. 'That's a shame,' he replied.

Rachel felt Sally settle down behind her. The chain loosened and she watched the young man's eyes narrow as Sally manoeuvred herself on to his penis.

'Ooh!' trilled Sally, 'I didn't realise how much I'd missed this.'

Rachel had a sudden thought. 'I suppose you're not allowed to come either?' she asked.

'Well, actually I am,' he admitted. 'We've been given permission.'

'That's just typical,' retorted Rachel. 'How are you doing, Sally?' she asked as her friend began to ride the young man in earnest.

'It's lovely,' replied Sally. 'But I wish we could climax.'

'I know,' agreed Rachel. 'It's not fair. Still, we can have the second-best thing.' She looked down at the young man. 'How well can you control yourself?' she asked, recalling Michael's prodigious ability to hold back his orgasm.

'I can delay for quite a bit,' he answered.

'So there's no danger of you coming until we're both ready?'

'No, that's all right,' he replied.

'OK,' she said, rising from his chest. 'Let's see how quickly you can fuck the pair of us. Are you ready?'

The young man took a deep breath and nodded. Despite his promise to control himself, it was obvious that he was in the last stages of pre-orgasm, which, thought Rachel, was hardly surprising. After all, if you were a red-blooded male and two naked women jumped on you in search of some serious fucking, your reaction was pretty well preordained.

Rachel knelt behind Sally. Her young friend was bouncing up and down, throwing her head from side to side, her breath escaping in short sharp bursts. It was obvious that she was sailing very close to the wind. A few more energetic thrusts and she would be unable to hold back.

'All right,' shouted Rachel, addressing the young man. 'Let yourself go!'

Brother Adam squirmed between Sally's thighs, his hips wriggling. He reached out with both hands and seized hold of Sally's hips. She threw her head back and bit her lower lip. Brother Adam thrust his pelvis upwards, driving himself deep against Sally's womb. He let out a shuddering groan and shook his head from side to side, screaming, 'Yes, yes, yes!' as the first of his semen jetted into Sally.

Rachel knew that she had to time her own move to perfection. She reached forward and took hold of the base of Brother Adam's penis, allowing him four thrusts, before shouting at Sally to dismount. The young blonde threw herself to one side, face buried in the grass, moaning and grinding her thighs into the damp earth. Without her vulva to restrain it, Brother Adam's penis jerked left and right, stabbing through the empty air. A tear of semen spilt from the eye of his urethra, before Rachel straddled his trembling shaft in mid-thrust, pulling it inside her. She felt Brother Adam's seed flood her channel as her vulva engulfed him. Tightening the muscles of her vagina, she rode him furiously, determined to milk every last drop of semen from his body. Brother Adam twisted his head sideways, burying his face in the grass, moaning his delight into the damp soil. He bucked his hips twice more, arched his back, then seemed to utterly collapse, weeping with exhausted delight. Rachel quickly dismounted, sitting back on her haunches. She had almost come. She knew she had been so very close. Her breasts rose and fell and swung gently from side to side as she tried to get her breath back. Brother Adam reached out and pressed the palm of one hand over her left nipple. She took hold of his wrist and pushed his hand away. She was too excited to take any more. Sally was sitting to her left, her breathing almost back to normal. Brother Adam lay quite still for a moment or two longer, apparently more exhausted than the two women. Then, as if suddenly recovering himself, he leapt to his feet and retrieved the fallen binoculars.

'That was fantastic,' he declared.

'We must do it again sometime,' smiled Rachel, 'only next time we get to come, too!'

'I have to go,' explained Brother Adam. 'The Masters will be looking for me.'

The two girls watched as the young man turned and scrambled uphill. Just before they lost sight of him altogether he turned and waved. Before they had a chance to respond he had vanished.

'We're going to be in trouble now,' said Rachel. 'Everyone else must have finished. I don't know how we're going to explain this.'

Sally grinned, rubbing herself gently between the legs. 'I don't care,' she replied. 'It was worth it.'

'I wonder if we'll feel the same when we've lost all our credits and been thrown out of The Hall on our very first day,' reflected Rachel sombrely.

Covering the last mile in fits and starts, Rachel and Sally sprinted the final one hundred yards in the desperate hope that it might impress Madam Janet and deflect attention from the fact that they had finished last, some half an hour behind everyone else. They finished in a tangle, exhausted, and collapsed on the lawns near to where they had begun. Madam Janet towered over them, a stopwatch in her hand.

'Fifty-six minutes,' she said. 'Not bad for beginners. Oh, yes, and congratulations. You're the first to finish.'

Neither Rachel nor Sally could believe their ears. How could they have finished first after what had happened?

Madam Janet consulted a clipboard. 'Which Brother Initiate did you surprise?' she asked.

Madam Janet's question came like a bolt out of the blue. She knew what had happened!

'Initiate Adam,' confessed Rachel, still confused by this unexpected turn of events.

'And did you both have him?' asked Madam Janet.

'Yes, Madam,' replied Rachel.

'In which order?'

'I took him first, Madam,' admitted Sally, 'and Rachel finished him off.'

Madam Janet ticked a couple of boxes on her clipboard and smiled. 'You may sit on the ground and rest now,' she told them, waving the two women to one side. They huddled together, their breathing still noticeably laboured. Rachel watched Sally's breasts bob up and down and felt a warm tingle spread between her legs. She looked up and realised with some embarrassment that Madam Janet had been watching her while she had been watching Sally.

It was some time before the next pair, the two blonde girls, Helga and Candie, arrived. They were followed closely by the long-legged brunette, Rowena, and her partner, Kimberley, the two girls who had performed so well in the early stages, just ahead of the freckled redhead, Maria and her partner, Shirley. It came as no surprise to Rachel and Sally to learn that all four teams had encountered a Brother Initiate. The last group, Evie, Tina and Ruth staggered home a few minutes later. Rachel wondered which lucky Brother had had the pleasure of coping with three women in quick succession. He deserved to have all his credits restored.

The formalities completed, Mistress Katrina addressed them again.

'Today was meant as a little light relief, both for yourselves and for your Brother Initiates. However, though these runs will be a regular part of your training, I am sorry to inform you that this part of the exercise will not be repeated.'

Rachel sighed. And just when it looked as if things were beginning to look up, she thought forlornly.

After a light breakfast, the day's academic routine began. The first class, art history, involved an introduction to the Pre-Raphaelites, and was given by a Madam Jullienne. Rachel found it hard going, though Sally seemed to enjoy it, and even asked a question or two. A short break for coffee was followed by an hour of Madam Della's speciality, European party politics, which soon had Rachel pining for the Pre-Raphaelites. After lunch, there was an hour of Shakespeare, followed by forty minutes of Modern Etiquette, with Madam Anita.

The last lesson of the day was the first of the sex classes, with a Master Devlin. For Rachel, her head bursting with academic niceties, this class couldn't come soon enough. Indeed, by now there was little doubt that all the girls were ready for it. Master Devlin, bare-chested like all the Masters, was waiting for them when they entered his classroom on the ground floor. He was a man of medium height and stocky build, but with a finely muscled body and a healthy shock of red hair.

In the centre of the room stood a small round table on top of which had been placed a large rubber phallus. It was about fifteen inches tall and some three inches in diameter. Rachel looked at it with a mixture of lust and terror. She hoped none of them were going to be asked to use it on themselves. She had a capacious vagina, but even she would struggle to get that inside her, she decided.

Master Devlin gathered them around the table. He read the concern and curiosity in the girls' faces and immediately put their minds at rest.

'The phallus is here purely for academic purposes,' he assured them.

They peered at it more closely now, and with a little more relief. It was a truly magnificent specimen, an exact replica of the male penis, right down to the tiniest detail. It had a soft, rubber foreskin that could be retracted, and large, round testicles covered in a thick mesh of dark, artificial hair. Master Devlin spread the fingers of his large hand and encircled the base firmly. Even he was only just able to encompass the penis's vast girth.

'You are all familiar with the male appendage,' he began. 'It is an instrument capable of both giving and receiving pleasure. But I doubt that many of you have examined it in close detail.'

He looked around to see if anyone disagreed with him. They did not.

'Note its shape, the way the stem is hard along the underside of the shaft. Note the veins and the way the foreskin is attached here.' He pointed to the stretched band of flesh at the base of the glans. 'Also how, when erect, the balls tighten against the body and the whole shaft feels warm to the touch as it engorges.'

The girls took it in turns to reach forward and hold the rubber phallus. It did indeed feel warm to the touch. They were encouraged to stroke it gently, examining every inch of its fake surrounding.

'This penis has been constructed to reflect every detail of the male member,' said Master Devlin. 'I want you to familiarise yourself with it, to see how it bends, how it stiffens. Examine too the way the balls hang at the base, the soft texture of the flesh between the penis and the anus. All this you must familiarise yourself with.'

As Rachel fingered the base of the penis she felt herself lubricating between the legs. Though she was sure it was impossible to accommodate such a monstrosity, she began to wonder what it would actually feel like to take it inside her. She closed her eyes for a moment and spread her fingers as far as they would go. A brief image flashed across her mind's eye – of the phallus stretching her vagina to limits it had never experienced before.

'Once you are familiar with every contour of this penis, you will have a more solid base on which to build your sexual knowledge of the human male. This will enable you to please him in previously unimaginable ways, which will in turn enhance your own pleasure immeasurably.'

The redheaded girl, Maria, raised her hand to ask a question.

'Yes?' inquired Master Devlin.

'No man has got a penis like this, so I don't quite see how it's going to help us,' she said.

Master Devlin shook his head sadly. Rachel was glad she had not raised the question herself.

'As I said,' he reminded her, 'it is purely to practise on and to enhance your knowledge. Here, let me show you.'

He placed both his hands around the phallus, closed his eyes and began to gently stroke the shaft, kneading the rubbery flesh as if he were preparing dough. Rachel licked the corners of her mouth and felt her sap leak out on to her thigh. Her tummy began to tingle. She glanced across at another Initiate, Rowena, who was standing open-mouthed. A dribble of saliva fell from the other woman's lips and she pressed her legs tightly together. Rachel was pleased to see that she wasn't the only woman who was finding this whole episode unexpectedly arousing.

'It is important to be aware of the feel of the penis as

it stiffens,' explained Master Devlin. 'In this way you can judge the moment of orgasm.'

He squeezed hard and suddenly the phallus erupted, a lush milky white stream of liquid emerging from its artificial eye. Rachel remembered the black phallus at Lady Frances's house but this was altogether more dramatic. The cream ran down the shaft and coated Master Devlin's hands. He stepped back and wiped his fingers with a handkerchief.

'There is a small electronic sensor which simulates the reactions of the excited male organ,' he explained. 'When the fingers press all the right places the penis will ejaculate like a real one. But the point is not to make the penis ejaculate, it is to keep it at a subdued level, high enough to sustain arousal, low enough to restrain orgasm. In this way, a woman will maintain her mastery over the male penis and, ultimately, if she wishes, the male himself.'

One after the other, the girls were shown how to masturbate the giant phallus. The electronic sensor proved as sensitive as Master Devlin had suggested. When rubbed fiercely, the penis stiffened and 'came'; when stroked more carefully, it hardened and throbbed, though still spurting white liquid when the rubbing went on for too long. Master Devlin gave each girl two minutes in which to practise her skills, while registering the results on a small electronic recorder. As they all took roughly the same time to make the phallus eject the sticky white cream, Rachel assumed they had all scored roughly the same marks on this introductory test.

When they had all finished and tidied themselves up – the semen was a mixture of honey and cream and they were allowed to lick their hands clean – Master Devlin made them all sit down, and continued the lesson from a flipchart. The girls were shown several drawings of the male penis in different stages of arousal and from all angles. They were advised how to hold it; where the pressure points were; how to prevent an orgasm by squeezing with finger and thumb at the root of the shaft or just below the glans. They were told how the slit in the cock-head was particularly sensitive, but how it should be wetted with the tongue first for maximum effect. They were shown how it was possible to extract a pearl of pre-come by careful manipulation and how this could be used both to lubricate the penis for further play and to stimulate the male with his own smell. In short, felt Rachel, they were told everything there was to know about masturbating the male penis. What she wanted to do now, however, was to get to work on a real one. If she were to cross paths with Brother Adam again, she decided, she would enjoy putting her new-found skills to the test.

It was late in the day when the class ended. Though it had been by far the longest class, it had been the most interesting, and the time had flown by. Supper followed: poached salmon, steamed vegetables, salad, strawberries, cream, and coffee. The food, as always, was both welcome and delicious. The girls chatted more freely this time, exchanging background details and light banter about the day's events. They were all visibly relaxing. Rachel learnt that Rowena was a lawyer, and Maria a publishing director's PA. Maria had a wicked sense of humour and a loud voice. Of all the girls she seemed to be taking matters least seriously. By contrast, Rowena was clearly determined to learn as much as possible. After supper, in what was now becoming a familiar routine, the Madams escorted each group of girls back to their rooms.

As Madam Janet detached the reins, Rachel suddenly realised how stiff and tired she was. At that moment, more than anything else, she wanted to throw herself flat out on the bed and savour the luxury of doing nothing at all. However, until Madam Janet left the room she felt it was diplomatic to refrain from so obviously unwinding.

Madam Janet circled the two girls. Something trailed down between Rachel's shoulderblades and, with a start, she realised that it was the hilt of Madam Janet's tawse.

'You both did very well today,' she said. 'Not as well as I would have hoped, but not bad.' She paused. 'You may thank me.'

'Thank you, Madam Janet,' intoned the two women simultaneously.

'You may also speak freely,' she added. 'I'm sure you could do with a break from the tension.'

Rachel and Sally breathed a combined sigh of relief. All this minding your p's and q's was as tiring as galloping around the quadrangle three times.

'Thank you,' said Sally, without thinking.

There was a blur of black and she fell forward, her backside burning furiously.

'I said you might speak freely,' said Madam Janet. 'But that doesn't mean you depart from the rules of obedience, one of which is that you address your Madams formally at all times.'

Madam Janet's tawse whistled through the air a second time, lashing cruelly across Rachel's bare bottom. She fell to her knees and screamed.

'That's not fair,' she squealed. 'Madam Janet,' she added quickly. 'I didn't do anything wrong.'

'Sister Sally is your friend,' retorted Madam Janet cruelly. 'I'm sure you wouldn't want her to suffer alone, would you?'

Rachel buried her face in the satin sheets. Her bum was stinging like hell. She wanted to jump up and run cold water over it, anything. She also wanted to leap up and punch Madam Janet in the face, but that was another matter altogether.

Madam Janet crossed to the bedside cabinet. She opened a drawer and took out a large white tube. She handed it to Rachel, who was staring up at her with tears welling in her eyes.

'This will help ease the pain,' said Madam Janet. 'You can apply it to your partner's backside.'

Rachel took the tube and looked at it blankly.

'Do it at once,' commanded Madam Janet, her hand tightening around the hilt of her whip.

Rachel undid the top of the tube and squeezed some gel on to the palm of her hand. It felt cold and wet. If it did work, she thought, it would have been nice to apply it to her own bottom first. It was still hurting like mad.

'You'll want more than that,' said Madam Janet. 'Give it to me.'

Rachel handed the tube over.

'Hold out your hands,' ordered Madam Janet.

Rachel did as she was told, and Madam Janet squeezed a large amount of gel on to her outstretched palms.

'Now,' she said, directing her attention towards Sally. 'Face down on the bed with your legs apart.'

Sally did as she was told, burying her face in the warm satin. Her body was aching all over and, like Rachel, all she seemed to want was to fall asleep. There was little chance of that, however, while their backsides stung the way they did.

'Apply the gel all over the affected area,' instructed Madam Janet.

Rachel pressed her hands into Sally's warm flesh, spreading the gel into her reddened buttocks.

'Round and round,' advised Madam. 'Work it all in or it won't have any effect.'

Rachel's hands flowed smoothly over Sally's skin, and she quickly realised that she was becoming aroused. Behind Rachel, Madam Janet squeezed gel on to the palms of her own hands and knelt between Rachel's legs. Rachel shuddered as Madam's fingers pressed into her backside, but continued as if nothing had happened. Though she was shocked to feel another woman rubbing her buttocks, the fact was that, at the first touch of the soothing gel, the stinging began to abate, and that was really all she cared about at that moment.

Sally began to squirm on the bed as Rachel's hands went properly to work on her. For her part, Madam Janet's fingers were working a magic of their own, spreading first outwards, then inwards, covering Rachel's larger buttocks and kneading the soft flesh. Almost instinctively, Rachel realised that she was beginning to mirror Madam Janet's movements. As the latter's fingers spread outwards, so did Rachel's. When they moved up and down, so did Rachel's. Like Sally, face down on the bed, she began to luxuriate in the cool of the soothing gel. There was something else, too, a vaguely heady and aromatic smell that the gel gave off. She had no idea what it was, but it was definitely adding to her excitement.

Suddenly, Madam Janet's fingers slipped into Rachel's crack, down the crease between her buttocks and on to her tightly rounded anus. Rachel lurched forward, and at the same time her own hands slipped, whether deliberately or accidentally now hardly seemed to matter, between her friend's cheeks. She felt Sally's buttocks part, the warm rounded globes small and light against her hands. Madam Janet's fingers pressed against Rachel's bumhole and she whimpered shamelessly, mirroring the action as she pressed the forefinger of her right hand into the well of Sally's smaller, tightly closed opening. Sally opened her mouth and groaned into the sheets. The sound of her whimpering only heightened Rachel's pleasure. She shouldn't have been enjoying this, she told herself, she shouldn't. And yet she was. It was wonderful. Madam Janet was speaking, her words adding to Rachel's excitement.

'Rub your hands around, the way I am; put your fingers into Sally's bottom the way I'm doing it to you.'

Rachel felt debauched and excited all at the same time. Her hands began to move further down, in time to those of Madam Janet behind her. Now they were at Sally's clitoris, rubbing, probing, scissoring open the swollen flesh of her cunny. Sally lifted her small, boyish buttocks off the bed, allowing Rachel more room for manoeuvre. Behind her she could feel Rachel's body heaving with excitement.

'Oh my God,' muttered Rachel, 'I'm going ... I'm going ...'

'No!' barked Madam Janet. 'Not yet!'

Suddenly she pinched at Rachel's clitoris, holding it tight between her forefinger and thumb. Rachel's climax froze in her belly. Madam Janet reached into the black pouch at her waist from which she extracted a large, double-pronged dildo. With amazing agility she strapped it to her waistband, then pushed Rachel forward, her other hand still clasped tight against her warm pussy.

'On top,' she ordered, pressing her palm into the small of Rachel's back. Instinctively, Rachel resisted. But Madam Janet was strong and manhandled her until she was straddling Sally's back. Rachel felt Madam Janet push the dildo forward between her legs, the rounded head nudging between her thighs. She was immediately aware, from the groan of delight emanating from Sally, that her friend was being entered, too. Now the fingers at her clitoris were no longer tight, but gentle, stroking and teasing. It was almost too much. She reached down, her own fingers rubbing at Sally's pussy one last time before Madam Janet pushed her forward and she lost contact with her partner's quim. But it hardly mattered, for at that moment, Madam Janet drove in as deep as any man, pumping the dildo in and out with her powerful hips, fucking both girls simultaneously. All three women screamed together, as the base of the double-pronged dildo ground itself against the nub of Madam Janet's clitty. At this rate they were all going to climax, and nothing could restrain them. A warning bell sounded at the back of Rachel's brain. She remembered Madam Janet's injunction when they had first met: *No Initiate is allowed to orgasm without the permission of her Madam*. Did that still apply now, with their Madam orchestrating their excitement? Rachel was so close that she hardly cared. She could feel the familiar glow of delight tightening in her belly. She dug deep, holding back.

'Madam!' she cried. 'Please – may I have permission to come?'

Madam Janet laughed loudly. 'No!' she cried. 'Permission denied!'

It was the last thing Rachel had expected to hear. Now it was Sally's turn.

'Please, Madam, please may I come?'

Madam Janet's reply was cruel beyond belief. 'Yes,' she answered. 'Permission granted!'

Rachel could hardly believe her ears. She was being denied her release. But she was desperate for it. It wasn't fair, it wasn't fair!

'Please, Madam!' she screamed, the need between her legs almost completely overpowering now. 'Please let me come, oh God, please! Please!'

'No!' screamed Madam Janet, pumping more furiously than ever.

'I'm going to come!' cried Rachel. 'I can't help myself!'

'You'll be punished, you disobedient bitch!' screamed Madam Janet, giving one final thrust that took her over the edge.

Behind her, Rachel was aware that Madam Janet was climaxing happily, humping Rachel's pussy and enjoying the hardness of the dildo against her own cunt. Beneath her, too, Rachel was aware of Sally's orgasm, her small body threshing left and right, her mouth biting into the satin sheets as she emptied herself on to the bed. Sandwiched between them, Rachel tried desperately to empty her mind. She mustn't come, she knew that, and yet she desperately wanted to. It was unbearably cruel to be held between two climaxing bodies and be told that you couldn't come yourself. Madam Janet withdrew almost at once. The dildos emerged with a delicious plop. Rachel groaned and bit her lip, drawing blood, sending her mind into the clouds, away, far away from her earthly body, which still teetered on the brink of ecstasy. Madam Janet reached between Rachel's legs, gathering the two dildos, squeezing them tightly together. She pushed slowly forward, wriggling the two artificial shafts into Rachel's cunt. Rachel thought she would pass out. The combined girth was huge, and she could only just take it. Madam was gentle, probing, easing Rachel's labia apart, and filling her to the limit. Rachel could take no more. She had believed that she could hold out, just, but this was too much. She emitted a wild, animal-like roar, threw her head high and came, driving her buttocks backwards, meeting Madam Janet's gentle forward thrusts, allowing her pussy to be filled to the limit.

Suddenly Madam Janet withdrew. The twin dildos plopped from Rachel's vagina. She fell forward on to Sally's back and lay there, panting, her hands clawing into the soft, warm satin.

Madam Janet stood up and returned the dildos to the pouch at her waist. 'Are we feeling a little better now?' she asked quietly.

Rachel and Sally struggled to their feet. This time they did not forget their manners.

'Yes, Madam Janet, thank you Madam Janet,' they replied together. It was still hard to believe what had happened. Rachel found herself wondering if this were a breach of the rules. After all, Madam Janet had told them that sex with Madams and Masters was permissible if both parties agreed. They had not agreed, though neither had they demurred. But Rachel knew that she had broken one rule. It was cruel and unfair, but she had broken it nonetheless. Madam Janet was looking at her with a cruel smile playing across her lips.

'I warned you what would happen if you disobeyed me,' she said.

Rachel lowered her eyes. Madam Janet tightened the belt around her waist, and her hand closed firmly around the hilt of her tawse. The fingertips of her glove still glistened with Rachel's juices.

'You will have to be punished,' she said. 'You understand that, don't you?'

'Yes, Madam,' replied Rachel softly. Madam Janet was obviously enjoying her moment of triumph.

'The question is – how?' reflected Madam Janet.

Rachel had little doubt how. She could feel the whip slicing across her bare bottom already. It would be worse than the first time, she was sure of that. Why didn't the sadistic bitch get on with it? This was cruel beyond belief.

'Back on the bed, both of you!' barked Madam Janet suddenly. 'On your backs, side by side.'

Rachel was nonplussed. Nevertheless, she and Sally obeyed at once. Madam Janet moved to Rachel's side. Her hands were at her waist. Rachel's heart skipped a beat. She had imagined that she would be whipped across the bottom. Her buttocks were heavy and fleshy and would at least absorb some of the pain. If she were to be beaten across the front of her body that would be much worse. Madam Janet was staring at her breasts. Rachel shuddered. Madam Janet removed her waistband and placed it on the floor. Her fingers moved towards her hips and the small bows that held her shiny black thong in place. She undid them quickly and flung the material to one side. It was the first time either girl had seen Madam Janet's vagina. Her vulva was shaven, her labia pink and puffy, and glistening with her recent excitement. Rachel swallowed hard. She could smell the come on Madam Janet's warm flesh.

Madam Janet swung her meaty thighs on to the bed

and across Rachel's chest. She straddled Rachel's head, facing her feet. Reaching back with both hands she dug her fingers into her own buttocks and clawed them apart. Rachel stared upwards into Madam Janet's exposed backside. Her anus was dark and damp, like a small starfish at the heart of her deep divide. She wondered what was going to happen next. She suddenly remembered Michael and the Amazon, and had a dreadful image of Madam Janet sitting on her face, whipping her clitoris. Then she remembered that Madam Janet had discarded the tawse and she temporarily relaxed.

Madam Janet dipped her hips and pushed her bottom backwards so that her bare vulva came into position just above Rachel's mouth. Rachel could smell the other woman's excitement, and realised that she had never been this intimately close to another female, not even with the Amazon at Michael's flat. Still, she reminded herself, until yesterday she had come to realise what a sheltered life she had always led. She watched as a bead of moisture ran down from the nub of Madam Janet's pink clitty and rolled unchecked along the length of one out-turned pussy lip, from where it hung like a tiny translucent pearl.

'Kiss me,' instructed Madam Janet. Rachel swallowed hard. She had never done anything like this before. She took a deep breath and raised her head slightly, planting a hurried and clumsy peck on Madam Janet's fleshy mound, just to the side of her open labia.

'That really won't do,' protested Madam Janet. 'You will kiss me properly. Now! And to make it easier for you I will lower myself fully on to your face.'

Madam Janet was true to her word. She dipped lower so that her cunt came to rest just above Rachel's mouth. This time Rachel knew there was no escape. Madam's tone had made it abundantly clear that if she did not do as she was instructed there would be worse in store for her.

Rachel pressed her lips to Madam Janet's cunt and felt the salty mixture of come and sweat on her tongue. She ran her lips up and down, and was surprised that the taste was so musky and sweet. She wondered whether Madam perfumed herself in this most intimate of places.

'Use your tongue,' urged Madam Janet. This time Rachel obeyed without protest, extending her tongue and running it up and down the length of Madam's vagina, then flicking at the swollen labia, just teasing the nub of her clitoris. She could sense Madam's renewed arousal.

Above her, Rachel heard Madam speaking to Sally. 'Play with her,' she instructed. 'Squeeze her breasts.'

Immediately, a pair of small, warm hands made contact with Rachel's nipples, touching and kneading. Rachel pushed upwards, meeting Sally's touch, enjoying the feel of her friend against her body. Sally squeezed Rachel's nipples and she felt her pussy moisten as it always did when that part of her was teased.

Above her, Madam was moving faster, backwards and forwards, rubbing her cunt from side to side. She was soaking wet and Rachel's mouth was filling with Madam's taste and lubrication. Suddenly Madam moved again, dragging her sweet cunt away from Rachel's mouth. A new smell and sight assailed Rachel's senses, as Madam's anus eased into view.

'Now my bumhole,' ordered Madam Janet.

This was not something Rachel had expected. But, she concluded, it was time to give up expecting anything. Raising her head ever so slightly she flicked her tongue nervously across Madam's anus, withdrawing almost at once, recoiling with embarrassment and shame.

'Properly!' cried Madam Janet. 'Or it will be worse for you! No need to be shy. We're all girls here!'

Rachel took a deep breath and pushed her reluctance to one side. She raised her head a second time, before closing her lips around the small puckered opening of

Madam Janet's anus. Madam responded by immediately dropping her full weight on to Rachel's face, squirming herself into position so that her anal crack was locked tight around Rachel's nose and mouth. Rachel could hardly breathe. Somewhere far away she heard Madam Janet issuing more instructions. Now there were hands at her breasts, big strong hands squeezing her flesh. She knew at once that they were Madam's. At the same time, fingers were probing at her pussy, rubbing her up and down, intruding and teasing. A fingerpad rubbed round and round on her clitoris while two or three smaller digits entered her now well-oiled vagina. She knew these were Sally's. Above her, Madam Janet was riding her like a bucking bronco, driving her hips back and forth. Suddenly her powerful thighs clamped tightly around Rachel's head. Madam Janet screamed her release, pushing back, filling Rachel's mouth with her cunt again, where her backside had been only a moment before. Ecstatically, she emptied her juices into the depths of Rachel's throat. Rachel's head was spinning. She could hardly breathe. Her hands were smacking at Madam's hips, trying to tell her that she couldn't hold out much longer. Sally's fingers dug deep into Rachel's quim and once more she came, giving herself up to the most wonderful release. Immediately, her left hand was pulled away from Madam's hip and she felt her own fingers pressed against something warm and soft and wet. She realised that it must be Sally's cunt. Somewhere in the darkness, Madam was barking more orders even as she climaxed.

Suddenly, Madam rose and Rachel could breathe again, gasping in huge lungfuls of air. Madam climbed off the bed and quickly replaced her thong. Rachel lay on her back, still panting, her breasts rising and falling. Sally sat upright, rubbing her hand against her thighs, her fingers still glistening with Rachel's juices.

With renewed horror, Rachel realised that she had not asked permission to come. But this time Madam was smiling. 'It doesn't count when it's a punishment,' she said. 'Not unless I tell you in advance.'

She crossed to the far side of the room, her fingers on the door handle. 'You have a lot to learn,' she remarked, 'but this is a very promising start.'

Neither Rachel nor Sally was sure whether they were meant to respond. They kept silent, just in case. Madam Janet smiled.

'My charges usually emerge the best. I hope you won't let me down.' She paused as if waiting for a response. Rachel and Sally had learnt their lesson, however, and were not about to give Madam another chance to use her whip.

'It's lights out in an hour,' she reminded them. 'Until then you may indulge yourselves in any way you please. As long as you don't break any more rules, of course.'

After Madam Janet had departed, the two girls quickly washed, brushed and climbed wearily into bed.

'What a day,' reflected Rachel, thumbing idly through a book on Futurism. 'I'll never get the hang of modern art. It's all cubes and squiggles.'

Sally wriggled her head on the pillow and yawned. Rachel dropped the book on the floor and settled back. She was too tired to attempt any late-night studying.

'I quite liked school,' admitted Sally, 'but I got sidetracked.' She grinned. 'I found boys more interesting.'

Instinctively, Rachel leant over and kissed Sally gently on the cheek. Sally reached up and brushed the side of Rachel's face with her fingers. Then she turned her back and nuzzled into Rachel's tummy. Rachel pressed close, her arms curling protectively around Sally's shoulder. It felt nice and so very natural, in a way she had not anticipated. The two girls chatted on and off, mostly about nothing in particular, drifting in and out of a vague half-sleep, until, at last, the automatic lights went out.

On the other side of the two-way mirror, Madam Janet switched off the tape-recorder and made one or two notes in her record book. Then, turning to the man standing beside her, she asked, 'So what do you make of our new girls?'

Master Stéfan's face was expressionless. 'Initiate Rachel interests me.'

'I'm sure she does,' replied Madam Janet. 'Just remember to be careful.'

'What do you mean?'

'Master Daniel was careless and look what happened to him.'

Master Stéfan sniffed disdainfully. 'Master Daniel was unable to control his emotions.'

'Something that no one could accuse you of, Master Stéfan.'

He faced her and smiled. She reached forward and unzipped his trousers.

'You seemed to be enjoying your time with them,' he observed.

'True,' admitted Madam Janet, 'but I enjoy this more.' She extracted his penis and squeezed it gently. It was already upright and engorged with blood. She parted her legs, pulled her thong to one side, and let him advance, entering her in one fluid movement. Of course she had enjoyed the girls, but there were times when a woman needed to be fucked. She fastened her legs around Master Stéfan's waist, closed her eyes and surrendered to the pleasure of the moment. On the far side of the mirror, Rachel and Sally drifted peacefully off to sleep, oblivious to the moment when Madam Janet dug her fingers into Master Stéfan's tight buttocks, held him fast and screamed.

Five

It was the start of their third week at The Hall, and a regular pattern had begun to emerge. Madam Janet would arrive at 6.30 each morning and expect to find them washed and ready. She would escort them outside where they would meet up with the other girls and run three times around the grounds. After a light breakfast the day's activities would begin. Academic classes – art, languages and politics – nestled alongside more physical activities such as circuit training and weightlifting. Master Devlin's sex classes were held at the end of each day, when the girls were most in need of a break from their more rigorous pursuits. They studied masturbation techniques, and methods of delaying the male orgasm. There were also regular sessions designed to enhance their oral sex abilities. One such exercise involved having thin rubber strips fitted around their mouths. The material was strong but flexible and, by pushing against the rubber, the girls found that they were gradually able to increase the strength of their tongues. They performed strenuous arm and leg stretching exercises, too, as well as simulating a staggering variety of positions from numerous sex manuals. Master Devlin appeared to be not so much double as triple-jointed, judging from the positions he was able to achieve. More incredibly, Rachel observed, was the fact that not once did he appear to develop an erection, despite his regular close contact with eleven, heavily sweating, hormone-charged women.

The Initiates grew closer as they adjusted to their new surroundings. At the same time, both they and their tutors began to gradually get the measure of each other. Rachel's fears regarding Master Stéfan had not been realised, though she remained uneasy in his presence. After the first class, acting lessons had followed a more traditional approach. The girls had practised voice control, posture and movement. There had been a small amount of improvisation, but nothing out of the ordinary. Nevertheless, there were times when Rachel would glance at Master Stéfan and catch him staring at her. Though he invariably turned away, it left her puzzled and confused. Had he forgiven her or not? What was he thinking? More than once she wanted to ask him outright, but she knew that was impossible. One thing she did learn early on, however, was that physical punishment was not administered by their tutors. It was the responsibility of their individual Madams or the so-called Discipline Master. The Discipline Master, they quickly discovered, was none other than Master Stéfan. Rachel realised, belatedly, that this was the dual role he had hinted at prior to their first acting lesson.

On the fourth day of the first week, while acting out a short scene from *The Tempest*, one of the girls, Kimberley, had forgotten her lines. Master Stéfan had made her bend over in front of the entire class and proceeded to whip her several times on the bottom. Unfortunately for Kimberley, she had a full bladder and had embarrassed herself by peeing on the floor halfway through. Master Stéfan immediately doubled the number of strokes and deducted her ten credits. Another girl, Shirley, who had failed to identify a painting by Martinetti as a leading work of the Futurist movement, had been called out of the art class for a similar punishment. On this occasion, however, Master Stéfan had placed her over his knee and spanked her twelve times on the buttocks. On the very last stroke, she climaxed loudly and was immediately deducted thirty credits.

It was just after supper one evening, when Rachel received the summons she had been dreading. Back in their room, Madam Janet unclipped the reins that held her and Sally together.

'Master Stéfan wants to see you,' she said, 'for special instruction.' She looked Rachel up and down. 'I wonder what you've done to warrant such treatment so early on.'

Rachel kept her thoughts to herself. She knew she must not speak without permission. Madam Janet smiled.

'Master Stéfan usually takes only the brightest pupils under his wing. This may be a feather in my cap, so don't let me down, will you?' Madam's hand tightened around her tawse as it always did when she wished to impress something on her charges.

'No, Madam,' replied Rachel. She felt her spirits slump. She was pretty sure she knew why Master Stéfan had chosen her for so-called special instruction. He wanted to punish her for the way she had made him lose control on her first day at The Hall. He had left her dangling all this time simply to enhance her suffering.

They left Sally under strict orders to spend her free time studying the Pre-Raphaelites. Rachel wasn't sure which was worse: two hours with Holman Hunt and his friends, or five minutes with Master Stéfan. She concluded, ruefully, that it was probably no contest.

Madam Janet paused outside Master Stéfan's office.

'A word of advice,' she cautioned. 'Don't annoy Master Stéfan. He's not a man to cross swords with.'

Although the advice seemed superfluous in the

circumstances, Rachel allowed herself a half-smile of thanks. She was convinced that Madam Janet was not someone to cross swords with either. It seemed to be a case of the pot calling the kettle black.

Madam Janet knocked sharply on the door, turning the handle without waiting for a reply. Master Stéfan's office was big and airy, with a large window overlooking expansive grounds. It contained a tall Victorian desk, a few chairs, and two walls covered with small, dark watercolours. Master Stéfan glanced up from the book he was reading as the two women entered. It was a thick, dog-eared tome with faded, gilt lettering on the cover and spine.

'Good evening, Master Stéfan,' began Madam Janet. 'Sister Rachel is here for special instruction.'

'Indeed,' he remarked carelessly, pushing the volume to one side. He glanced over some sheets of paper in front of him. Without looking up, he continued: 'I have decided to instruct her in some of the aspects of dungeon duties.'

The word 'dungeon' made Rachel's ears prick up. There was something at once both very sexy and very sinister about the word.

'I'll leave her in your very capable hands, Master,' said Madam Janet, retreating towards the door.

Master Stéfan looked up and his eyes noticeably narrowed. 'You may be sure I will take good care of your charge,' he replied.

The door closed with a loud click and Rachel suddenly felt very alone. She lowered her eyes to the floor, afraid that looking Master Stéfan in the face would be interpreted as a mark of insolence. His voice broke into her thoughts.

'Look at me, please.' It was a command not a request. She raised her head and stared directly into his cold, blue eyes.

'While you are under my private instruction you may

speak freely at all times, unless I tell you otherwise, is that clear?'

Rachel nodded her understanding. 'Yes, Master Stéfan.'

'Good. Now, tell me, how are you enjoying your time at The Hall?'

The question took Rachel by surprise. She wasn't quite sure how to respond. 'It's – well – interesting,' she replied, which, in the circumstances, wasn't far from the truth. She was aware of Master Stéfan's eyes scanning her upper body. Her breasts rose and fell, swinging gently as she shifted nervously on the balls of her feet. He quickly averted his gaze, but his eyes had lingered long enough to confirm his weakness. So she hadn't been mistaken, reflected Rachel. She would have to remember that. There might come a time when the knowledge would prove useful.

Rachel glanced at the book on Master Stéfan's desk. Though it was upside down, she could see it was open at a page of sketches: drawings of what could only be described as sado-masochistic practices. There were scenes involving whips and chains and various pointed implements that Rachel did not really care to dwell on. She averted her eyes at once, but it was too late. Master Stéfan slammed the book shut.

'You will say nothing about what you have seen here, is that understood?' he barked.

'Yes, Master,' promised Rachel, nodding furiously. More than ever, she was convinced that Master Stéfan was not a man to meddle with.

'Here at The Hall we are involved in many projects. They are all classified. If you speak of these matters, you will be expelled at once. Is that clear?'

'Yes, Master!' repeated Rachel. She was shaken by the vehemence of his response. She wondered if the book really related to his work at The Hall or to something more personal.

Master Stéfan pushed his chair back, stood up and crossed to a far door. 'This way,' he announced curtly, twisting the handle, and preceding Rachel into the adjoining room. Her eyes opened wider and she inhaled sharply. His outer room was modern, with telephones, bright lights and a computer. In here, it was as if she had travelled back in time to a darker, more hostile environment. She was standing in a carefully constructed mock-up of a medieval dungeon. The walls were rendered in dark green stone, investing the chamber with an eerie chill. Electric firebrands, cleverly designed to resemble the real thing, jutted from all four sides at realistically irregular intervals. Chains, hoods and a variety of leather hoops hung from the walls, as did several metal contraptions and spiked containers that Rachel decided it was best not to dwell on. In the centre of the room was a low wooden bench. At first glance, Rachel thought that there was someone lying on it. But as she peered closer, she realised that it was a large male-shaped dummy. It was very realistic, other than for the fact that it possessed a massive erection, jutting upwards at an anatomically incorrect right-angle to the groin.

Another equally blessed model stood propped up against the far wall. Close by was a low table on which was laid out a motley collection of whips, chains and leather restraints. Rachel felt the hair stand up at the back of her neck. She wasn't sure if she wanted to know what all this meant. At the same time, however, she was aware of a tingling sensation spreading downwards across her belly. It was all so dangerous and forbidden, and yet curiously exciting.

Master Stéfan walked across to the far wall, picked up the dummy and set it down firmly to the left of the low wooden bench. He turned it around, so that its back was towards them, and proceeded to lock the dummy's feet into two footholds set into the dungeon floor.

Rachel noticed that there was a series of thick, coloured lines drawn around the dummy's torso. Master Stéfan crossed to the large table and selected a small-handled whip with a long lash. He came back and stood beside Rachel.

'In the handle of this whip is an electronic sensor,' he explained. 'You will see that there is a series of coloured buttons, matching the colours on the dummy.'

Rachel leant forward and examined the whip handle.

'Choose a colour,' he instructed.

'Red,' replied Rachel, without any serious thought. It was a colour she liked.

'Watch,' he said, standing with his feet apart and holding the whip loosely in his right hand. His arm flashed forward; there was a blur of black and the end of the lash made contact with the dummy's buttocks.

'A perfect hit,' observed Master Stéfan.

Rachel said nothing. It had all happened so fast that she only had Master Stéfan's word for it that he had hit the red crease and not the blue one below or the yellow one above.

Master Stéfan smiled. Rachel knew he had read her thoughts. She felt she could not hide anything from him. She hoped she had not made an enemy of him. If she had, then her days were surely numbered.

'I will now show you what happens if you miss the target.'

He lashed out a second time, whipping the dummy sharply across the head. There was a loud buzz and Master Stéfan visibly winced.

'When the whip is tuned to red,' he explained, 'you must strike the red colour on the dummy. Miss it and you receive a low-voltage electric shock. The result is somewhat uncomfortable, though not dangerous.'

Rachel felt distinctly uneasy. When Master Stéfan smiled, it was like looking a hungry lion in the face.

'Which colour will *you* choose?' he asked.

Rachel froze. This wasn't fair. She wanted to protest, but realised that that was probably what he wanted her to do. Instead, she took a deep breath, defiantly lifting her breasts. It pleased her to see him avert his eyes again.

'Brown,' she decided, concentrating on a thick dark line over the dummy's right buttock.

'A good choice,' conceded Master Stéfan. His voice was unsteady, as he struggled to keep his eyes away from Rachel's bosom. He pressed a button on the hilt and passed her the whip. His hand was trembling slightly.

Rachel took a deep breath. She knew she was going to miss, and found herself wondering how much it would hurt. The whip felt warm and clammy in her hand; she was afraid and yet, at the same time, excitement gnawed at her belly. She was enjoying the act of venturing into uncharted territory. The effect she was clearly having on Master Stéfan only increased the thrill. She took aim and lashed out with the whip. There was a loud crack and a beep from the whip handle. Rachel flinched, waiting for the shock to hit her. But it never came. She was astounded, she must have hit the target after all.

Master Stéfan grinned cruelly. 'If that had been a real man you would have taken his penis off. I don't think he would have been very pleased.'

'But I must have hit it,' protested Rachel. 'I didn't get a shock.'

'Only because I switched off the power,' replied Master Stéfan. 'It would not have been fair for you to have suffered on your first attempt, would it?'

Rachel didn't know what to say. She was disappointed, of course, yet it was a relief to discover that Master Stéfan had been lenient with her. Perhaps he wasn't as cruel as she feared. On the other hand, he had not told her that he had switched off the power. He had still meant to frighten her, and he had succeeded.

'I'm sorry,' said Rachel. 'I've never done this before.'

'Don't worry,' replied Master Stéfan, 'you will improve. Everyone does. Try again.'

Rachel took careful aim a second time. She concentrated very hard. She was about to let fly when Master Stéfan intervened.

'You are not standing properly,' he admonished her. Immediately, he went down on one knee and placed his right hand between her legs, his fingers spread across the smooth flesh of her thighs. His fingers were warm and sticky and made her feel uncomfortable. But at the same time there was something wicked about being manipulated like this. He forced her legs further apart, the edge of one finger grazing the flesh directly below her hairy pudenda. She glanced down and saw that he was staring straight into her cunt, as if he were examining her. She heard him draw in a deep breath and realised that he was actually sniffing her pussy. The thought made her legs tremble, and an image floated into her mind: Master Stéfan was kneeling in front of her, his hands tied behind his back, his face buried between her thighs. She was holding on to him for dear life, thrusting with her hips, bending him backwards, making him struggle for breath. She felt her juices start to flow. With enormous difficulty, she dragged herself back to the present.

Master Stéfan stood up and moved behind her. Reaching forward, he took hold of Rachel's right wrist and pulled her arm back.

'You must hold the whip easily,' he advised, pushing her hand down slightly.

He was very close to her now, his chest up against her back. Rachel could feel his hardness between her legs, aware of his barely concealed excitement. She knew he wanted her and the thought made her heart beat faster. Without warning, he let go of her wrist and moved his hands so that they covered her breasts. Rachel felt her stomach churn with pleasure, and her knees wobbled girlishly. It was ridiculous, she told herself. She did not welcome his advances and yet at the same time the realisation that he wielded such power over her, that she had abdicated a part of her personality and freedom to the Sisterhood, aroused her beyond measure. Master Stéfan could do as he wanted and she would submit. The thought alone made her go weak inside and caused her to moisten further between her legs. Master Stéfan squeezed her breasts hard and she let out a low whimper, partly of pleasure, partly of distaste. She wondered if this was part of her training, or was Master Stéfan succumbing to something he should not? She wanted him to squeeze harder, because she loved having her breasts squeezed, even by a man she didn't trust.

Suddenly, he released his hold. Rachel swallowed hard, trying to regain her composure. She wondered if he knew the effect that he was having on her, and decided that he surely must. Master Stéfan stepped back and round to the side of her. Already, he seemed to have regained his former composure.

'Now,' he said calmly, as if nothing had happened, 'aim for the green line on the top of the left buttock'.

Rachel steadied herself and let fly with a quick flash of her right hand. The whip touched the outside of the dummy's rubber backside, and the whip handle beeped its message of failure.

'Not bad,' said Master Stéfan. 'Better than before. Try again.'

Rachel tried once more, and missed. She was made to repeat the exercise countless times over the next hour, the parts of the dummy's body being constantly varied. She missed every time and was beginning to despair. She believed she would never master this skill, if skill were the word it deserved. At last Master Stéfan took pity on her and called the exercise to an end.

'I'm not very good, am I?' she said.

'Rome was not built in a day,' he replied. 'Besides,

you did better than you think. And next time you will do better still.'

Rachel wanted to ask if he really thought so, but it seemed too friendly a response, and she wasn't sure that Master Stéfan would welcome so informal an approach. Besides, she still didn't trust him.

Back in the office, he pressed a button on his desk. Madam Janet entered almost at once. Rachel wondered if she had spent the entire lesson with her ears pressed up against the door waiting to be called. It was unlikely, she knew, but the thought amused her as Madam Janet clipped the rein to Rachel's neckband. Master Stéfan said nothing. It was as if she were no longer there.

On the way back to her room, Rachel found herself strangely confused. She had not thought that she would enjoy her introduction to dungeon training, but she had. Yet what was she to make of Master Stéfan? He had not punished her as she thought he would. Indeed, in his own way he had been quite solicitous. But the book on his desk told a different story. She was convinced that there was a sinister, sadistic side to Master Stéfan, a side perhaps that he was struggling to keep hidden. Rachel was so engrossed in her thoughts that at first she failed to notice that she was not being returned to her room. Instead, she was led out to the entrance hall and up the main stairs to the first floor.

Rachel knew better than to ask where she was being taken. Her next class was French and that was held on the ground floor, so there was obviously something going on. Madam Janet paused outside Mistress Katrina's office. Rachel felt her stomach churn. She must have done something wrong to be brought here. Madam Janet knocked once, then, as seemed to be her practice, opened the door without waiting for a reply. She stepped to one side and ushered Rachel forward. Rachel felt the breath catch in the back of her throat, for it was not, as she had expected, Mistress Katrina waiting to meet her, but Lady Frances De La Vie.

Six

'You may leave us alone,' instructed Lady Frances. Madam Janet bowed silently, unclipped the rein from around Rachel's neck and quickly withdrew.

Lady Frances smiled sweetly. 'Please sit down,' she said, waving Rachel towards a chair. She flicked through an open file on her desk. 'I've been studying your progress since your arrival at The Hall.'

Rachel felt a sinking feeling in her tummy. This was like being called before the Headmistress. Was it good news or bad news?

'I am pleased to say that your progress is everything we had hoped it would be,' smiled Lady Frances.

Rachel breathed a sigh of relief as Lady Frances went on. 'So tell me, Rachel, are you enjoying your time at The Hall? Is it everything you imagined?'

Rachel had to marshal her thoughts. She didn't want to disappoint Lady Frances.

'It's not what I expected,' she confessed after a moment or two's consideration, 'if only because I didn't know what to expect.'

Lady Frances smiled. 'But you are enjoying the training?' she asked.

Rachel nodded enthusiastically. 'Oh, yes,' she replied. 'Very much. I've learnt such a lot.'

'But is it exciting?' asked Lady Frances. 'I know it's hard work, but is it more than that?'

'Yes, it is,' replied Rachel truthfully. 'I like the idea that each day is going to bring something different.'

Lady Frances nodded approvingly. 'Yes, that is an important consideration,' she observed, then leant forward and looked Rachel straight in the eyes.

'I want to ask you something. It is not an easy request, so please think carefully before replying.'

Rachel sat bolt upright and gave Lady Frances her full attention. Oh dear, she thought, this sounded serious.

'It has been observed that one of the Masters has taken a particular interest in your progress.'

Rachel stiffened. She had a horrible feeling she wasn't going to like what was coming next. She wondered if complaints had been made, perhaps by Master Stéfan himself.

'You know who I'm referring to,' suggested Lady Frances.

Rachel took a deep breath. Her insides were quivering. 'Master Stéfan,' she replied quietly.

'Indeed,' said Lady Frances. 'Master Stéfan is one of our most experienced tutors and a respected member of our associate organisation, the Brotherhood. However, he is prone, shall we say, to certain weaknesses.'

Rachel had a sudden flashback: of the book on Master Stéfan's desk, of pages littered with a bewildering variety of sado-masochistic practices.

'We are concerned that Master Stéfan may have become a liability to the organisation.' Lady Frances paused. 'You must realise that what I tell you is strictly confidential. You are not to repeat our conversation to anyone, not even your Sister Initiate, Sally. Do you understand?'

Rachel nodded.

'If you do, it will mean instant expulsion – without any of the financial rewards promised. Not only that, but you will remain under constant surveillance for the rest of your life. One word to anyone about our activities, even the merest hint . . .' Lady Frances leant back in her chair. 'I don't think I need say any more.'

Rachel went cold. Lady Frances was threatening her. She shouldn't have liked it, but, in spite of herself, a warm glow began to spread out from between her legs.

Lady Frances smiled. 'Do you regard yourself as a dominant or a submissive?' she asked.

The question was so unexpected that Rachel was taken aback. 'I – I don't know,' she replied truthfully.

'Think about it,' urged Lady Frances. 'What are your feelings either way?'

Rachel frowned. It really wasn't that easy. 'I honestly don't know. There are times when I enjoy being in charge. I want to be in charge, I want to –'

'Make men do things?' suggested Lady Frances.

Rachel nodded. 'Yes,' she replied, then hesitated.

Lady Frances smiled, 'And not just men, perhaps?'

Rachel bowed her head a little and blushed.

'There is no aspect of life that goes unnoticed at The Hall,' explained Lady Frances. 'Everything is monitored and recorded. It is important for us to be aware of everyone's weaknesses, strengths and peccadilloes.' She leant back in her chair and a weak smile played on her lips. 'We all have them,' she added.

Rachel looked up. She wondered what Lady Frances's were. Then she remembered the scene in the London dungeon, and the two men suspended from the ceiling undergoing perpetual sexual arousal. She began to have an inkling of what Lady Frances's own personal peccadillo might be.

'I think there are times when you wish to be dominated,' suggested Lady Frances, returning to the earlier theme.

'Yes, I – I suppose there are,' admitted Rachel. There seemed little point in trying to hide anything from Lady Frances. Besides, she knew that being at The Hall was all about exploring herself, finding out what made her tick, what turned her on. 'It's nice not to have to worry sometimes.'

'And it's exciting, too, isn't it?' suggested Lady Frances. 'I still remember when Madam Karen had you in that half-nelson at my house. You almost wet yourself, didn't you?'

Rachel lowered her eyes and blushed again. This time she was genuinely embarrassed.

'Don't worry,' said Lady Frances reassuringly. 'It's more common than you'd imagine. But that's not why I wanted to speak to you. This matter with Master Stéfan is more important, though your own sexual orientation may have some bearing on the matter.'

Rachel looked up. The words seemed laden with meaning. What *was* her sexual orientation? She wasn't sure even she knew the answer to that one. She had thought it was obvious before she had met Lady Frances. But since then her eyes had been opened to many experiences. She had found nothing, except possibly Master Stéfan's secret predilections, off-putting.

'Master Stéfan is probing into matters that are better left alone. Not that there is anything wrong with sado-masochism in its right place,' conceded Lady Frances. 'But it should be a matter between consenting adults. It has no place at The Hall, where we aim to teach a more subtle appreciation of the sexual psyche.'

Rachel wondered where all this was leading. What had all this to do with her?

'Master Stéfan is developing a weakness for you,' continued Lady Frances. 'I want to exploit that weakness for the good of the Sisterhood.'

'How?' asked Rachel, feeling a little more relaxed now she knew she wasn't there to be punished.

'You must gain his confidence, and find out what he's up to.'

'I don't understand,' confessed Rachel.

'We believe that Master Stéfan is straying from the straight and narrow in more than one respect,' explained Lady Frances. 'We believe he is gathering information about the Sisterhood and that he intends selling it to the highest bidder.'

Rachel shot forward in her chair. 'But he can't do that!' she cried. 'It would ruin everything!'

Lady Frances smiled sweetly. 'So much enthusiasm already,' she remarked. 'It's very pleasing to see.'

Rachel sat back. 'I'm sorry,' she murmured, 'it's just that I'm enjoying myself here and I want to go on. I like it.'

'Excellent,' said Lady Frances. 'If you maintain that attitude there is a bright future for you in the Sisterhood. Unless, of course, Master Stéfan has his way.'

'But I don't understand,' said Rachel. 'Can't we just confront him? Hire a private detective or something?'

'We could,' replied Lady Frances, 'but this way we get to test your own abilities. It will take considerable skill to win Master Stéfan's confidence, to make him think you're on his side.' She paused, then added, 'But it may be dangerous. He is a violent man. If he should believe that you have been sent to spy on him . . .' She left the sentence unfinished.

Rachel realised that she should have been worried, but, to her surprise, there was something about the idea that thrilled her.

'You like fear, don't you?' observed Lady Frances.

'Do I?' replied Rachel. It wasn't something that had occurred to her before. And yet she began to realise that Lady Frances might have hit on something. She did like the excitement of the unknown. After all, wasn't that what had drawn her to The Hall in the first place?

'So what exactly do you want me to do?' asked Rachel.

'Master Stéfan will certainly wish to see you again. For more of his "special instruction". You must go along with any of his suggestions. Get him to believe that you enjoy being with him. Find out what he's up to. Will you do this for us?'

'Yes,' answered Rachel unhesitatingly. 'I will.'

Lady Frances smiled. 'Excellent. I knew I could count on you.' She stood up and came over to Rachel's side of the desk. Rachel felt too nervous to turn round. Suddenly Lady Frances's hands were on her bare shoulders, her fingers pressing lightly into her flesh.

'You are a very beautiful young woman,' she told her. Rachel felt herself blushing again. Lady Frances's fingers pressed harder. Her arms swept low and her hands spread around Rachel's large, heavy breasts, fingernails scratching at her nipples. Rachel felt her insides do a somersault as Lady Frances squeezed her flesh tight.

'Does that feel good?' she asked quietly, bending down so that her face was close to Rachel's, her breath warm against the back of her neck.

'Yes,' mumbled Rachel nervously. She wasn't sure what was going on, but she liked it. Lady Frances's hand began to wander lower, exploring the flat plane of Rachel's tummy before her long fingers dipped into the thatch of curls that sprouted from between the two lengths of leather enclosing her vulva. Rachel let out a loud, deep sigh. Lady Frances breathed warmly into her ear and pushed her fingers hard between Rachel's legs. Rachel parted her thighs and raised herself ever so slightly, affording Lady Frances easier access. She felt her sap rising, oozing out from between her pussy lips, moistening Lady Frances's fingers. Suddenly, Lady Frances withdrew her hand and stepped away.

'Stand up,' she commanded, and Rachel immediately jumped to her feet.

'Kneel,' said Lady Frances. She reached down and pulled the black material of her long dress to one side, baring her legs. Rachel saw at once that she was wearing sheer black stockings and suspenders but no panties.

Her vulva was shaven, the lips of her vagina plump and well pronounced. Rachel looked away, lowering her eyes. She felt that she should not look upon Lady Frances's nakedness unless given express permission. Lady Frances laughed lightly, aware of Rachel's misgivings.

'Look at me, Rachel,' she ordered. Rachel turned her face upwards, gazing into Lady Frances's dark brown eyes.

'You will go far, Rachel,' said Lady Frances. 'You may now swear your loyalty and your silence.'

'I do,' promised Rachel quietly.

'Then seal our bargain with a kiss,' instructed Lady Frances.

Rachel's frown betrayed her lack of understanding. Lady Frances smiled, pushing her hips forward so that her vulva was almost hanging over Rachel's nose.

'Pay homage to me,' she commanded.

This time Rachel was left in no doubt as to Lady Frances's meaning. She pressed her face forward, her nose nuzzling into Lady Frances's warm slit. Her vulva was damp and there was a faintly perfumed smell, not of pussy but of some expensive scent. Rachel pressed her mouth reverently to Lady Frances's labia and savoured her salty, musky taste. Without being asked to, she extended her tongue. Lady Frances's vagina was soft and warm and wet, and Rachel entered it with the greatest of ease.

'Make me come,' instructed Lady Frances. 'I wish to orgasm inside your mouth.'

Rachel didn't know if Lady Frances was being deliberately provocative, but the effect was the same: her belly glowed and she felt a trickle of juice at her own pussy. Pushing upwards with her tongue, Rachel located the hard nub of Lady Frances's clitoris, stabbing at it lightly. She was blissfully aware of Lady Frances's hands clawing through her hair, holding her tight, mewing softly and driving her hips forward. It was all over in a matter of seconds. Lady Frances gave a sudden squeal and her whole body shook from top to toe. She emptied herself into Rachel's mouth, her labia engorged and mushy with her spendings. Then she pulled back and let her dress close around her. Though she seemed suddenly calm again, that was more than could be said for Rachel, whose breath was coming in short, fast bursts.

Lady Frances looked down at her and smiled. 'Are you excited?' she asked. Rachel lowered her head and felt her cheeks burn with embarrassment.

'Then masturbate yourself,' said Lady Frances. 'No, better still,' she added after a moment's reflection. 'Come here.'

Lady Frances beckoned Rachel towards her, around the side of the desk. Opening a drawer, she extracted a large strap-on dildo and quickly tied it about her waist.

'Bend over the desk,' she instructed.

Rachel did as she was told, flattening her breasts across the warm oak. Gripping the edge of the desk, she opened her legs as far as she could, closed her eyes and waited for the shock of penetration. Lady Frances positioned herself between Rachel's thighs and pushed gently, the dildo sliding home with ease. Rachel pushed back, matching her invader thrust for thrust, her head giddy with excitement. It thrilled her to realise that Lady Frances, the head of the Sisterhood, was using her like this. Suddenly, she gave a short sharp scream and came, moaning into the green blotter, dribbling on to the desk and driving her hips back as hard as she could. She knew now that she would be Lady Frances's for ever, and that loyalty to the Sisterhood had become her overriding concern.

It came as a shock when Lady Frances announced, 'I am sorry, Rachel, but you will have to be beaten.'

Rachel looked suddenly and understandably mystified.

'People will wonder why I have asked to see you. This way we can say that you were to be punished. It's the only way, I'm afraid. Please resume your kneeling position.'

Lady Frances reached forward and pressed a buzzer on her desk. A minute, perhaps two passed, then there came a knock at the door and Master Stéfan and Madam Janet entered. Lady Frances extended her arm in Rachel's general direction.

'Master Stéfan,' she began. 'I have spoken to Sister Rachel about certain aspects of her progress. She is promising Sisterhood material, but may go wrong if not properly governed.'

Master Stéfan lowered his head reverently. 'I understand, High Mistress.'

'I knew you would,' said Lady Frances. 'I will leave her chastisement to you.'

'Should it be public?' he asked.

Lady Frances fell silent for a moment or two as if considering the options.

'Again, I leave that to you,' she said at last. 'Though perhaps on this occasion, a private humiliation would be more appropriate.'

'I will see to it at once,' replied Master Stéfan.

'Or you could delay,' suggested Lady Frances. 'Not knowing when the punishment is to take place will add to her suffering.'

Master Stéfan looked at Rachel and grinned slyly. It was obvious that this suggestion greatly appealed to him. 'An excellent idea, High Mistress,' he acknowledged.

Rachel felt her blood run cold. Lady Frances had surely delivered her into the hands of the devil himself.

Rachel had expected to be taken back to her room, or at least to another class but, instead, she now found herself being escorted along an unfamiliar corridor on the second floor.

'It's time for your psychological profiling,' explained Madam Janet. 'All the girls go through it. It's to check your suitability as a potential Sister. Everyone is interviewed. It will be Sally's turn after dinner.'

Madam Janet took Rachel down two more interlinked corridors, past several doors and across a large oval area bordered with wide, stained-glass windows. Eventually, they came to a large oak door, with the words, MADAM LAURA embossed on a gold-edged plaque.

Madam Laura smiled as she flicked through a sheaf of papers on her desk.

'You are here for assessment,' she began. 'I expect Madam Janet has explained.'

Rachel nodded. 'Yes Madam,' she replied.

'It is very important that we discover our Initiates' inner psyches. We all have longings, desires and fantasies. It is these which mould our personalities and lend us both our strengths and weaknesses.'

Rachel wondered where all this was leading. She had never considered how her sexual character might have affected the rest of her. All she had ever thought about was that she enjoyed sex, didn't like to go for long without a man and, well, that was it, really.

'I have a questionnaire,' said Madam Laura, 'which I would like you to answer as truthfully as possible.' She smiled, pushed her chair back and stood up.

'Please lie down,' she said, waving towards a nearby black leather couch. Rachel was aware of a series of restraints loosely hanging from both ends, and a raised protrusion midway along its length. Examining the latter more closely, she realised that it was a thick, phallus-shaped extension, about eight inches long. A wire ran out from the base, feeding into a small, brightly coloured control panel sitting beside Madam Laura's loudly humming computer.

'Please lie down and I'll fasten you to the apparatus,' said Madam Laura.

Rachel did as she was told, though she was uncertain how to negotiate the leather phallus until Madam Laura reached past her and pulled it to one side. As she settled down, however, Madam Laura pushed the phallus forward again, so that its rounded tip nudged the entrance to her vagina. Rachel sighed and felt butterflies tickle her tummy.

'Are you comfortable?' asked Madam Laura.

Rachel nodded happily. 'Yes thank you, Madam, very comfortable.' If this was anything to go by, she reflected, it was going to be the nicest visit she had ever made to a medical establishment.

Madam Laura fed the phallus into Rachel's vagina. When it was lodged fully inside her, Rachel settled back and closed her eyes. It was such a lovely, delicious feeling. She had to fight not to push down and enjoy the feel of riding the warm intruder. Finally, Madam Laura took the straps and looped them around Rachel's wrists and ankles, tightening them until she was secured in place. Her arms were stretched back past her head and her legs were pulled wide apart.

Madam Laura drew up a chair and wheeled the small computer table forward. She examined the monitor screen for a moment or two, then pressed a button on a control panel. The phallus began to throb between Rachel's legs. Rachel let out an involuntary whoop of pleasure and surprise.

'I just needed to confirm that the tantaliser was working properly,' explained Madam Laura, smiling.

The tantaliser was well named, thought Rachel. She was wondering how much more of this she would be subjected to, when she realised that Madam Laura was speaking again.

'We like to back up the psychological profile with physical data,' she explained. 'The tantaliser will monitor your vaginal reactions to the questions I am about to ask.'

Rachel breathed deeply but said nothing. Her pussy had already begun to ooze at the realisation that she was so utterly helpless. She didn't need additional stimulation. Madam Laura's eyes were fixed on her screen.

'I see that you're beginning to secrete quite heavily,' she remarked. 'Excellent. You show a very high arousal level even before we begin.'

Rachel said nothing. She didn't need to be told how aroused she was. She could happily take this sort of examination until the proverbial cows came home.

'Right, let's begin,' said Madam Laura, turning to her page of questions. 'You may answer each question as fully as you like or with a simple yes or no as appropriate. Question one: do you regard yourself as a dominant or a submissive?'

Rachel felt a sudden sense of *déjà vu*. And yet oddly, though Lady Frances had already asked her the same question, she remained just as unsure of her response.

'I don't know,' she replied truthfully. 'I've never given it much thought. I like both really. I suppose it depends on the mood I'm in.'

Madam Laura tapped the keys on her keyboard and entered some unseen details.

'Question two,' she continued. 'You are walking home late at night when you come across a man you have found physically attractive for some time but who has never shown any interest in you. His hands and feet are handcuffed, he is gagged, blindfolded, and in all respects utterly helpless. Would you (a) untie him at once, (b) walk on by just to teach him a lesson, or (c) aware that he had no idea who you were, undo his trousers, remove your knickers, straddle his penis and take him without mercy, bouncing up and down until you had successfully milked him?'

Rachel swivelled her hips from side to side, bearing down on the leather phallus. Had Madam Laura simply asked, 'Would you fuck him?' the image would have proved exciting enough. But the way she had dragged out the description was clearly designed to effect maximum arousal. Rachel could feel the fluids oozing from her body and soaking into the leather lining of the couch. She had been thinking of Michael, of course – presumably everyone supplied their fantasy man in this situation.

'I'd fuck him senseless,' she moaned, twisting her hips and allowing the phallus to work its magic inside her.

'We'll take that as a (c),' replied Madam Laura. 'By the way, though I can tell how much you're enjoying this, I must warn you that if you climax you'll be deducted thirty credits.'

Rachel took a deep breath and pulled herself up short.

'According to the monitor, you were very close to coming,' observed Madam Laura, scanning a swathe of coloured lines on the computer screen.

Rachel felt her belly shimmer. She began to wonder how close she could take herself and still hold back, and whether she might be awarded extra credits if she reached higher levels without climaxing.

'Next question,' continued Madam Laura. 'Do you fantasise about any of your fellow Initiates? And if so, which ones?'

Rachel took another deep breath before responding. Something had occurred to her. It was late in the day, but it was something she could use. She suddenly cursed herself for the answers she had given to the two previous questions. Master Stéfan was a dominant. Surely, what he would want most in a woman would be submissiveness? Rachel was fairly certain that her submissive tendencies were weak. She liked being taken over, of course, or else she wouldn't have volunteered to join the Sisterhood. But her real self was more independent. She liked being in control. In fact in her quiet, dreamy moments she often wondered what it would feel like to adopt the guise of a dominatrix and wield the whip with some spineless male slave.

Madam Laura's voice broke into her thoughts. 'Well?' she asked again. 'Do you ever fantasise about your fellow Initiates?'

'Yes,' replied Rachel, honestly, though she had now taken the decision that whatever else she said, she must do her best to manipulate her psychological profile. She was certain Master Stéfan would be privy to the results and this might well be one way to gain his trust.

'I fantasise about Sally.'

Rachel felt the phallus turn inside her and she shut her eyes, surrendering herself to the pleasurable vibrations.

'And what is the nature of your fantasy?' asked Madam Laura.

'I imagine that we're at school together. She's so petite. She's wearing little white socks and a short skirt that keeps riding up and showing her knickers.'

'What are you wearing?'

'The same, except that I'm wearing stockings and suspenders because I'm –' she was about to add something like, I'm a prefect, and Sally's been very naughty, before realising that this would not further her cause. She paused, thinking hard for a moment, then modified her response. 'I'm bad,' she continued. 'I'm not supposed to be wearing clothes like this. And Sally's a real goody two-shoes. She's a prefect. So she can tell me off.'

'And does she?' inquired Madam Laura.

'Yes, she does,' replied Rachel, opening her eyes. She could see Madam Laura monitoring her reactions on the computer. Rachel knew very well that what she was saying and what the machine was recording were not matching up. If she failed to rectify matters promptly, Madam Laura might guess that she was lying. She might lose credits and be no further advanced with her plan to entrap Master Stéfan. Rachel closed her eyes and concentrated. She imagined Sally bending over in front of her, with her little bottom raised high, on full, public display. She saw herself with a cane in her hand, striking Sally's bare backside and watching with delight as her little white cheeks swayed and reddened. Between her legs she felt her juices begin to flow.

'She – she grabs me by the hair and pulls me over,' murmured Rachel.

'Even though you're bigger than her?' interjected Madam Laura. There was an uncertain edge to her voice, as if Rachel's answers were not adding up, despite the fact that the computer was now registering more normal arousal levels.

'Yes,' replied Rachel, 'because I don't want to be bigger. It's not fair. When you're bigger people think you want to be in charge and, and ...' She was struggling and it showed. She allowed a vision of Sally to float though her mind. She was bound and gagged and Rachel was smacking her bare bottom. Sally was wet between the legs and Rachel was bending down to lick her pussy. On the computer, the arousal levels went into overdrive.

'What are you trying to say?' asked Madam Laura.

'I – I ...' spluttered Rachel. Well, what was she trying to say? 'I want her to – to – to humiliate me.'

'Interesting,' murmured Madam Laura. She looked at Rachel and frowned. 'I would have imagined you to be more dominant.'

'It's just a front,' lied Rachel, twisting her head from side to side, her eyes still firmly shut as she thought hard. Now she was in black dominatrix gear. She thought of Michael in his flat and imagined it was *her* sitting on his face whipping his penis. She felt her lubrication flow more heavily and Madam Laura was forced to accept that either the computer was malfunctioning or she had got it very wrong on this occasion.

'So, what happens next?' she asked, studying the data and jabbing at a few keys. She examined a pie graph in one corner of the screen.

'She – she makes me stand in front of the entire class and pulls my panties down and everyone can see my bottom.'

'And do you feel embarrassed?'

'Yes, yes I do,' admitted Rachel truthfully. She realised that she would feel distinctly embarrassed. And yet at the same time there was something very exciting about the prospect. She was becoming confused. This was not supposed to be part of her fantasy, it was supposed to be a ploy to confuse Madam Laura and further her scheme to ingratiate herself with Master Stéfan. Something was going wrong. Madam Laura whistled as the arousal levels hit a new high, then frowned as they dropped almost as quickly. She leant forward and slammed the monitor with the side of her hand. Rachel jumped.

'Sorry,' said Madam Laura. 'Sometimes it's the only thing that works. This is supposed to be state of the art, yet I sometimes think I was better off with a pen and paper.'

Rachel had a sudden, unnerving thought. Perhaps she was not quite the dominant she thought she was. This was all terribly confusing. She closed her eyes sleepily and allowed herself to drift. Madam Laura was speaking again. Her voice was low and melodious and helped to put Rachel at her ease.

'What happens next?' asked Madam Laura.

Rachel did not reply. She had drifted so far away from her original concept that she could hardly remember where she was.

'She has pulled your panties down in front of the entire class,' Madam Laura helpfully reminded her. 'Now what does she do to you?'

'She – she tells me to reach back and part my buttocks so that everyone can see me properly.'

'And do you?'

'Yes. Yes, I do. I reach back and open up my bottom, and the whole class can see my – my –' She was struggling to commit herself.

'Anus?' suggested Madam Laura helpfully.

'Bum – bumhole,' groaned Rachel, lifting her hips and feeling the phallus shift inside her. 'And I feel so embarrassed . . .'

Rachel began to move her hips gently left and right. In her mind's eye, the fantasy had shifted again. Now it was Sally bending over and exposing her small behind. Rachel was kneeling between her legs and licking at the soft flesh of her buttocks.

The phallus between her legs seemed to have taken on a life of its own, twisting and turning in her capacious vagina. Somewhere at the back of her mind she realised for the first time that Madam Laura was probably operating it in some way, sometimes to stimulate her, and sometimes to bring her down again. She felt her arousal levels spiralling dangerously and it took a supreme effort to bring them under control. She wanted to come, hard and suddenly, but she knew that if she did she would lose credits and that wouldn't help her at all.

'And then what happens?' asked Madam Laura.

'I beat her,' said Rachel. 'I smack her on the bottom with my bare hand, again and again, until it gets really red and she's crying out, begging me to stop.'

Rachel twisted on the phallus, bearing down harder than ever. She felt as if she were lying in a pool of her own wetness, all warm and sticky. She could smell her juices wafting up and realised that Madam Laura must be able to smell them too. Madam Laura suddenly reached out and cupped Rachel's nearest breast in her left hand. Rachel's eyes flashed open. She hadn't expected this.

'Do you mind if I play with you while we talk?' asked Madam Laura.

'No, no, not at all, Madam,' stammered Rachel. In fact she had already warmed to Madam's touch.

'Lie back and close your eyes,' encouraged Madam Laura gently. Rachel did as she was urged and once more surrendered herself to her fantasy.

'Once you've beaten her bottom, would you rub it a little to soothe the pain?' asked Madam Laura, rubbing her own hand gently around and around Rachel's big bare breast.

'I would, Madam,' replied Rachel. 'I'd rub it around and around.'

'And would you ease your fingers into her little crack and push her buttocks apart, perhaps?'

'I would, Madam, because it's such a sweet little bottom.'

'And the anus would be quite small, very small probably and pink and shaped like a little mouth, wouldn't it?'

'Yes, Madam, such a sweet little mouth, just shaped to be kissed.'

'But you wouldn't kiss it, would you?'

Rachel's head was swimming. Something which had begun as her fantasy had been taken from her. She thought she had regained control of it but Madam Laura was leading her again.

'No, Madam, no,' she replied, allowing herself to be carried along wherever Madam Laura wanted her to go.

'So what would you do with it?' asked Madam suddenly.

Rachel froze. She had no immediate reply. There were any number of things she might have said that she wanted to do with it, but none of them were true. What she really wanted to do was to kiss it, to lick it with her tongue and feel the warm, wrinkled skin against her lips. She wanted to sniff it, and to enjoy the musky aroma and sour-sweet taste of Sally's tiny little rosebud. But she had just told Madam that she didn't want to kiss it. Something had gone wrong.

'Next question,' said Madam Laura.

Rachel suddenly realised that she had been tricked. Between her legs the phallus twitched, but now, instead of exciting her, it served only to lower her arousal levels. She felt stupid and embarrassed. She had not been true to herself. Madam Laura removed her hand from Rachel's breast and tapped more entries on to the screen.

The questions continued. Questions about her clothing likes and dislikes, whether she preferred fellatio to cunnilingus, whether she had ever been buggered, whether she liked to be taken against her will, which positions she liked best and so on. Some questions left her flat and unmoved, while others, such as when she was asked to describe in detail one of her favourite sexual experiences, left her so excited that she nearly climaxed more than once. At last the session was over, she was untied and the phallus removed. Rachel glanced down at the leather couch and felt embarrassed when she saw how wet she had made it. If she had peed herself she felt she could hardly have left it in a worse state.

'Perhaps we should get Sally to lick it dry with her tongue,' suggested Madam Laura. Despite the fact that the phallus was no longer caressing her secret places, Rachel almost stumbled with excitement.

Madam Laura smiled and made another note on the computer.

Seven

Rachel landed on her back with a sickening thud. It was not for the first time and, she reflected ruefully, it was unlikely to be for the last. She had not expected wrestling to be on the agenda at The Hall. It had been introduced into their schedule at the start of the fourth week, since when Rachel had learnt how to fall on her front, on her back and on her side. What she had not yet grasped was how to remain on her feet for any great length of time. She had learnt a variety of complicated wrestling holds: among them, the half-nelson, the body press and the neck-lock. These proved occasionally effective when fighting one of her fellow Initiates, and so far utterly useless when fighting her instructor, Madam Kyra, who now reached down to help her to her feet for the umpteenth time in as many sessions. Six weeks into her training and, like all her fellow Initiates, Rachel was now fitter, stronger and leaner than she had ever been in her life. But wrestling, she had come to suspect, was not her forte.

Madam Kyra was tall and slim, though her muscles, like those of all the Madams, were firm and well defined. Her breasts were large and heavy, with long, strawberry-shaped nipples set in the centre of her wide, dimpled areolae. Her waist was slender and served to accentuate the flat plane of her tummy. Her legs were long and well muscled, her calves strong and firm. She had the most muscular buttocks Rachel had ever seen on a woman, while her thighs looked as if they were capable of cracking coconuts. When they wrestled, Rachel had learnt quickly – and from painful experience – to avoid getting her head caught between them. Madam Kyra's uniform was even more meagre than that of her fellow Madams. She wore only a small leather thong, tied at each hip in a delicate little bow. There was a noticeable bulge between her legs. More than once, Rachel mused that Madam Kyra had either a very plump vulva or a generous abundance of pubic hair. The almost obscene skimpiness of her thong appeared to suggest the former rather than the latter.

'Wrestling,' Madam Kyra had announced at their first class, 'will teach you agility and swiftness of movement. It requires firmness and strength, and will serve as an excellent form of self-defence should you ever need it. It is not only a fine sport, but a surprisingly popular male fantasy. One of my aims will be to show you how to wrestle a man into submission, without necessarily hurting him.'

That was two weeks and fifteen two-hour sessions ago. Rachel, the wide-hipped brunette Rowena, and the tall blonde Helga, had proved themselves the most consistently successful fighters, but there had unfortunately, as yet, been so sign of any men on whom to test their new-found skills.

Madam Kyra clapped her hands loudly, and waved the Initiates into a semicircle around her. Stepping forward, she took hold of the large exercise mat and dragged it back several feet. Then she crossed to the door of the gymnasium, opened it and called to one of the attendant Madams, before returning to the centre of the gym and addressing the girls again.

'You've all worked very hard over the last fortnight, so I've laid on a small entertainment which I hope you'll enjoy.'

Two Madams entered the gym. Walking ahead of

them, securely attached to a short rein, was a well-built young man. He was immediately recognisable as a trainee Brother, dressed as he was in the familiar leather harness. Rachel and Sally had more reason than most to be aware of his identity. It was Brother Adam, the young man they had surprised on their first morning at The Hall. He seemed different, however. His muscles were bigger, his deportment more impressive and now his head was held high. Like his Sister Initiates, he had improved out of all recognition as a result of several weeks of rigorous training.

'Brother Adam and I will demonstrate the noble art of hand-to-hand combat,' explained Madam Kyra. 'The Brothers are more advanced in their training so the contest will hopefully not be too one-sided,' she added, grinning slyly at her opponent.

Rachel shifted from one buttock to the other. Her eyes were glued to Brother Adam's penis, which hung long and limp between his legs. She remembered what it had felt like to straddle it. The memory sent a frisson of delight upwards from her vulva, from where it rolled across her lower tummy. It took a supreme effort to drag her attention back to what Madam Kyra was saying.

'Brother Adam and I will wrestle until one of us forces the other into submission. Are you ready, Brother Adam?'

'Yes, Madam,' he replied, bowing slightly. As his head rose, his gaze met Rachel's. Wickedly, she parted her legs, and was happily aware of his eyes lowering for a moment, enjoying the sight of her scarcely covered vagina. It was wicked, she knew, to try to excite him like that, for if he were about to fight Madam Kyra, he would need all his wits about him.

Brother Adam and Madam Kyra stepped on to the large, foam-filled mat. Madam Kyra let her arms hang low, shaking her wrists lightly to relax her muscles.

Brother Adam raised and lowered his shoulders a number of times, and breathed deeply. His face was tight with concentration. The two combatants circled tentatively, their arms occasionally swinging from side to side, their weight shifting from one foot to the other as they first closed in, then stepped back as if awaiting the right moment to attack. Suddenly, Madam Kyra leapt forward. She seized hold of Brother Adam's hands, their fingers locking, and pushed him backward, trying to unbalance him. He lurched sideways but managed to remain upright, twisting hard and pulling Madam Kyra quickly from side to side before releasing her and jumping away. They were clearly testing each other, searching for any sign of weakness. Again, Madam Kyra leapt forward, her right arm across Brother Adam's shoulder, her left hand suddenly around his wrist. This time she pulled him towards her, throwing herself on to the mat. Bending her leg, she brought her foot up into his tummy and sent him spinning over so that he landed on his back with a dreadful thump. She rolled over in one fluid movement, her thighs splayed, wrapping her legs around his chest and squeezing tight. He brought his arms up to try to shift her, but that only enabled Madam Kyra to slip her own arms around his right shoulder which forced him back on to the mat. Brother Adam let out a squeal of pain as she stretched the ligaments in his forearm. Pinning him down with her legs and one arm, she allowed her other arm to shoot forward, towards his groin. Her fingers encircled his shaft, pushing down so that his foreskin rolled back and his penis jumped into life. Rachel leant forward, the struggle on the mat appearing suddenly more interesting. Brother Adam arched his back and rolled sharply from left to right, trying to dislodge his opponent, but she held on firmly, her long fingers still tugging at his erection.

'Submit!' she cried. 'Or I spill your seed!'

He pushed back with all his strength, forcing his buttocks up from the mat, in a desperate attempt to shift her.

'Never!' he retorted, driving upwards a second time, knocking the wind out of her. Madam Kyra's grip loosened, and Brother Adam twisted around, sensing a chance to free himself. He brought his elbows high, drove his arms outwards and broke her grip. Immediately he lunged forward, pushing Madam Kyra on to her back, executing a textbook body-press and pinning her to the mat. The match was taking a further unexpected turn. The Initiates had all assumed that Madam Kyra would triumph quickly, but her opponent was evidently making a fight of it. Well, either that, thought Rachel, or Madam Kyra was having fun at everyone's expense, especially Brother Adam's.

Almost immediately, Madam Kyra arched her well-muscled back. The tendons in her neck stood out like whipcords as, incredibly, supporting herself on one arm, she brought the other one up, wrapped her fingers around Brother Adam's nearest wrist and pulled him off balance. They were suddenly locked together, a writhing mass of flesh, each struggling for the upper hand, aware that victory was now tantalisingly close. Brother Adam brought his forearm up and pressed it across Madam Kyra's throat. His other hand shot down between her legs, searching for her panties. His fingers found the bow at her hip and scrabbled furiously. Evidently there were no limits to this fight. Again, Madam Kyra bent her legs and drove her thighs towards the ceiling. Brother Adam was caught completely off balance and, as he reached down for the bow holding her thong in place, Madam Kyra brought her legs up and wrapped them around his head, trapping him between her thighs. Rachel and the others leant forward excitedly, aware now that Madam Kyra was in a position to deliver the *coup de grâce*. She leant forward, locking her fingers at the back of Brother Adam's head, and hugging his face to her groin. Then she rolled him on to his back. Brother Adam wriggled like a landed fish, his legs kicking uselessly whilst his hands clawed at Madam Kyra's powerful thighs. He slammed his palms against her flesh several times to no avail. Madam Kyra twisted to her left, dragging her beaten opponent with her, then swung sharply right, and straddled him. Lying full length on top of his body, she took hold of his arms and forced them back, winding him with a powerful body slam. She repeated the assault twice more, before jumping to her feet. She stepped forward, grabbed his wrists and walked him across the mat, like a rag doll, before turning round and dropping her full weight on to his chest, pinning his arms to his sides with her thighs. Her panties were now hanging loosely from her hips, exposing her vulva for the first time. Rachel had been right. It was unusually plump and shaven, the labia pink, parted and glistening. Madam Kyra leant forward and took a firm hold of Brother Adam's wrists, ending all resistance.

'Submit to the Sisterhood!' she barked, looking back over her shoulder. He wriggled uselessly once or twice, but was aware now that all was lost.

'Submit!' she cried again, shifting her weight back. 'Or I will sit on your face.'

Despite the threat, Brother Adam continued to struggle, whether out of a mistaken belief that he could shift Madam Kyra or out of a desire to be sat on it was hard to tell.

'Very well!' she cried. 'You will pay the price for your continued defiance!' She shifted backwards, dropping her bottom on to Brother Adam's head, ending all further protest. Madam Kyra reached down for the bow at the left-hand side of her thong and quickly undid it. Rising for one brief moment, she tugged on the thin stretch of leather, pulling it free and tossing it aside, before dropping back on to her defeated opponent's face. Brother Adam arched his buttocks and his hands clawed the empty air. As Madam Kyra pressed down with all her weight, her beaten opponent went suddenly still. Madam wriggled from side to side, then leant forward and slapped him hard on his right hip.

'Have you given up the fight, Brother Adam?' she asked. 'Has the Brotherhood taught you nothing? Or are you enjoying yourself too much? Is that it?' She slapped him again, harder this time, and he whimpered forlornly. Madam Kyra reached out and took her victim's penis in both hands. She began to pump viciously, up and down, driving his foreskin back and forth. He arched his hips a second time, threshing his legs from left to right.

'Let's see you fountain, shall we?' cried Madam Kyra. 'I'm sure the Initiates will enjoy this, even if you do not!'

She squeezed her fingers tight around the base of his manhood and jiggled her palm up and down one last time. From somewhere between her buttocks came a muted wail of despair. Brother Adam's battle was over. Suddenly, Madam Kyra released her hold on him and sat up. Brother Adam drew in huge lungfuls of air, his chest heaving. Before he had a chance to recover further, however, Madam Kyra took hold of one of his arms and one of his legs and rolled him on to his side, wrapping her legs around his thighs and securing him in a half-nelson. Brother Adam's erect penis bobbed excitedly in the direction of the Initiates, who leant forward, greedy for a closer look.

'Sister Rowena,' said Madam Kyra, somewhat breathlessly. 'Would you finish him off for me, please?'

Rowena's face lit up. She rose and crossed to the mat, squatting beside Brother Adam. His face turned pink with embarrassment at this sudden escalation of his predicament.

'Empty him,' ordered Madam Kyra. Brother Adam

began to struggle, but Madam Kyra held him tight. Rowena reached forward and wrapped her long fingers around his penis. She began to move her hand gently. Rachel felt her stomach shudder. She was certain that she was not the only girl who wished it was her masturbating Brother Adam. He writhed about, then arched his back and swivelled his hips furiously. Rowena looked him in the eyes, smiled sweetly and squeezed one last time. With a wild flurry, his shaft began to jerk between her fingers. His semen jetted out in a series of long milky arcs, splattering his belly in big white dollops. It seemed that he would never stop coming. Even after the last violent flurry had ceased, thin gobbets of sperm wept from the eye of his shuddering cock. Rowena did not stop pumping until every last drop had been drawn.

'That's enough,' said Madam Kyra at last. Rowena reluctantly let his penis slip from her spunk-smeared hand. Madam Kyra released her powerful grip and rolled Brother Adam on to his tummy before standing up and smiling down at him in triumph. She was still the teacher and he was still the pupil. She reached down and took his outstretched hand, helping him to his feet. He was still a little groggy from his experience.

'You fought well, Brother,' she said. 'But you have a long way to go before you will best me.'

Brother Adam bowed silently. His face was damp with effort, with sweat and with Madam Kyra's juices. His penis was limp between his legs, a stark testament to his defeat. Madam Kyra picked up her thong and put it back on, tying the bows carefully.

'You may leave us now,' she said.

Brother Adam stepped back, the two Madams took hold of his arms and escorted him from the room. Rachel was sorry to see him go. She would have liked to have wrestled Brother Adam herself. Watching the contest had made her feel so randy that she wouldn't have minded if she had won or lost. Being subdued, she reflected, was evidently not without its compensations.

Rachel was aware of Master Stéfan looking her up and down. It was early evening, just after supper, and she had been unexpectedly summoned to his room. It was the first time they had been alone since her brief introduction to dungeon duties. That was the day Lady Frances had given him permission to punish her at some unspecified date in the future. She wondered if he had deliberately avoided her since then as a means of enhancing her torment. Of more concern to her, however, was that as a result she had been unable to make any progress in her attempt to unmask him as a traitor to the Sisterhood. Lying in bed at night she had mulled over a variety of approaches and had finally fixed on one.

'Master,' she began tentatively.

Master Stéfan raised his eyebrows. 'Yes?' he asked.

'I would like you to punish me, Master,' she continued, adding quietly, 'please . . .'

Master Stéfan was silent for a moment as if taken aback by Rachel's request.

'The time of your punishment is for me to decide,' he said.

'No, Master,' explained Rachel. 'I don't want you to punish me because you've been told to. I want you to punish me anyway.'

'I cannot punish you other than as already determined,' replied Master Stéfan. 'You have not committed a breach of the rules.'

'But you are a Master and I am a mere Initiate. It is your right to punish me if you wish.'

Rachel registered a slight movement in Master Stéfan's trousers, aware that he was stirring at the thought of what he might be able to do to her.

'There are rules,' he said. 'If you do not break them, I cannot – and I will not – punish you.'

Rachel fell silent. Very well, she decided, if she must break the rules to engineer an extra punishment, then she would break the rules. She stepped back and pressed her bottom up against the edge of his desk, spreading her legs wide. Master Stéfan did not disappoint her. He lowered his eyes towards her belly as Rachel reached down and pressed the fingers of her right hand up against her pubis. She probed for the small opening in her harness and found it. She felt her labia part and was surprised at how wet she actually was, her fingers slipping home easily. This whole charade was turning her on. She felt like a spy, behind enemy lines. This was a fantasy of her own making, and she was enjoying it immensely. Fear, she was discovering, could be a heady drug.

Master Stéfan stepped forward. 'What are you doing?' he asked.

'What does it look like?' she replied. 'I'm playing with my pussy. I'd rather you played with it but that's against the rules, I suppose.'

'I would advise you to stop this at once,' he said, but she knew from the tremor in his voice that it was the last thing he wanted her to do.

'I'm not going to stop,' she replied, then winced as if in pain. 'Ooh,' she moaned, 'that was good. I think I hit a nerve there all right.'

'You are making a big mistake,' he continued, moving closer and drawing himself up to his full height.

'I'm going to frig myself,' she said. 'I'm going to play with pussy until, until – oh God, this is so good!'

Rachel pushed her fingers in and out. They made little squelching noises – proof, if proof were needed, of her genuine excitement. What she was doing was so brazen, so wicked. And what's more, she was doing it in front of a man she believed to be dangerous. What if he lost control? What if she pushed him too far? It didn't bear thinking about. But even as she thought about it she found her juices flowing more freely than ever.

She withdrew her hand, raised her moist fingertips to her face and rubbed them against her nose. At the same time she pressed her other hand between her legs and continued to masturbate herself. She watched Master Stéfan's Adam's apple pump up and down. For a man used to exercising an iron control over himself, she thought, he appeared to be weakening fast.

She stretched out her arm towards him. 'Would you like to smell them?' she asked, curling her fingers in the air. 'I'm really hot now, you know. Ooh!' She bent forward slightly. 'Getting closer all the time!'

Rachel's voice shot up a notch, her eyelids closed and she rolled her head from side to side. She covered her left breast with her pussy-soaked hand, took hold of her large pink nipple and tugged it taut, before releasing it in order to palm the heavy flesh of her breast. She knew that Master Stéfan was a breast man; this whole act was meant to trap him, but suddenly she went too far. Aware of the reaction in his tight leather trousers – it looked for one awful moment as if he had a live animal in his pants – she sloshed her fingers home one last time and came without warning. Rachel threw her head back, the tendons in her neck standing out like cords as she gasped out her climax. She pumped her fingers in and out, and fell forward, mouthing obscenities, a final touch which she was certain would appeal to a man like Master Stéfan.

He reached out, took hold of her head and pulled her forward. Rachel yelled in real pain as his fingers twisted her hair into clumps and he dragged her away from the table. He pushed her to her knees, then pulled her head sharply up, so that she was forced to look into his face. His eyes blazed with a look of pure anger. And yet, behind that look, she was sure that there was another look, one of unbridled lust.

'Very well,' he declared, 'you have broken the rules. You have had an unauthorised orgasm and that is a very serious offence'.

'So you'll punish me, Master?' asked Rachel. 'Please . . .'

'Get up,' he barked.

Rachel rose to her feet, her head bowed, shifting awkwardly from foot to foot. She was a perfect picture of someone who had committed a serious wrong and knew that retribution was to follow. A fleeting image of Sally in a gymslip being beaten senseless came into her head. She was astonishing herself with the thoughts that seemed to occur to her these days.

'Very well,' conceded Master Stéfan, 'I will punish you. You are aware, I am sure, that the worst punishment, however, is the deduction of credits.'

'Yes, Master,' replied Rachel, hoping she wouldn't lose too many. If she did, it meant that a future accidental breach of the rules might render her vulnerable to further punishment.

'You will be deducted twenty-five credits.'

Rachel groaned inwardly. That was bad enough. Still, it was worth it if it helped her unmask Master Stéfan as a traitor.

'Now, as to your physical punishment, you must be taught a lesson you will not forget.'

'Yes, Master,' she replied, meeting his steely gaze with a smile. Suddenly his arm lashed out and Rachel fell backwards, stunned by the severity of the blow as the flat of his hand whipped across her left cheek and sent her flying.

'Do not cheek me, Sister!' he roared. 'I have broken more stubborn girls than you!'

Rachel fell to her knees, her head bowed subserviently. 'I'm sorry, Master,' she said. 'It won't happen again.'

'Get up,' he said, then changed his mind. 'No, wait. Remain where you are.'

He reached down and she heard the sound of a zip. 'You may raise your head,' he instructed her.

When she looked up she saw that his penis was

already erect and almost flat against his tummy. She suddenly realised how much she had excited him.

'May I kiss your manhood, Master,' asked Rachel, 'as part of my punishment?'

Master Stéfan smiled grimly. 'So you believe that kissing my penis is a punishment, do you?' he said. 'I should be insulted.'

Rachel tried backtracking quickly. 'I'm sorry, Master, I didn't mean... What I meant –'

'I know what you meant,' interrupted Master Stéfan sharply.

Rachel realised that she had gone too far. Her approach had been too blunt. She did not like the look on his face. With unexpected abruptness he replaced his penis and zipped up his pants. She wondered if it was because he was angry with her or whether he had exposed himself because it genuinely afforded him a perverse sense of pleasure. Master Stéfan was hard to fathom.

'Follow me,' he said. Rachel felt uneasy as he led her into the dungeon. What was she letting herself in for?

'Lie down,' he ordered, pulling at an array of chains attached to the ceiling. Rachel shivered as she settled herself on the cold stone floor. Master Stéfan tied a series of thick cords around each of her legs in turn, pinning her calves against her thighs. Then he dragged her back to her feet.

'Move forward,' he commanded. Rachel tried, but could only manage an awkward waddle. She fell forward on to her face and heard him laugh. Taking hold of the ends of the cords, he tied them in a secure knot, then pulled at three ceiling chains. He attached the centre one to the joined cord. The remaining two chains were fitted with small clips and these he now fastened over each of Rachel's long, pointed nipples.

'Have you perhaps changed your mind?' he asked, grinning cruelly, watching her eyes narrow with pain.

For a long moment, Rachel remained silent. There was no longer any question of her backing out. The die was cast. If she could not ensnare him now, she never would.

'No, Master,' she replied defiantly. 'Never.'

He smiled, but it was like the smile of a hungry wolf before it devours its prey.

Master Stéfan stepped back and began to turn a handle. Rachel was suddenly swivelled upside down and hoisted three or four feet into the air. The cold metal clips pulled cruelly at her nipples, bringing tears to her eyes. The blood rushed to her head and made her a little dizzy. She adjusted the angle of her neck to relieve the queasy feeling in her tummy. As Master Stéfan stepped forward and looked down at her, she realised with acute embarrassment that the manner of her suspension had opened up her vagina. He reached out his hand and palmed the heat of her vulva, before pushing two fingers inside. She mewed with genuine pleasure. The pain in her breasts had subsided and now all she was aware of was the heat welling up in her pussy. Master Stéfan stepped out of her sight for a moment. When he came back into view he was holding a long rubber tape which he proceeded to fasten around the lower half of her face. There was a ball-type device attached to it that stopped up her mouth, so that she was unable to cry out. He was holding something else in his hand, too – a double-headed duplex, presumably the female version Lady Frances had hinted at in her London dungeon. Rachel's eyes widened in horror as he attached it around her waist, easing one plug into her bumhole and the other into her vagina. He pressed a button on a small hand-held device and the two plugs whirred into action. Rachel jerked in mid-air, and the clips wrenched at her nipples. The pain began to grow, alleviated only by the pleasure in her quim and – incredibly – in her rectum.

Master Stéfan took hold of a small whip. Rachel

threw her head from side to side as she swung between extremes of pain and pleasure. The whip struck her across the left buttock, and her body shook violently. The clips tugged at her breasts. Again and again the whip struck home as she fought the rising tide between her legs. Just as she thought she would climax, the duplex switched off. Rachel began to get some inkling of the suffering Lady Frances's dungeon slaves must have endured in her service. The whip cracked home several times more. Her skin burned, the blood rushed to her head, and she would have filled the dungeon with her screams if it were not for the ball in her mouth. The duplex began to work its magic all over again. Blow upon blow rained down on her backside. Suddenly, she lurched in mid-air and came, her vulva bubbling with her juices, an indescribable sensation clawing at her belly and her bowels. Rachel was still shaking as she was lowered to the floor. She hugged herself into a small ball for a little while as Master Stéfan untied her and removed the clips and the rubber gag.

'Get up!' he ordered. Rachel struggled to her feet. The sweat was pouring from her face and she was trembling. Her nipples were swollen and throbbing and her bottom felt as if it were raw. Glancing down, she saw that her buttocks were bright red, though the skin had not been broken. Master Stéfan was an expert. He leant forward and closed his mouth over each of her breasts in turn, licking the cruelly abused flesh. She felt him suck as if he were a baby at the teat and, as he moved close, she was aware of his stiff penis pushing against the inside of his pants. She wanted to reach out and touch him but decided that, for the moment at least, she had taken things as far as she dared. It was up to Master Stéfan to make the next move.

He led her back into the office, stabbed at a button on his desk and Madam Janet appeared on cue.

'Take her away,' he instructed, with a dismissive

sweep of his hand. Rachel felt her spirits sink. All she had done, she suddenly feared, was to antagonise Master Stéfan without getting any closer to him.

'No, wait,' he added. 'I almost forgot.' He pulled open a drawer and removed two blue plastic folders. 'It's time for them to begin learning their lines.' He handed the thin binders to Madam Janet.

'Of course,' she grinned, reattaching Rachel to her rein. 'Shall we say one week?'

'One week will be most acceptable,' replied Master Stéfan.

Rachel watched as the pair exchanged a weak enigmatic smile. Sometimes she got the feeling that there was something going on between them. No, that was daft, she told herself, and dismissed the thought at once. For there to be something going on, one of them would have to have feelings, and she doubted that was very likely.

After Rachel had been taken back to her room, Master Stéfan got up, walked quickly over to the door and locked it. Crossing back to his desk he dropped to his knees, pressed his face to the warm oak and took a deep breath. It was where Rachel had begun to masturbate herself, and though the wood was now dry her musky scent still lingered. He reached down between his legs and unzipped himself. His heart began to beat more rapidly. A bead of sweat broke out on his forehead and ran down the side of his face. He had wanted to take her in the dungeon, while she had been trussed up and helpless, and had so nearly succumbed to his baser instincts. Perhaps Madam Janet was right. He would have to be careful. It was a dangerous game. It always was. He breathed again, savouring the last traces of Rachel's aroma as he took his penis between his strong fingers and began to pump himself fiercely.

Eight

Helga and Candie had gone missing. Well, that was not strictly correct. They were not so much missing as just nowhere to be found. Five days earlier, Maria and Shirley had been absent for a whole day, and on Monday it had been the turn of the trio, Evie, Tina and Ruth. They had been absent for only twenty-four hours, but it had sent a buzz through the rest of the group. No one knew where the first pair had gone, and though Sally and Rachel mentioned it in private, there was no open discussion. They had assumed at first that the girls had been expelled, for there seemed to be no other explanation. When they had reappeared the following morning, their revised guess was that they had been punished in some way. The girls said nothing and no one asked. No one said they couldn't, it just seemed to be accepted that some matters were not up for public debate. When the second pair had temporarily disappeared, the curiosity of the remaining Initiates went into overdrive. It was developing into something out of an Agatha Christie novel. There were only four of them left now, and they wondered whose turn it would be next.

Meanwhile, Rachel had received no further summonses from Master Stéfan. Six days had passed without any contact. There had been no acting classes pencilled into the syllabus for the past week and Rachel had not wanted to press her cause too hard by engineering a breach of the rules in case she ruined her plan by appearing over-eager. Nonetheless, as each day passed, the fear that she had already overstepped the mark began to weigh more heavily with her.

At the same time, she and Sally had been hard at work. The folders that Master Stéfan had handed to Madam Janet contained detailed scripts designed to put their new-found skills to the test in a carefully staged and supervised setting. They were to act out a private, tailor-made fantasy, written, they were told, by an associate Brother, one of a small group of client contacts who helped finance the Sisterhood's work in return for the fulfilment of their own particular requirements.

'It's absolutely vital that nothing goes wrong,' emphasised Madam Janet, handing over the scripts. 'This is not just a bit of fun: this is part of your course work and you will be rigorously assessed on it.'

They had read through the scripts quickly and had been surprised by both the storyline and detail.

'On no account will you discuss this with your fellow Initiates,' warned Madam Janet. 'They will have their own assignments in due course.'

Finding the time had not been easy. There was no let-up in their normal classes, which had grown increasingly more intense as the weeks passed.

'If I hear one more word about Kierkegaard's analysis of the Socratic paradox, I'm going to hold my breath until I pass out!' groaned Sally, flopping down on to the bed beside Rachel. It was the evening before they were due to act out their playlet. Neither girl was happy she had yet mastered her lines and certainly neither had the energy to do any more work.

'I think, therefore I have a headache,' laughed Rachel, lying back and stretching her legs. 'I bet you're looking forward to tomorrow,' she added.

Sally grinned sheepishly. 'It should be fun.'

'More fun for you than for me,' complained Rachel. She turned to Sally, raising herself on one arm, looking into her friend's soft, blue eyes. 'It's great here, isn't it?' she said.

Sally's face lit up. 'Yes it is,' she replied. 'I didn't think it would be at first, but now I'm here, I just know it's what I've always wanted.'

Rachel leant over and kissed Sally on her cheek. 'Will you do something for me?' she asked. She felt her heart beginning to race.

'What?' asked Sally quietly.

Rachel lowered her face so that their cheeks brushed softly together. 'Will you bring me off?'

Sally looked startled and Rachel immediately regretted what she had asked. 'I'm sorry,' she said, pulling away, 'I don't know what came over me.' She felt her face turn the colour of beetroot. If they hadn't been linked together, she would have got up and hidden in the other room for the rest of the evening.

'Don't be daft,' said Sally. 'I'm not offended. I'm just surprised it's taken you so long to ask.' She snuggled up close. 'We've been sleeping together for the last six weeks, silly. Don't you think I've wanted to ask you the same question?'

'I didn't know,' confessed Rachel. 'I just thought, well, neither of us are, well . . .' She didn't quite know how to finish the sentence, so Sally did it for her.

'Lesbians?' she smiled. 'No, of course we're not. It doesn't mean to say we can't have a bit of fun together, though. Especially as the men are a bit thin on the ground these days.'

Rachel put her arm around Sally and held her close. She had wanted to do that for ages and, now that she had finally had the courage to do so, it felt good. Very good.

'Sisters are supposed to have open minds about everything,' Sally reminded her. 'As long as it doesn't hurt anyone, where's the harm?' She raised her head and whispered, 'I'd love to bring you off.'

Rachel's heart had begun racing all over again. A familiar feeling clawed at her belly and her pussy was beginning to throb.

'There's just one thing,' cautioned Sally. 'We're not supposed to have orgasms without permission, are we?'

'I'll be very quiet,' promised Rachel.

'You will not,' retorted Sally, grinning. 'Or I'll think I haven't done it properly.'

They rolled apart, laughing out loud. Rachel sat up. 'I suppose we'll have to ask Madam Janet,' she said, looking at the red button on the wall. They had never had to use it before. Still, there was a first time for everything. Their concern proved academic, however, for as if on cue the door suddenly opened and Madam Janet came in. They jumped up at once, as if they'd been caught in some illicit act which, Rachel realised, they almost had been. She suddenly realised that, if she hadn't let Sally talk her out of it, they'd have been threshing around at that very moment.

Before either of them had a chance to speak, Madam Janet stepped forward and removed the chain linking them together. She snapped her rein to Rachel's neckband and said, 'You have an appointment, my girl. With a man who does not like to be kept waiting.'

Ten minutes later, Rachel was standing in the middle of Master Stéfan's private dungeon, ruefully reflecting that, without this unwanted interruption, Sally might now be bringing her to a climax. On the other hand, if Master Stéfan had deemed it necessary to summon her to his room at this time of the day, and the night before her acting assessment, he must have wanted to see her very much. And if she were to expose him as a traitor, the more she was in his loathsome company, the better.

'I have been considering how we might improve your

ability with the whip,' he began, preceding her towards the low bench in the middle of the dungeon. She recognised the familiar sight of the dummy, laid out on its back. She had not previously seen its penis at such close quarters and was pleasantly surprised to note how much it resembled the real thing, even down to its carefully crafted veins and swollen glans. She indulged in a moment's wishful thinking and imagined herself astride it, bouncing up and down and generally enjoying herself.

'I would like you to straddle the dummy's face,' said Master Stéfan.

Rachel had not expected this. The head, too, looked very real, and it was obvious that whoever had designed it had gone to great pains to create something as lifelike as possible. It could almost be a real man's face she thought, as she swung one thigh over its head and assumed a squatting position. Master Stéfan's right hand lashed out, striking her hard across the right buttock. Rachel yelped.

'Please sit on the face properly,' he commanded.

Rachel settled back. She felt a little embarrassed. Acting like this in front of Master Stéfan was mildly degrading but then, she reminded herself, it was all part of her training. She must put such thoughts aside if she were not only to progress through the Sisterhood, but also unmask Master Stéfan.

'That's better. Make yourself as comfortable as possible,' advised Master Stéfan, his attention fixed on the electronic monitor.

Rachel shuffled back and forth, but trying to find a relaxed position was almost impossible. There was no give to the dummy's head and its nose kept sticking into her. In the end she wriggled back, so that the nose nudged gently between her labia, penetrating her vulva like a miniature penis. That was definitely the most comfortable position, she decided, if a little naughty.

She felt quite moist already and hoped she wasn't going to embarrass herself further.

'Are you sitting comfortably?' There was a sarcastic edge to Master Stéfan's voice, which Rachel suspected was intentional. Of course she was not sitting comfortably, far from it. Yet the longer she sat there the more her juices began to flow and, the wetter she became, the easier it was to straddle the hard plastic protrusion that passed for the dummy's nose.

'Yes, thank you,' she replied quietly.

'Please rock back and forth,' he said, surveying her with his cold blue eyes. Rachel allowed her own eyes to alight for the briefest moment on Master Stéfan's trousers. There was an unmistakable bulge that had not been there before. It was obvious that he was becoming aroused. He stepped out of sight, though she could tell from the sound of his breathing that he was close behind her.

Suddenly there was a harsh slap across her back and Rachel yelped out in pain.

'I said rock back and forth!' he repeated, loudly this time, the anger in his voice undisguised.

Rachel began to move more vigorously. It was so humiliating. She was lubricating freely now, soaking the dummy's artificial face; aware that each time she slid forward, Master Stéfan was able to view the evidence of her excitement. Each time she moved back she aroused herself further still as the hard plastic pressed against her clitoris and made her little nubbin tingle with pleasure. Master Stéfan placed his hands firmly on her hips. Rachel wondered what was going to happen next. Her eyes were transfixed by the fake phallus, and she began to imagine what it would feel like to lower herself on to its hard, plastic length. Master Stéfan pushed down, holding her firmly in position. She could feel the strength in his arms. The dummy's nose was now firmly embedded in her vagina. Had she wished to raise herself off it, which she didn't, it would almost certainly have proved impossible.

'I want you to wriggle,' he said, 'from side to side. Imagine you are sitting on a real man's face and are trying to arouse yourself. Imagine it is his tongue inside you if that helps.'

Rachel's heart began to pound against her ribcage. She felt giddy with pleasure, but embarrassed, too. She kept telling herself that she mustn't be so self-conscious and that this was all part of her training. If she wanted to rid herself of all inhibitions then she must empty her mind of all thoughts other than those that gave her pleasure. Master Stéfan's hands moved around her hips, pulling at her flesh, gently massaging as she rocked to and fro. Her tummy felt as though it were melting and a familiar warm glow began to spread across her groin. She clutched the whip handle hard as she fought to ward off the rising tide of pleasure. Master Stéfan was speaking. Wrapped up in the joy of the moment, Rachel had to concentrate hard on what he was saying.

'I want you to try and hit the red line on the dummy's phallus,' he instructed. Rachel took a deep breath. He must be joking, she thought! Her mind was on other things. Much more of this and she would definitely climax. Master Stéfan's fingers dug hard into her flesh. He pushed violently back and forth and her bottom shook, pressing the dummy's nose hard against her clitoris, dragging her towards the brink. She moaned and let her head loll back. This was madness! What was he up to? Did he want her to lash out with the whip or did he want to make her come?

'I can't think straight,' she whimpered. 'Oh, God, this is so good!' Her head fell forward and she bit into her lower lip in a desperate attempt to steady herself.

'It is essential that you retain full control of your body at all times,' said Master Stéfan. 'A Sister can always pull back. It is vital to your training that you learn to act while experiencing near-orgasmic feelings.'

That was easier said than done, thought Rachel. At this moment, all she wanted to do was let herself go. Far from wanting to whip the dummy's penis she wanted to impale herself upon it. Master Stéfan released one buttock, but only so that he could crack the flat of his hand across Rachel's quivering flesh. It did the trick, bringing her up short, clearing her mind for one brief instant. She threw her right hand forward. The whip curled through the air, flicking the tip of the fake penis, missing the red line completely. The handle buzzed and this time a small shock stung her flesh. Again she lashed forward, but missed once more. The electric shock burnt her arm. She took a deep breath and tried to steady herself, shutting out the blend of pain and pleasure that was wracking her body. She tried for a third time: her right hand flashed forward and the black threads whipped at the dummy's huge erect shaft. This time there was no buzz and no shock. Rachel froze. She had hit the red line exactly. She felt so pleased with herself that she wanted to jump up and punch the air. Master Stéfan's hands left her hips and wormed their way around her breasts. His fingers dug into her flesh, his nails scratching at her nipples. Through his pants, Rachel felt his penis press into the small of her back. It was big and hard and she could feel it throbbing against her.

'Excellent!' declared the voice at her ear. 'Excellent.'

Rachel leant back, enjoying the sensation of Master Stéfan's hands roaming over her flesh. At that moment she didn't care how much she loathed or feared him, she just wanted to be pleasured. She desperately wanted to orgasm and if it had to be with Master Stéfan, so be it. Besides, she was certain that if he fucked her once, it would strengthen her hold over him.

Master Stéfan's hands left her breasts, swooping low around her waist and thighs. He hoisted her into the air with surprising ease, carried her across the room and set her down in front of the second upright dummy on whom she had first practised her less-than-perfect whipping skills.

'Do not move,' he told her, reaching towards the ceiling. Rachel looked up and saw him unwind two familiar chains from somewhere above her head. There were cuffs on the end of each chain. He snapped them around her wrists then pulled on the chains, raising her arms until she was on tiptoe. He moved to Rachel's rear, cupped her buttocks in his hands and lifted her legs up, walking forward with her towards the dummy. Rachel's vulva was now at the same level as the dummy's penis and, as it touched the warm rounded plastic, she whimpered with unembarrassed delight. Master Stéfan had not finished with her, however. Incredibly, he continued to walk her forward until she had taken the dummy's entire length inside her.

'Wrap your legs around its waist,' instructed Master Stéfan in a very matter-of-fact voice. Rachel sometimes felt that he possessed less emotion than a machine, but at this moment she was enjoying herself so much that she didn't care.

'We will now test your strength and flexibility,' said Master Stéfan.

Rachel wondered what he had in mind, apart from any perverse satisfaction he might get from watching her hanging in mid-air, impaled on an artificial penis.

'Grip tightly,' he ordered. 'I am about to let go.'

Suddenly she was hanging in mid-air, her arms stretched towards the dark roof of the dungeon, her neck bent backwards, her eyes staring straight up. The blood ran to her head and made her feel dizzy. She could feel the muscles straining in her neck and she wondered how long she could sustain this position. Master Stéfan reached for his clipboard and made a few notes. He came back into her line of vision and looked her up and down.

'Push towards the dummy, please,' said Master Stéfan.

Rachel took a deep breath and urged her lower half forward. It wasn't easy and she quickly realised that if she pushed too hard there was a reverse shunt that pulled her in the opposite direction. Gentle rocking motions were necessary, though they badly stretched the muscles in her arms and shoulders. Rachel found that, by squeezing her vaginal muscles, she was able to maintain a tighter grip on the rubber shaft, which was just as well because, perversely, her increasing wetness now worked against her. It didn't help that she had not been given permission to jettison the whip which felt increasingly heavy in her hand.

'Are you becoming excited again?' asked Master Stéfan, continuing to make notes on his clipboard.

'Yes,' gasped Rachel truthfully.

'What does it feel like?' he asked.

'It – it feels good,' she stammered.

Master Stéfan slipped the pen into a sheath at the top of the clipboard, brought his right hand up and smacked her hard on the left buttock.

'Ow!' she cried. 'That hurt!'

His hand flashed out a second time and Rachel's bottom quivered like jelly. He's damn well enjoying this, the bastard, she thought.

'Answer the question,' he insisted calmly, taking out the pen and making a short note as he spoke. 'I wish you to be specific about the pleasure you feel. Are you close to reaching an orgasm?'

'Yes!' replied Rachel angrily. She had almost lost her hold on the artificial penis in the aftermath of the blow from Master Stéfan, and had to tense her vaginal muscles hard to prevent herself breaking contact.

'Then please control yourself,' he said.

'I'm not sure that I can!' Rachel's voice rose an octave as she swung towards the dummy, surrendering to the sheer delight of the thick rubber wedge filling her to the hilt.

This time Master Stéfan did not pause to put his pen away, but instead brought the underside of the clipboard down across her left hip. It was a vicious blow. Rachel squealed and swung sideways. The muscles in her vagina went into spasm, clamping and unclamping about the rubber penis. She screwed up her eyes and bit her lip hard, drawing blood; the pain of her self-inflicted wound cutting in only a moment before she would have allowed herself to climax.

As her body began to loll back into position, she chewed her bruised flesh and tried to steady herself. She started counting backwards to lower her arousal. She dreaded to think what punishment Master Stéfan would mete out if she were to have an unauthorised orgasm.

'While maintaining your present position,' continued Master Stéfan, stepping out of her line of sight, 'I wish you to attempt another stroke on the penis of dummy number one.'

Rachel was stunned. This was ridiculous. She could hardly hit the target in an upright position. How was she expected to do better with it now located behind her, while she hung suspended from the ceiling, impaled on the second dummy's penis? She turned her head slowly, the only part of her body she could move, and even that was difficult. Master Stéfan was standing to one side of her. He had placed his clipboard under one arm, unzipped himself and was stroking his penis between his fingers. Rachel could smell his warm skin as she took aim. Her arm movement was very restricted and all she could really do was flick her hand. She was unable to get her full strength behind the blow and the lash fell short by several inches, sparing her the pain of an electric shock.

Master Stéfan held the tip of his penis between forefinger and thumb. He squeezed, and a tiny pearl of pre-come oozed out. He rubbed his finger over the top of his cock, smearing it with the tiny jewel of semen, then reached forward and wiped it across Rachel's lower lip. Instinctively, she ran her tongue around the outside of her mouth. Her pussy was wetter than ever, her grip on the dummy's penis increasingly fragile.

'Try again, please,' he ordered. His voice wavered and she heard his sharp intake of breath as he shifted awkwardly from one leg to the other, struggling now to control his own arousal.

Rachel tensed herself, drew her right hand back as far as she could and let fly with all her strength. The whiplash touched the dummy's left thigh, just missing her intended target and the shock hit her with unexpected force. She gripped the whip handle tightly and groaned, her body shaking, her pussy spasming around the rubber shaft.

Master Stéfan made a hurried note on his clipboard. 'A very reasonable attempt,' he observed, 'in the circumstances. One more attempt and we will bring this lesson to a conclusion.'

Rachel stiffened, struggling to maintain her increasingly precarious position. Her arms were aching and the muscles in her shoulders trembled with exhaustion. The rubber penis had aroused her to such a degree that she desperately wanted to climax now. She might not trust Master Stéfan, but she wanted him. She wanted him to pull her off the dummy and enter her with his large, erect weapon before it was too late. There was nothing like fatigue to dampen sexual ardour and she was tiring fast.

Rachel drew her arm back, gathered all her wits and let fly one last time. The tip of the lash struck the second dummy's penis and this time there was no electric shock.

'Excellent,' said Master Stéfan. 'You are to be congratulated.'

Praise from Master Stéfan? Rachel could hardly

believe her ears. Yet it was hardly more surprising than the fact that she had hit the target. Perhaps she had a talent for dungeon duties, after all.

'You deserve a reward,' he continued. 'I'm sure you are very excited so if you can finish yourself, you have my permission.'

Rachel knew that all she had to do was wriggle once or twice on the rubber phallus and she would come. Yet the thought of doing it so coldly and clinically in front of Master Stéfan made her hold back. It was, she realised, absolutely ridiculous, and yet once again she felt embarrassed.

Master Stéfan, it appeared, could read minds. 'You have a problem with this. Very well,' he said, 'do not worry.'

He reached for his pen and Rachel went cold. She could see the report now. *The girl is too inhibited to continue as an Initiate.* Well, she wasn't, and she would show him she wasn't.

'No!' she exclaimed. Master Stéfan looked up in surprise, his pen poised in mid-sentence.

'I want to finish myself off,' she said. 'If that's all right with you, Master.'

His eyes narrowed for a moment and he put the pen back into its clip. 'Very well,' he said quietly. 'Please continue.'

Rachel felt suddenly very bold. It was time to bait the hook. 'May I ask a favour, Master?' she said.

'By all means,' he replied.

'Would you let me fellate you while I masturbate myself on this thing? It would be nice to include a human touch.'

From the way his eyes suddenly widened, it was clear that Master Stéfan had not anticipated Rachel's request. She realised she had caught him off balance and it pleased her.

'I see no objection,' he answered quietly.

'Will you come in my mouth?' she asked him.

'Would you like me to?' he responded, a little too quickly thought Rachel, for a man truly in control of himself. She paused for a moment before replying.

'Surprise me,' she said.

A weak smile flitted briefly across Master Stéfan's chiselled features and Rachel knew she had given him the right answer. He was circling her baited hook and was about to bite. She parted her lips as wide as she could and Master Stéfan pushed himself into her in one fluid movement. It was not the first time she had fellated him, yet she was as impressed as ever by the size of his penis. She hoped he wouldn't thrust too much. He was already touching the back of her throat. If he went much further she would gag. She began to rock back and forth on the rubber phallus. Her body was hurting all over but, by raising herself from time to time, she could use different muscles in her arms and was able to keep up a regular rhythm. Master Stéfan remained motionless, content to rely on Rachel's mouth movements to stimulate his penis. She enjoyed the realisation that it was she who was in control now. Instead of his cock fucking her mouth, she was using her mouth to fuck his cock. It was a fine distinction, but one she relished. Suddenly she was coming. Though she hadn't thought it would take long, the abruptness of her release still took her by surprise. She would have opened her mouth to shriek but it was filled with Master Stéfan. Instead, she sucked in her breath furiously, emitting delighted whooping squeals around his penis. Whether the moment was of his own choosing or whether it was the sight of Rachel swinging back and forth in the throes of orgasm that took him over the edge, she couldn't be sure, but suddenly Master Stéfan exploded, too. Thick wads of semen jetted into the back of her throat and she almost gagged as it struck her tonsils. As her own orgasm began to subside, Rachel recovered herself enough to begin sucking gently, milking the huge penis until, though it still pulsed with excitement, it had given up its complete store of cream.

At last Master Stéfan pulled away, and allowed her off the dummy, releasing her arms. He threw her a sudden glance as she rubbed her aching wrists, then looked away like an embarrassed schoolboy. Did he want to say something to her? She wasn't sure. Perhaps he didn't know what to say. His feelings had been aroused; he had crossed the divide and didn't know what to do next. Rachel's heart skipped a beat. She had made no plans for this moment, simply content to plot her way into his presence and hope that nature would take its course. On the spur of the moment she raised her hands to her breasts, cupping them in her palms. She watched him struggle to avert his eyes as she squeezed her nipples, palming her flesh up and out, deliberately flaunting herself. She knew that one of the most exciting things a woman could do was to stroke herself in the presence of a man who was unable to touch her yet wanted to. It was what made bondage games so exciting. And if she was sure about anything, it was that the Master was very much into bondage, and he wanted to touch her desperately.

'You must leave now,' he declared, turning away. They were back in his office. He reached out, his fingers hovering over the button that would summon Madam Janet. He hesitated. It was the first time Rachel had seen the Master unsure of himself. Would he, wouldn't he? Should she try to take it a stage further? But what could she do? It was out of the question to proclaim undying love, that was not what he would want. But he did want her, that much was obvious.

'Use me, Master,' she said softly. 'Please ...' The words were out before she had really given them much thought. It was just instinct, really. She saw his fingers draw back for a moment before he took a deep breath and regained control of himself. His index finger stabbed the red button. The door opened and Madam Janet entered. Master Stéfan sat down and opened his book, deliberately ignoring her. Rachel was dismissed. But as Madam Janet led her back to her room, she knew that she had taken a huge leap forward. Master Stéfan was no longer out of her reach. She had hooked him. Now it was surely a matter of time before she could begin reeling him in.

Nine

'Good morning, Madam Yolanda!'

It was the second class of the day. Rachel enjoyed music but had to admit that until recently her knowledge had been rather limited. Madam Yolanda had changed all that. Her lessons ranged widely, from jazz to hip-hop, from popular to baroque, and from blues to Stravinsky. Not that Rachel had taken to Stravinsky, a composer she felt would be better categorised under 'noises I prefer to the sound of fingernails scratching on a blackboard'. Still, she reflected, to have liked everything suggested a lack of discrimination. It was not necessary to like everything, as Madam Yolanda had stressed from the start, but it was essential to understand it. The circles in which they would move, should they graduate as full Sisters, required nothing less. Further reflection was abruptly curtailed as the classroom door opened and two women entered. Rachel recognised Madam Saskia and Madam Kaye at once. In the absence of Master Stéfan, as the girls were well aware, these two fulfilled a disciplinary role. The fact that they were putting in a joint appearance did not augur well. They exchanged a quick word with Madam Yolanda, who immediately turned and addressed the class.

'I am afraid it's been brought to my attention that we have a miscreant amongst us.'

A deathly hush descended. No girl wanted it to be her, and each feared that it was.

'Will you please stand up, Sister Sally,' said Madam Yolanda.

Rachel could hardly believe her ears. Sally rose uneasily to her feet. She was visibly shaking. Madam Saskia and Madam Kaye stepped forward. They unclipped Sally from Rachel, grabbed hold of her by the arms and marched her to the front of the class. Rachel felt herself stir in her seat. She suddenly felt very protective. Sally was her friend and she was in trouble. And yet she knew that there was nothing she could do to help her.

'You do know the rules about having an orgasm without permission?' enquired Madam Saskia loudly.

'Yes, Madam,' whispered Sally, her eyes nervously scanning the floor.

'Then why have you broken the rule?' asked Madam Saskia.

'I haven't, Madam,' protested Sally, 'I haven't!'

'Don't lie, girl!' exclaimed Madam Saskia. 'You masturbated yourself during your partner's absence yesterday evening!' Her hand shot out, catching Sally's left cheek. It was a sharp but relatively harmless blow, the shock of receiving it more disturbing than the pain it inflicted, but it confirmed that Sally was in serious trouble.

'I – I'm sorry Madam,' said Sally, her lips trembling. Rachel thought how small and vulnerable her friend looked. Madam Saskia reached out and took hold of Sally's chin, tilting it up so they were facing each other eye to eye.

'You were warned on your first day that such activities were forbidden. Is that not so?'

Sally nodded rapidly. There were tears in her eyes. 'Yes, yes, Madam,' she stammered.

'We are not insensitive to your needs. What we will not tolerate is deception!'

Sally's head flew round and her eyes met Rachel's.

There was a look of horror in her face, as if to say, help me, please!

Rachel felt dreadful. Sally had been asleep when she had returned from her meeting with Master Stéfan the previous evening. Now she knew why. She had left Sally in a state of arousal and the poor girl had clearly succumbed to her urges. It was *her* fault. If she hadn't asked Sally to masturbate her, she might not have become excited, and if she hadn't become excited she wouldn't be in trouble now. Rachel knew it should be her taking any punishment meted out, not Sally. But she also knew that there was nothing she could do about it. Her friend was on her own now, no one could help her.

Madam Saskia grabbed hold of Sally's chin and twisted her face round. 'Do you deny the offence?' she asked.

'No, Madam,' replied Sally softly.

'Very well, then you will accept the need for punishment.'

'Yes, Madam,' conceded Sally.

Madam Saskia turned towards Madam Yolanda. 'I'm sorry to interrupt your class like this,' she said. 'But if you will gather the girls and bring them along to the Punishment Room we can get this unpleasantness over with as soon as possible.'

'Certainly,' replied Madam Yolanda, turning and addressing the class. 'You heard Madam Saskia,' she said. 'We will adjourn to the Punishment Room where our miscreant will receive the treatment she so richly deserves.'

It was the first time any of the girls had heard of the Punishment Room. They had most of them had a taste of the tawse, either from their Madams or from Master Stéfan, but to learn that there was a room set aside for the express purpose did not seem to bode well. Several minutes later they had reassembled in a large, circular chamber on the far side of The Hall. The room was windowless, with plain pink walls and dull, concealed lighting. Sally was made to stand between two upright pillars. Her arms and legs were spread apart and her wrists and ankles strapped into thick leather hoops. Having satisfied herself that Sally was securely restrained, Madam Kaye stepped forward and began to fit something dark and black around Sally's waist. Rachel recognised the duplex at once. Sally yelped with surprise as Madam Saskia fed the twin protrusions into her body, before tightening a thin pair of straps and stepping back to admire her handiwork.

'I want you all to take note of what happens when you break the rules,' she said, turning towards the other Initiates. 'I trust this will encourage the rest of you to keep to the straight and narrow.'

Madam Kaye held a small remote control in her hand. At a nod from Madam Saskia, she grinned and pressed a button. The duplex suddenly whirred into life and Sally's hips swivelled from side to side.

Rachel was puzzled. She couldn't yet see how this constituted a punishment. From the little mewing noises she was making and the way her hips were jiggling, Sally was clearly in seventh heaven. In no time at all, she climaxed, throwing her head back and emitting a wild shriek of pleasure. Rachel felt her labia swell and moisten as her excitement mounted. Much more of this, she thought, fidgeting in her seat, and she would come, too.

The instant Sally reached orgasm, Madam Kaye lashed her across the buttocks with her tawse. Sally screamed and her body shook furiously. Her little breasts bobbed up and down and Rachel had a fleeting image of cupping and squeezing the seductive little orbs in her hands. Between Sally's splayed legs, the rubber plugs continued to whirr. Her breath was coming in short, sharp gasps now, partly the result of the whip and partly the aftermath of her climax. Madam Kaye stepped forward and addressed the class, while Madam Saskia took up a position at Sally's rear.

'As you know,' explained Madam Kaye, 'the duplex can stimulate orgasm and then cut off at the moment of climax. However, this can be overridden and the subject –' she turned back briefly to Sally – 'or shall we say, victim –' she added, smiling grimly – 'can be forced to spend herself whether she likes it or not.'

Rachel shifted uncomfortably in her seat. She squeezed her thighs together, surrendering to the warm feeling that was beginning to spread upwards across her belly. She had a bad feeling about her friend's fate. But in spite of her misgivings, the sight of Sally, helpless and tormented like this, was beginning to turn her on.

A series of shrill moans filled the air as Sally whimpered towards her second climax. She shook her head from side to side, dribble running from the corner of her mouth as the thrill of arousal coursed through her. Madam Kaye was still speaking, though Rachel knew she could not be the only woman finding it hard to concentrate on Madam's words while watching Sally writhe in front of them.

'We have cut out the override facility on the duplex. Sister Sally will experience the pleasures of unrelenting climax. However, every time she reaches orgasm, she will be beaten.'

Behind her, Sally cried out and came a second time. Her squeal of delight was replaced by a shriek of pain as Madam Saskia brought the tawse down across her exposed rump. Sally swore and whimpered. Tears ran down her cheeks as the duplex continued to whirr cruelly between her legs. Rachel felt sick to her stomach. This was inhuman. Sally was going to be made to climax time after time. It was obvious that, after the first two or three, the pleasure would turn to torment as it always did. Sally would surely crack under the strain.

'Sister Sally may end her ordeal at any moment,' continued Madam Kaye. 'Alternatively, she may fight the rising pleasure in her vagina. That may give her some respite. If she chooses to end her ordeal she will leave the Sisterhood forthwith.'

Madam Kaye turned back to Sally who was now squealing like a baby, her face contorted with pleasure and pain as she fought the onset of another climax.

'It's entirely up to you, Sister Sally,' said Madam Kaye.

Sally threw her head back. 'Oh my God!' she screamed and her entire body shook furiously as another orgasm ripped through her groin. Madam Saskia brought the whip down three times in quick succession.

'I forgot to tell you,' added Madam Kaye. 'Every time you climax, the whipping increases by one lash.'

Sally was shaking horribly and her breath was escaping in short sharp gasps. Her little breasts were swinging left and right as she swayed under the lash of the whip and the aftermath of orgasm. Rachel saw the look of intense concentration in Sally's face as she tried to steel her body to resist the next wave of pleasure already clawing at her vulva. Her eyes narrowed and she bit hard into her lower lip. Her cheeks were wet and her eyelashes matted with tears. As the duplex continued to vibrate cruelly in Sally's pussy and rectum, Rachel found herself both horrified and excited at the same time. Though she felt sorry for Sally, she could not deny that the sight of another woman trussed up so helplessly, willingly submitting to such an outlandish torture, was arousing her. She felt her oily secretions ooze out on to the seat. Looking at the other girls she could see that they were every bit as excited as she was. Rowena was staring open-mouthed and seemed to have stopped breathing, Maria was rocking gently from buttock to buttock, while Helga pulled idly at her left nipple. Rachel felt her tummy perform several somersaults while, in front of her, Sally began to lose the battle to control her own arousal.

'Oh, no, no, please, no, dear God, no!' she screamed, then shuddered pitifully as yet another orgasm tore through her belly. Again and again Madam Saskia rained down whip strokes on her raw backside.

Madam Kaye pressed her face to Sally's, extended her tongue and licked a running tear from her cheek. 'Just say the word and it's all over,' she whispered.

Sally screwed up her face and took a deep breath. 'No!' she spat back. 'Never!'

Madam Kaye smiled grimly. 'Your arm must be tiring, Madam Saskia,' she said, turning towards her colleague. 'Let me relieve you of your task.'

Rachel lost count of how many times Sally came after that, and of how many times her backside was cruelly flogged. Yet she would not submit, in spite of both the pain and the pleasure sweeping through her tiny, tormented frame. Then suddenly, it was over. Incredibly, Sally was in the throes of yet another climax when Madam Kaye pressed a button on her remote control and the duplex fell silent. Sally's orgasm died in mid-flow and her neck flopped forward, her eyes blood red, her face soaked in her own tears.

Madam Saskia and Madam Kaye untied her quickly and helped her down. Now that her ordeal was over, they became immediately concerned and solicitous. It was hard to believe they were the same two Madams who had exulted in torturing Sally for the past hour. They lay her flat on the floor, propped up her head with cushions and applied a soothing gel to her tender backside.

Madam Yolanda stood up and addressed the class. 'The punishment is over,' she declared. 'We will now return to the classroom and complete our lesson.'

Rachel didn't see Sally for the next two days. Madam Janet told her that she was recovering in another part of The Hall. She was well, but needed rest before returning to her training. Sally's 'misbehaviour', as Madam Janet described it, meant a slight rescheduling of events. The staged assessment had had to be postponed for forty-eight hours. Still, reflected Rachel, at least it gave both girls some extra time in which to ensure that they had learnt their lines properly. It was important to be positive, Rachel told herself, before quietly adding that she was positive she would never indulge in any secret masturbation during her remaining time at The Hall.

Ten

Rachel and Sally were completely naked. No reins, no chains, no harnesses. They were standing in an unfamiliar room, somewhere below ground level. Madam Janet was seated at a crescent-shaped control area, studying an array of monitors. She was flicking switches and pressing buttons, satisfying herself that all systems were functioning correctly. Rachel and Sally looked past her to a wide expanse of glass, a window into a second, larger chamber. It was the stage on which they would act out the client's fantasy: an everyday sitting room, with settee, telly, stereo and all the familiar rubbish strewn across chairs and floor. The sole departure from normality was the inclusion of four leather straps fixed into the floor beside the coffee table.

'Are you sure you've mastered your scripts?' asked Madam Janet, stabbing at a keyboard and adjusting the brightness levels on the nearest monitor.

They both nodded and replied together, 'Yes, Madam.'

Madam Janet looked up and smiled. She enjoyed having their respect, even if it was forced upon them. She crossed the room and opened the doors of a large white cabinet.

'Here are your costumes,' she said, pulling out two hangers of clothes. 'Remember,' said Madam Janet, as they dressed. 'Your actions will be video-recorded and assessed by the Examining Tutors. Though you're both doing well so far, at least one of the other groups has achieved almost maximum marks for this exercise. You must give it your best.'

Sally was playing a role that Rachel felt was made for her. She had on a tight black tank top that hugged her breasts and emphasised her small, firm curves. Her midriff was bare and below that she wore a wide, pleated skirt that ended just above the knees. Madam Janet lifted up the hem and examined the thick, green cotton panties she was wearing underneath.

'Excellent,' she remarked. 'And how old are you?' she asked, dropping the edge of the skirt.

'Sixteen, Madam,' replied Sally, lowering her eyes shyly in character.

Madam Janet smiled approvingly. At that moment, it was hard to believe that Sally was anything other than a wide-eyed teenage innocent. She turned her attention to Rachel, whose outfit was less striking, but all that the client required. Make-up lines had been etched in around her eyes and cheeks, her long auburn hair hidden beneath a wavy, black wig, laced with hints of grey. She might easily have been in her late thirties or early forties. She wore a long, see-through nightdress, no underwear, and in her hand she carried a small wooden paddle.

'You know the scenario,' said Madam Janet. 'There's no point in wasting any more time. Let's get on with it.'

Madam Janet pressed a button on the console and the door into the adjoining chamber opened. It was a short walk along a narrow corridor and then Sally went through a second door at the far end into the sitting room. Madam Janet waved Rachel into a chair beside her as Sally skipped into the room, kicked off her shoes and sprawled out on the settee. She reached for a remote control and switched on the TV. There were some magazines nearby. She picked one up and began flicking through it. After about a minute, the client came in; a man, not very tall, and in his mid to late thirties. Like Sally, he was dressed to deceive, wearing a schoolboy blazer and short trousers, an image strangely not altogether unconvincing given his diminutive stature. His shirt was open at the neck and his tie askew. He threw a satchel on to the carpet and took off his blazer.

'Hello, Sally,' he said, a noticeably nervous edge to his voice.

'Hello, Darren,' she responded quietly, looking up from her magazine. 'I didn't know you were coming round tonight. Did mummy let you in?'

'Yes,' he replied, crossing to the settee. 'She said I could watch telly with you as long as we didn't do anything naughty.'

Sally swung her legs down so that Darren could sit beside her. He threw himself into the chair and pulled at his tie.

'Mummy always thinks we'll do something naughty if we're left alone,' laughed Sally nervously. 'She said that the first time she and daddy were alone he tried to put his hand up her skirt and touch her you-know-what.'

'Did he get away with it?' asked Darren, stretching his arm out across the settee so that it rested on the top of the sofa, just above Sally's head.

'No,' she replied. 'Mummy said she had to sit on him and give him a good hard spanking though, just to show him who was boss.'

Back in the observation room, Rachel flipped through the pages of her script. It wasn't her place to criticise, of course, but she felt she could have tightened up the dialogue in several places and removed some of the more over-the-top lines. Still, it was the client's fantasy, not hers. She returned her attention to the events unfolding in the next room. On the sofa, Darren snuggled closer and put his arm around Sally's shoulder.

'Do you mind if I kiss you?' he asked quietly. Sally looked up at him, her eyes wide and innocent.

'Will it be tongues?' she asked.

'If you want,' he replied.

Sally nodded sweetly. 'Yes, please. I've never had a boy's tongue in my mouth before. Mummy says it's not very nice.'

'Well your mother's not here now, is she?' he retorted. 'So we can do what we like.'

'What else do you want to do?' asked Sally demurely.

'This for a start,' replied Darren, reaching across and cupping her covered left breast with his hand.

'Ooh!' gasped Sally. 'That's very naughty. I don't think you should do that.'

'It's what boys do to girls,' said Darren.

'Is it?' replied Sally. 'I don't know. I've never been with a boy before.'

'And I've never been with a girl,' confessed Darren.

'That means we're both virgins,' giggled Sally. 'Isn't that nice? I want to stay a virgin until I get married.'

'Have you ever masturbated?' asked Darren abruptly.

Sally looked shocked. 'No, never!' she replied. 'Mummy says it's very bad. She says I must wait until the right boy comes along and he'll do it for me.'

Darren placed his hand in his lap. 'I masturbate,' he said quietly.

'Do you?' asked Sally. 'Is it nice?'

'Yes, it is,' replied Darren, fumbling for the zip in his trousers. 'Would you like to see what it looks like?'

'Ooh, yes, please,' replied Sally excitedly. 'I've never seen a boy's willy before.'

Darren reached into his flies and pulled out his penis. Though not erect, it was already beginning to fatten as he threw himself into his fantasy.

'It's very small, isn't it?' observed Sally. 'Can I touch it?'

'Yes, please,' said Darren, his voice rising with his excitement.

Sally stretched out her fingers and wrapped them

lightly around Darren's shaft. Her touch was cool and smooth and brought an immediate response as Darren's penis stiffened and raised itself several degrees.

'Goodness me!' shrieked Sally, letting go of it at once. 'It's getting bigger!'

'That's what it does when it's near a girl,' he said, 'or when I wank myself.'

'It must be very uncomfortable,' suggested Sally.

He ignored her. 'Would you like to play with it?' he asked.

'I've heard that white stuff comes out if you press it too hard,' said Sally. 'I wouldn't want it all over my hands.'

Darren's penis was now standing rigidly to attention and he was having some difficulty in controlling himself long enough to remember his lines. Back in the observation room, Rachel shifted uncomfortably on her seat.

'Are you becoming moist?' asked Madam Janet.

'Yes, Madam,' admitted Rachel truthfully. 'I can't help myself. I'm sorry.'

Madam Janet reached sideways and placed a warm hand on Rachel's inner thigh, stroking her fingers up and down.

'Are you looking forward to joining in?' she asked.

'Yes, Madam,' replied Rachel, raising her left buttock ever so slightly to increase her comfort. She was sticking to the leather upholstery, which was simply adding to her arousal as it squelched free of her skin.

'Remember, Rachel, become as excited as you like, but no unauthorised orgasms, otherwise it will be lost credits and a severe thrashing.'

'Yes, Madam,' replied Rachel. 'No unauthorised orgasms.'

Heavens, thought Rachel, even saying it was exciting enough. She would need to keep a firm grip on herself if she were to avoid losing some marks here.

Rachel turned her attention back to events in the theatre, which had moved on a few lines while her attention had been elsewhere. Sally was speaking.

'So, are we going to do naughty things to each other?'

'I'd like to,' said Darren.

'What would you like to do?' asked Sally, allowing her hand to stray on to the inside of his thigh.

'I'd like to touch you here,' he said, pushing his hand between her legs. She opened them a little wider to allow him easier access.

'Oh, I don't know,' she said. 'That sounds very naughty.'

'I know it's naughty,' he continued. 'That's why I want to touch you there.' He manoeuvred his fingers up under her skirt and began to fiddle around. His breathing was growing louder and more laboured. He moved closer and pushed his chest close to hers, pressing his lips against her mouth. If Sally hadn't known better she'd have sworn that he really was a virgin. Fumbling around as if unsure of himself, Darren pushed his tongue deep into her mouth, licking her gums and her teeth. With his right hand he squeezed her nearest breast rather inexpertly while his other hand began to roll around outside her thick cotton panties. Sally saw his fingers scurry up and down, trying to find the elastic of her waistband. With some difficulty, he tried to work his fingers under the hem around her thighs, closer to the crotch. It seemed as though he would never find a way in and he began to grunt with frustration. Suddenly, his fingers pushed up under the hem of her knickers, scurrying across her fluffy, baby-soft mound. His body stiffened as his fingers found her slit. It was her cue to pull back.

'No, you mustn't!' she objected. 'Not there!'

He broke away for an instant, staring at her in some confusion, but with his hand still firmly ensconced inside her knickers. 'What do you mean?' he asked.

'That's my wee-wee hole,' she replied. 'It's where I widdle, you mustn't touch me there!'

His face clouded over. 'I'll touch you wherever I want to,' he declared, suddenly grabbing her tight.

'No, no!' she protested, forming her hands into little fists and pummelling his shoulders with light, ineffectual blows. 'Not my wee-wee hole! Leave my wee-wee hole alone, you horrible boy!'

'It's too late for that,' he announced, climbing on top of her. 'I'm going to fuck you, I'm going to put my willy inside you and have my first come with a girl, you little bitch!'

From behind them came the sound of a door slamming shut. The young pair froze. Sally looked over Darren's shoulder, her eyes wide, her hand raised suddenly to her mouth. Darren stopped in his tracks and twisted around. Standing behind them, framed in the doorway, was Rachel. Her see-through nightdress left little to the imagination. It was clear that beneath the flimsy silk she was completely naked. Darren's eyes flashed from her head to her darkened pussy and back again.

'Mrs Harper!' he muttered and his eyes dropped sharply.

Rachel folded her arms and did her best to sound censorious.

'So what's going on here, then?' she asked sternly, tapping the paddle against her thigh.

Darren's jaw dropped. 'Nothing, honestly; we were just playing, weren't we Sally?'

Sally nodded, sitting up straight and trying to straighten her dress. She looked hopelessly dishevelled.

'Is that true, Sally?' asked Rachel. 'You know what will happen to you if you lie to me, don't you?'

'Yes, mummy,' replied Sally quietly. 'You'll smack my bottom very hard until it's red all over.'

'So tell me the truth, Sally, and you won't be punished, I promise.'

Sally went quiet for a moment or two as if weighing up her options. Then she raised her head and looked Rachel straight in the eyes.

'He was trying to touch me in a naughty place,' she said. 'Down here,' she added and lightly touched herself between the legs.

'Is this true, Darren?' asked Rachel, her voice loud and frightening.

Darren was silent. He lowered his head and began to sob quietly.

'You've been very wicked, Darren,' said Rachel. 'I can see that we are going to have to tell your father.'

Darren's eyes widened with horror. 'No, Mrs Harper, please don't tell my father, he'll beat me. I don't want him to beat me.'

'Well, that's all very well,' replied Rachel, 'but if we're not going to tell your father, what are we going to do?'

'You'll have to punish me instead,' suggested Darren.

'Will I?' asked Rachel, as if she were considering the matter. 'Well, I suppose I could, but you might not like what I would do to you.'

'I don't care, Mrs Harper, you can do anything you like to me, only please don't tell my father.'

'Very well,' replied Rachel. She turned to a sideboard, put down the paddle, opened a drawer and pulled out a complicated set of leather straps.

'Sally,' she said, gathering up the straps and paddle, 'get down on the floor.'

Sally dropped to her knees, lowered her head and pushed out her bottom so that her skirt rode up around the tops of her thighs.

'Darren, pull down your trousers and underpants and kneel behind Sally,' instructed Rachel.

Darren did as he was told and undid his belt and pulled his Y-fronts down around his knees. His cock sprang free at once. Rachel noticed with an admiring glance of approval that it was very far from being the penis of a randy adolescent schoolboy. It was long and firm and bobbed hard against his tummy. Darren's hands and feet were near the leather hoops that protruded from the floor. Rachel bent down and clipped them over his wrists and ankles so that he was held fast. Next she coiled one end of the leather strap she was holding around his neck, up, over the top of his head and then down between his legs. Finally, she attached the end of the strap around his testicles. He winced as she drew the knot tight. At the base of the straps was a series of small metal spikes, pointed and very sharp. They dug lightly into the soft underside of Darren's testicles even if he remained absolutely still. Rachel knew that if they were tightened any further and he moved his head back, the pain would become excruciating.

Rachel took another set of straps and wound them around the underneath of Sally's waist. 'Bend your head lower,' she instructed Darren.

'I can't, Mrs Harper,' he protested.

'What do you mean you can't?'

'If I lower my head any further it will be in Sally's bottom.'

'Of course it will,' replied Rachel, 'that's the whole idea.'

'Oh please, Mrs Harper,' he murmured. 'Please don't make me do that, it's rude.'

'You wanted to be rude,' replied Rachel. 'Now you're getting your chance. Sally, lift up your skirt.'

Sally reached back and took the hem of her short skirt between her fingers, pulling it up to her waist.

'Now take your panties down,' instructed Rachel. 'Just enough to expose your little botty-hole.'

Sally took hold of her panties and tugged them halfway down her buttocks.

'That's enough,' said Rachel. She felt the breath catch at the back of her throat. Sally's anus was small and pink and faintly shiny. She had such a delectable little arse, reflected Rachel excitedly. Each time she saw it she wanted to cover it in kisses. Despite their play-acting she suspected Darren now felt the same.

'Right, Darren,' said Rachel. 'I want you to kiss Sally on her bottom.'

'Please, Mrs Harper,' pleaded Darren, 'don't make me do that.'

'It's either that or we tell your father,' Rachel reminded him.

Darren was quiet for a moment. Then, he leant forward and planted a quick kiss on Sally's left buttock, drawing back almost as quickly.

Rachel admonished him sharply. 'That's not what I meant, as well you know. If I'd wanted you to kiss her bare behind I'd have said, "Kiss her on the buttocks", but I didn't, did I? Kiss her properly – on her botty-hole.'

Darren's eyes widened in horror. He really was very good, thought Rachel. Anyone would have thought that he really didn't want to kiss Sally so intimately.

'If you don't do as I say,' warned Rachel, 'I'll beat you first and then tell your father. Or –' she added quietly – 'I might even sit on your face and make you kiss *my* bumhole. And I can tell you now, boy, that you won't shift me in a hurry!'

Darren looked from Rachel to Sally and back again. Rachel tapped the paddle in her hands and straightened her back. She really did feel very officious and realised, not for the first time, how much she enjoyed the role of dominant.

'Well, boy?' she asked at last. 'What's it to be? A bumhole or a beating?'

Darren turned back towards Sally. Rachel knew that there was no doubt in his mind. This was what he wanted, after all. This was his fantasy. His cock was rigid, almost flat against his belly, and Rachel was pretty sure that if she bent down and gave it a gentle squeeze he would empty himself over the floor. But that was not the object of his fantasy. Darren took a deep breath as if reluctantly preparing himself for the inevitable. Slowly, he leant forward until his mouth was poised over Sally's anus. Rachel wondered what was going through his mind. She half wished she could swap places with him. Sally's anus pouted like a small mouth, pursed for a lover's kiss. It was hard to believe that any man would be reluctant to press his face between her tight little cheeks.

Darren dipped his head and planted a kiss on the soft, distended ring. Immediately, Rachel brought the straps up and tightened them around the back of Darren's head, effectively pinning him to Sally's bottom. She reached down between his legs and gave the testicle strap a final tug. Darren's body jerked awkwardly. Now, if he lifted his head away from Sally's behind, the movement would stretch the strap and force the needles into his scrotum.

Rachel's hand tightened around the paddle. She wondered if this were the feeling Madam Janet experienced just before she administered a beating.

'I'm going to have to spank you on the bottom, Darren,' she said. 'I'm sorry, but it's for your own good.'

Darren grunted inaudibly. With his mouth clamped tight over Sally's anus it was difficult for him to say anything. Rachel brought the paddle down across his buttocks. His skin trembled, his body jerked and he let out a sudden muted shriek. His head had shifted ever so slightly and the needles had dug cruelly into his flesh.

Rachel struck him a second time. He groaned, but this time did not move. He was learning, thought Rachel.

'Now,' she said, kneeling down beside him, 'I want you to do something very special for me. I want you to put your tongue into Sally's botty-hole.'

A muted wail of protest broke from Darren's lips.

'If you don't, I'll have to tell your father that you were rude with my daughter,' said Rachel. 'I'll have to tell him that you touched her little pussy. And that after that you kissed her on the bottom. I don't think he'd approve, do you?'

Darren let out another wail of abject despair. He really was playing his role to perfection. They all were, thought Rachel. She hoped that they would get good marks for this performance. They deserved to, she told herself, as she leant closer to Sally.

'What's he doing?' she asked quietly. 'I want you to describe it to me so that I know if he's doing what he's been told. If he doesn't do it properly, I'll have to spank him again.'

'He's not doing anything, mummy,' answered Sally. 'Apart from kissing me in a very rude place.'

Rachel reached down between Darren's legs and felt his penis. It was rock hard. His subservient position and just listening to Sally were enough to keep him in a permanent state of erection. Indeed, if anything, he seemed to be growing bigger and harder. Rachel allowed her fingers to graze his balls. They were very large and very heavy. He winced. They were hurting. That meant they were full. She wondered how much more seed could possibly flow into them before he reached orgasm.

'Wait, mummy!' cried Sally. 'I can feel his tongue. He's trying to push it into me. Oh, mummy, it's going into my bottom. It's going into my bottom!'

'Is it going very far?' asked Rachel.

'Not at the moment, mummy,' said Sally. 'Oh, wait a minute, it's going further. It's so hard. Oh, mummy, it's up me. It's up my bottom!'

Rachel leaned closer to Darren. 'Wiggle your tongue around,' she ordered him. 'I don't care how difficult it is, I want you to move it inside my daughter's bottom.'

She struck him on the buttocks and his head bobbed. The straps tightened and the needles dug into his already damaged flesh. He would have screamed out loud but for the fact that his mouth remained closed around Sally's bumhole, his tongue trapped inside her. Rachel felt his cock and was astounded to discover that it was harder than ever.

'Oh, mummy,' sighed Sally. 'It's wriggling inside me. It feels so good. Oh, mummy, what's happening to me? It feels – it feels – oh, mummy!' Sally wailed and drove her hips back hard, ramming herself into Darren's face as she came. His head was forced back, tightening the straps around his balls. The needles dug home and he screamed horribly, dragging his face out of Sally's backside. The pain instantly redoubled. He thrust his face back between her buttocks, desperately trying to alter the angle of his head and stem the dreadful torture between his legs. It was too late. The pain was excruciating and there was nothing he could do to lessen it, screaming pitifully into Sally's wriggling backside. Rachel reached down and undid the straps around Darren's testicles. Then she untied the straps around his feet and hands. She pulled him back until he was lying on his back on the floor, huddled into a near-foetal position, hugging himself, biting back the tears caused by the stinging in his groin.

Rachel got up, crossed to the drawer and took out a tube of ointment. She handed it to Sally, who was trying to steady herself as the last waves of her climax washed over her.

'You're a very naughty boy,' admonished Rachel. 'You gave my little girl an orgasm. You made her pussy come for the first time ever. Now she'll have a taste for it. She'll want to do even naughtier things to you, won't you, Sally?'

'Yes, mummy. I want to be really rude now. I want to lose my virginity on his big stiff pole.'

'Did you hear that?' asked Rachel, breathing into Darren's ear. 'Now you're in trouble, my boy. But first things first. I think we'll have to attend to your sore testicles.'

She handed Sally the bottle of ointment. Darren's scrotum was red and raw. The damage wasn't as serious as it looked, but there was always the chance of infection. It would have to be sterilised and that would be painful; probably more painful than what he had already endured.

Sally opened the bottle as Rachel prised Darren's legs apart. His eyes widened nervously.

'This is going to hurt,' warned Rachel. She reached up and pulled her dressing gown to one side, scooping out a large breast and pushing it towards him.

'Would you like to suck on me?' she asked him. 'I'm nice and firm and it might stop you crying out too loudly.'

Darren buried his face in her cleavage, his mouth closing over her wide dimpled areola. Rachel held him close, wrapping her other breast around his face, sandwiching his head in her bosom. She nodded to Sally, then whispered into Darren's ear. 'Here it comes, my darling. Be brave and don't cry.'

Sally dabbed ointment on to Darren's reddened flesh. His body went into spasm and he screamed into Rachel's bosom and bit on her nipple. She winced but held him close as Sally dabbed more of the ointment on to the damaged part of his scrotum. He sucked furiously, like a small child, tears rolling down his cheeks and soaking Rachel's breasts. She held him tight, rocking his head from side to side like a baby at the teat. Only when, after several more minutes, she judged that it was safe to move on to the next stage of the proceedings, did she release him and lower him on to his back.

'Spread your legs,' she ordered, though doing so

evidently caused him considerable pain. 'Feel his balls,' she instructed Sally, 'but don't squeeze them or he might spend himself.'

Sally reached forward and cupped her fingers around his scrotum, cradling Darren's large testicles in the palm of her hand, rolling them like marbles. They were warm and heavy and he whimpered weakly into Rachel's bosom.

Rachel pressed her lips to Darren's ear. 'You're heavy with seed, Darren,' she said, 'I think it's almost time for my daughter to mate with you.'

Darren looked up into her eyes, his mouth pulling away from the nipple it had been suckling on. 'What will she do?' he asked weakly.

Rachel smiled. It was obvious that Darren's particular turn-on was hearing the words. 'She'll take her panties off. In fact, she's taking them off now. No, don't look!' she ordered, forcing his head back between her breasts as he tried to turn and watch Sally divesting herself of her knickers.

'You mustn't look at a girl when she undresses, Darren, it's very rude. She has naughty bits that she doesn't want men to look at. Don't you understand that by now?'

Rachel pushed a nipple towards Darren and he returned to sucking her wet, rubbery teat. She cradled him tenderly in her arms, rocking gently on her buttocks, her pussy throbbing with renewed excitement.

'When she's got her knickers off, she'll sit on your willy. She'll take it right up inside her and squeeze it with her pussy until lots of white stuff comes out of you.'

As Rachel spoke, Sally mounted Darren's midriff and manoeuvred her pudenda over his penis. She reached down and took hold of his shaft, positioning it at the entrance to her vagina. Darren's hips rocked from side to side and he gurgled loudly into Rachel's bosom. He moved his feet so wildly that Rachel was forced to hold him tight, muffling his tortured response. By now she was as excited as anyone. It was obvious that Darren was close to climaxing and was desperately trying to hold back in order to extract the maximum pleasure from his experience. Rachel wanted to take hold of one of his hands and place it between her legs. She wanted his fingers inside her, playing with her, stroking her, probing her until she came, too. But that was forbidden. It was not part of Darren's fantasy. She tried to dismiss the lustful feelings raging inside her, though watching Sally's small, fluffy vulva swell around Darren's member did not make it any easier for her. With difficulty, she managed to recall her lines.

'What does it feel like, my darling?' she asked.

'It feels really nice, mummy,' replied Sally. 'It's filling me up and making my tummy go all warm inside.'

'That's good,' observed Rachel. 'Now feel his balls again.'

Sally reached down and grazed her fingers along the underside of Darren's scrotum. He jerked inside her and Rachel could sense that he was close to coming, closer in fact than Sally was. She knew Sally would have to be very careful.

'They're rolling in my hand, mummy,' she said.

'That means they're very full,' explained Rachel, hugging Darren's face hard against her breasts. She felt his teeth tighten around her nipple. Her pussy was sopping wet. This was all so unfair. One touch now, in the right place, and she would climax like nobody's business. Holding back was so difficult. She wanted to be on top of Darren. It took an effort to drag herself back to the matter in hand.

'What do you want to do now?' asked Rachel.

'I want to bounce up and down, mummy. I want to ride him like a horse and make the white stuff come out of his willy and fill me till it runs down my legs!'

Darren kicked out with his feet and rubbed his face violently from side to side. He had written every word of this, it was what he wanted to hear, and Rachel could tell that he was almost at the point of no return. But they had to take him to his limit, that was the way to earn maximum marks. He was close now, so close. Rachel was holding him so tight she wondered how she hadn't smothered him. She could feel the hot stickiness of her own skin, his nose and mouth pressed flat against her flesh. If she were to allow him the slightest room and wiggle her breasts from side to side she was certain that he would climax.

'Bounce, my darling!' she cried. 'Show him no mercy!'

Sally reached down and pressed her clitoris with the flat of her thumb. It was enough to take her over the edge. Darren had insisted that he and Sally must reach orgasm simultaneously. He had made no such stipulation for Rachel. She bit her lip and tried to empty her mind as a flood of pleasure threatened to unleash itself across her belly.

Sally was riding Darren like a madwoman, threshing about and bucking up and down. Darren swivelled his hips one way, then the other, hollowing the small of his back as the first wave of semen jetted from his shaft. He twisted his head sideways, breaking contact with Rachel's bosom. She pulled him back at once, covering his nose with her left breast, squashing her nipple between his lips and hugging him so hard that this time she was sure he couldn't breathe. He kicked and threshed as he emptied himself happily. Sally's joy, too, was unconfined; her release spilling from her as the muscles in her vagina worked to milk his penis dry.

Rachel leant close and whispered into Darren's ear. 'Be brave, my darling,' she murmured. 'My daughter is raping you. She's taking your virginity. There's no escape for you now . . .'

Darren kicked again as a second wave of pleasure

broke through the dam of his resistance. Rachel bit her lip hard. She wanted his fingers between her legs. Just one touch and she would come. But there was to be no release for her. She swallowed hard, holding him close as the last eddies of his pleasure ebbed away. Sally fell forward, utterly exhausted, her small breasts grazing Darren's chest. Then she rose, dismounting quickly. Rachel released his head from the prison of her breasts and lay him gently on the floor. He curled up in a foetal position, his legs and arms huddled against his tummy and his head bowed low, his eyes closed.

It was over and he was sated. Rachel and Sally were no longer part of the proceedings. A red light blinked on and off over the observation window and they knew it was time to withdraw.

Eleven

Rachel and Sally were woken earlier than usual the following morning and, after a hurried shower and a light breakfast, Madam Janet escorted them to the front of The Hall. A large black van was parked outside, its rear doors wide open. Leading them by their reins, Madam Janet ushered them inside. They both wanted to ask what was going on and suspected that Madam was enjoying their obvious bewilderment. On the floor of the van were two long rectangular metal cages into which Rachel and Sally were quickly bundled. Thick cushions were placed beneath each girl's head and buttocks. A leather band was secured around their foreheads. Several more straps were tightened around their legs, tummies, chests and arms, so that, by the time Madam Janet had finished her work, neither girl could move a muscle.

'You will remain silent throughout the journey,' she told them. 'However, I am sure you'll be happy to know that Master Stéfan will be travelling with you in case of emergency.'

Rachel could hardly believe her ears. In her view, Master Stéfan and his sado-masochistic leanings *were* an emergency. From her prone perspective, his lean, angular features seemed to fill her entire vision.

'I do not wish to hear a word from either of you until we arrive. Is that understood?' said Master Stéfan, looking down at them.

'Yes, Master,' they replied together.

He turned to Madam Janet. 'You may leave us now.'

'Yes, Master,' she replied, stepping out of their line of sight.

Master Stéfan knelt down and released Rachel's right arm and Sally's left. 'I am going to blindfold you,' he explained. 'However, if you wish you may touch for comfort.' He leant forward and slipped something soft and dark over Rachel's eyes, fastening it tight. Then he placed something over her ears. It felt like a pair of headphones. He moved away and she guessed he was doing the same to Sally. Finally, she felt the top of the metal cage being lowered and snapped shut. Because of the cushions, her head and vulva pressed upwards through the cold metal bars. For what seemed like several minutes, Rachel's entire world was shrouded in darkness and silence. It was an eerie feeling and one that she realised both thrilled and frightened her. Then she heard the doors slam shut and felt the van begin to move off. She knew that they were on their way. But to where?

Almost immediately, she heard a fresh sound. It was music, very soft and gentle. It began to lull her, which was nice because it broke the monotony and made her feel a little less lonely. On a whim she reached out with her free hand. It was several minutes before she felt warm flesh against her fingers as Sally stretched out her own hand. They held on to each other and it felt surprisingly comforting and sexy all at the same time. Occasionally, Rachel would squeeze and Sally would squeeze back. After a while, the music began to fade, and now she could hear voices. They were moaning and sighing and at first Rachel thought they were people in pain. Then she realised that, far from being in pain, it was the sound of a man and a woman making love. They were sighing with ecstasy. Little cries of 'Yes, yes, yes', and muffled moans filled her ears. It was very exciting. She wanted to touch her pussy or to squeeze her legs together, but was unable to move a muscle, or at least any muscles that would enable her to enjoy herself. Madam Janet had done a good job. Rachel felt the warm metal against her vulva, squashing her pussy up and out, but nothing was touching her all-important clitty. Then she remembered that though her world was in darkness, Master Stéfan's was not. He was sitting there, looking at them. It was a strange feeling. He knew what they were listening to and could watch them shift in useless frustration. Again, it made Rachel feel simultaneously appalled and yet strangely aroused, too. When Sally began squeezing her hand very rapidly, she suspected that her friend was also listening to the unknown lovers and suffering her own torments.

After a while, Rachel began to lose track of how long they had been travelling. Sensory deprivation, an inability to move and a constant barrage of sexual mewing began to muddle her mind. She started drifting in and out of a sleepy twilight world, when something unexpectedly brushed the side of her face and a familiar smell invaded her nostrils. Warm flesh pressed down on her face and she realised that Master Stéfan – it must be him surely unless someone else was inside the back of the van – had straddled the top of the cage. When a familiar length of male hardness waved against her lips, all her doubts disappeared. It was Master Stéfan all right. He was lying over her, the warm edge of his shaft heavy against her mouth, his balls resting lightly on her forehead. Clearly, Master Stéfan wanted her to fellate him. It was strictly against the rules and she was within her rights to tell him to stop. She wondered whether he would. After all, she was completely helpless and if he chose to continue there was little she could do about it. On the other hand, this latest move of his was surely proof that she had wormed her way into his affections – or whatever passed for affections in Master Stéfan's world. Now wasn't the time to resist. Now was the time to show him what she could do for him.

Rachel opened her mouth wide. Master Stéfan needed no encouragement, sliding forward and spearing her to the back of the throat. She closed her warm lips around his huge girth, sucking gently on his flesh. He pushed himself in and out, enjoying the even rhythm of her mouth. She flicked her tongue around the base of his cock and felt his pubic hair tickle her nose. It was a strange angle and she wondered why he didn't take her towards her head. His next movement revealed why. Leaning forward, he nuzzled at her squashed-up vulva and she felt the butterfly caress of his tongue on her open labia. She tightened her grip on his cock, grunting with pleasure. She suddenly realised that Sally was squeezing her hand very hard. Heavens, she had been so carried away with what Master Stéfan was doing to her that she had forgotten all about her friend. She squeezed back, aware that Sally had no idea what was happening to her, a thought which excited her even more.

Between her legs, Master Stéfan was pleasuring her in a way that even Michael never had. She might not like him very much, he might even be a traitor to the Sisterhood, but she couldn't fault his cunnilingus. He stroked her slit up and down, flicking and teasing her labia, sucking gently on her clitoris and urging the tiny bud out from under its protective hood. Rachel wanted to cry out but his penis effectively stopped up her mouth. She began to realise how important movement was to the enjoyment of sex and how much she had always taken it for granted. Yet, at the same time, being unable to move lent a frisson of excitement that she had not anticipated. She was a helpless plaything, at the total mercy of another human being. Master Stéfan's thrusts into her mouth became more urgent, the sign of a man moving towards his inevitable release. Rachel prepared herself for the rush of seed into the back of her throat. She had experienced it only yesterday and was aware of the force of Master Stéfan's ejaculation. The sound of lovemaking in her ears continued to thrill as the man above her began to buck fiercely. Rachel felt his tongue worry her most sensitive folds and realised that she too, under his careful ministrations, was heading inexorably towards her climax. His penis froze, and she was aware of that moment of tautness that immobilised the male body immediately before orgasm. She tensed herself for the flood and, almost immediately, felt Master Stéfan empty himself into her mouth. Warm semen hit the back of her throat, tickling her tonsils and making her want to cough. He was flooding her so furiously that she found it hard to swallow fast enough to keep up. Then she too came as his tongue stabbed hard at her clitoris. She tightened her grip on his cock, whimpering with delight as her climax shook through her belly. She squeezed Sally's hand so tight that she realised her friend must have thought something had frightened her. She hoped she didn't ask afterwards, it might be difficult to explain.

As soon as her orgasm subsided, Master Stéfan gave Rachel's vagina a final lick as if attempting to scoop up her remaining juices. Then he moved away from her face. She swallowed the last drops of his semen and licked her lips clean, savouring his strong male taste. Gradually her breathing returned to normal.

Soon after, the van came to a halt and shortly after that she was aware of the cage being opened. The headphones and straps were removed but not the blindfold, then strong arms were lifting her up and carrying her down some steps. She was carried some distance, up stairs and into a building, the air grew suddenly warmer and she could hear voices murmuring nearby. Eventually she was placed down gently, on to her feet and, shortly afterwards, her blindfold was removed. The light stung her eyes and she rubbed them for several moments as they adjusted to the glare.

She and Sally were standing in a large well-appointed room. Master Stéfan was a few feet in front of them beside a large mahogany desk, twice as big as his own. There was a man sitting behind the desk who they had not seen before. He stood up and came round to join Master Stéfan. He was about forty-five, well built, bare-chested like Master Stéfan, with dark leather trousers and boots. Another Master, presumably. But where were they?

The man smiled. 'My name is Master Conrad,' he explained. 'Welcome to Brotherhood Manor.'

He paused while they digested this information. They knew that there was no need to reply, unless of course they wanted mild whipping which, at the moment, was not uppermost in either girl's thoughts.

'You know of the Brothers, of course. You have already met Brother Adam, I believe.'

He paused again. Rachel and Sally's memory of Brother Adam was still very vivid. Rachel, for one, hoped they might yet renew their acquaintance. She felt they had unfinished business.

'Though you should regard today as part of your training,' Master Conrad went on, 'we also want you to enjoy yourselves. With this in mind, two Initiate Brothers have been assigned to you.'

The fog had begun to lift from Rachel's befuddled brain. She suddenly realised that this was where the other girls had been vanishing to over the last week or so. She wondered what was in store for them. Master Conrad was still speaking.

'I won't spoil the day for you by giving you a detailed account of your duties. However, suffice it to say that it should prove fruitful both to yourselves and our Brother Initiates.'

Rachel wondered if the Brothers were as starved of

the company of women as the Sisters were of men. She suspected that the answer might be no. She assumed there were Madams at this establishment, too, and had little doubt that they made free with the young men under their control. She didn't pause long to consider whether any of the Masters did.

Master Conrad's chest was very broad, with a mat of dark hair, his muscles finely chiselled. He seemed even more powerful than Master Stéfan and, though at least ten years older, had clearly kept himself in excellent condition. He was very handsome, thought Rachel, and wondered whether it might be worth breaking a rule or two in his presence just to see what he would do to her. He wore a leather tawse at his waist, like all the Madams and Masters, but it was the object he kept in his trousers that was of more interest to her at that moment.

Master Conrad examined the two women carefully. He reached out and palmed Rachel's left breast. 'You are a very beautiful young woman,' he observed. Rachel smiled but said nothing. Turning to Sally, he spread the fingers of his large hands, enveloping her smaller breasts, closed his eyes and sighed deeply, squeezing at her flesh. Rachel felt jealous. She got the impression that she was always being left out and wondered why. Or was it just her imagination? Perhaps Master Conrad was like so many men, with secret schoolgirl fantasies that girls like Sally could help fulfil.

'Yes,' he repeated, stepping back and smiling again. 'You are both very beautiful women. Now, please take off your harnesses.'

Obediently, Rachel and Sally removed the various lengths of leather until they were quite naked, holding the harnesses in their hands because they didn't know what else to do with them. That problem was quickly resolved as Master Stéfan took hold of both outfits and placed them in a small drawer nearby.

Rachel felt that there was something very exciting about standing in front of these two men, completely naked, aware that they could do whatever they liked with them, and half hoping that they would.

Master Stéfan returned, holding some black and white material in his hands.

'Please put these on,' said Master Conrad. Rachel and Sally took the clothes and realised almost at once that the new outfits were maids' costumes, complete with little frilly hats, aprons and short, satin skirts. There was also a pair of stockings, suspenders and high heels in each kit. There was only one thing missing – there were no panties.

When they were dressed, Master Conrad pressed a small button on the top of his desk and a section of wall slid back to reveal a full-length mirror. Rachel was surprised to discover that she and Sally looked far sexier than she had imagined. Their breasts were completely exposed and their legs looked very alluring in the black fishnet stockings.

'Please bend over,' instructed Master Conrad. Both girls leant forward as far as they could, cheerfully presenting their posteriors to the two men.

'What do you think, Master Stéfan? Will they do?'

'I think they will do very nicely,' replied Master Stéfan.

Rachel flinched as a hand pawed her bottom. She wasn't sure which of the Masters it was, but it felt nice all the same. The fingers spread across her backside, pressing into her warm flesh, passing from one buttock to the next and back again several times. She felt warm breath fan her bare behind and had to grip her lower calves in order to steady herself as a pair of lips pressed into her crack, and a nose pushed up against her anus. A tongue thrust out, burying itself in her pussy, flicking up and down, teasing her clitoris. She let out a short whimper before screwing up her eyes and struggling to exercise some semblance of self-control. Master Stéfan's voice broke into her thoughts. It removed all doubt as to who was making so free with her backside. The words she heard were like magic to her ears. 'You have permission to reach orgasm,' he said.

Rachel hardly needed permission. The way Master Conrad was worrying her clitoris while burrowing his nose into her anus made it almost impossible to hold back. Master Stéfan had barely given her permission before she was gasping for breath and rotating her hips from side to side, her parted labia impaled on Master Conrad's tongue. As the waves of her orgasm subsided, she looked across at Sally. Her friend was gazing open-mouthed, having been no more than an envious spectator to the proceedings. Rachel felt the juices trickling down the inside of her thighs. She had wanted to keel over completely at the point of climax and was struggling to keep her legs straight.

'Remain where you are,' instructed Master Stéfan. Rachel felt her heart skip a beat as Sally let out a short, but familiar sigh. She knew without looking that Sally was receiving the same treatment that she had. Rachel had imagined Master Stéfan's cunnilingus could not be bettered, but she had been wrong. Master Conrad's tongue had been like a steel rod, yet at the same time long and eminently flexible. It had been like having a snake in her pussy. Alongside her, Sally was already flooding happily, her little breasts bouncing up and down.

'You may both stand up,' said Master Stéfan, when it was over. 'If you can,' he added rather drily.

With some difficulty, Rachel and Sally resumed their upright positions. Master Conrad was already sitting behind his desk as if nothing had happened.

'Your duties will begin shortly,' said Master Stéfan. 'The Manor is a large establishment and, like all establishments, it requires a certain amount of maintenance.'

Master Conrad pressed a button on his desk and the door opened. Two Initiate Brothers entered. Rachel had hoped that one of them might be Adam, having decided that a familiar face would be nice in these strange surroundings, but she recognised neither of the men who had just walked in. They were both tall, dark haired, very well built and lightly tanned.

'This is Brother Martin and Brother Duncan,' explained Master Conrad by way of introduction. 'They are Initiates like yourselves and will show you to your duties.'

The audience was clearly at an end, for Master Conrad now turned to Master Stéfan and began speaking to him on a completely different matter. Brother Duncan gestured with his open palm and Rachel and Sally preceded the two men out of the room. Once outside, the girls were led down a long corridor and back into the foyer. There were two marble statues positioned against a near wall, Greek-style gods, naked and typically muscular.

'These are a bit dusty,' said Brother Martin. 'Please clean them.'

As they set about their task, Rachel reflected that this was a bit of a comedown from what she had expected. She dallied around the statue's penis, which was hanging half erect from between its legs. She could not remember seeing a piece quite like this before and wondered if it had been specially commissioned. The two Brothers inspected their handiwork.

'All right, I suppose,' said Brother Martin, 'but I'd like you to go over this bit again, please.' He pointed to the statue's penis. Rachel couldn't see what was wrong with it but raised her duster.

'Not with the duster,' said Brother Martin. 'I'd like you to clean it with your breasts.'

Rachel was taken aback.

'Yours is dirty, too,' said Brother Duncan to Sally. 'I'd like you to lick it clean.'

Rachel wasn't sure whose request was the more peculiar. On reflection, she decided that cleaning anything with a pair of breasts took first prize in terms of daftness. She approached the statue and cupped her bosom in both hands. Carefully, she placed her fleshy mounds either side of the penis and began to rub. The marble was cold and, at first, the sensation was uncomfortable. After a minute or so, however, the feeling changed into something unmistakably exhilarating. Rachel closed her eyes and imagined that it was a real penis, and that she was masturbating it. She imagined it was Michael's penis and she felt her pussy pulse and lubricate. Out of the corner of her eye she watched as Sally's mouth closed around the other statue's long, marble erection. Brother Martin came up behind Rachel and she felt his hands press against her buttocks through the thin gossamer of her maid's dress. His fingers slipped under the hem of her tiny skirt and dipped between her thighs. She felt the tip of one finger ease itself into the warm goo of her pussy and it almost took her over the edge. In the nick of time she pulled herself back. She didn't want to risk a punishment at this early stage. Brother Martin's mouth pressed against her ear.

'It's all right,' he reassured her. 'Orgasms are permitted. Well, as long as a Brother agrees.'

Rachel felt her heart thumping against her ribcage. She was so worked up that she didn't know how long she could hold out. No, that wasn't true. She knew she could hold out if necessary. Her training had taught her that at least. But all the training in the world couldn't stop her wanting to climax.

'May I come?' she asked him quietly, squirming against his invading fingers as she continued to cradle the marble penis between her breasts.

'Perhaps,' said Brother Martin.

To her right she heard Sally moan quietly. It was

obvious that she too was being teased to the limits. She heard Brother Duncan say, 'Shall we put them out of their misery?' and was desperate to hear her own tormentor's affirmative response.

'I'm not sure,' Brother Martin replied, cruelly prolonging the girls' torture. His fingers pushed deeper, spreading inside her, widening her labia. Rachel felt her knees wobble and mashed her breasts around the marble penis. Brother Martin whispered into her ear. 'Pity the man who gets his head between those two. You'd smother him alive!'

Rachel bent low, driving her backside into her tormentor's groin. She felt his penis, thick and hard, moving up and down between her buttocks. She could feel Brother Martin's heart thumping against her, and was convinced that he was close to spending himself over her bottom. At last she heard the words she had longed to hear.

'You may come,' he whispered. All it took was two further thrusts of Brother Martin's expert fingers and Rachel's orgasm coursed through her. She staggered forward, enveloping the marble penis in her warm flesh, while her oily juices spilled from her vulva and trickled down her thighs. To her right, she heard Sally emit a series of short sharp muffled squeals that left Rachel in no doubt that she too had climaxed. The two Brothers had clearly restrained themselves, however, though whether out of admirable self-control or under instruction it was impossible to say.

'I expect you could do with something to eat and drink, now,' suggested Brother Martin casually as the two girls caught their breath.

They were taken along a labyrinth of connecting corridors and eventually into a large, white-walled canteen area, very much like the one at The Hall. There were half a dozen circular tables set out, two of which had been laid with tablecloths. Brother Martin went over to the counter and picked up two trays, on each of which was set a small cup of coffee and a sandwich. Rachel was grateful for the opportunity to eat. They had had nothing since their early breakfast and she was beginning to feel hungry.

Rachel turned to Brother Martin and said, 'Does it matter which chair we sit on?'

'You won't be sitting on the chairs,' replied Brother Martin, raising the edge of one tablecloth. 'You are only a maid after all, Sister Rachel. You will sit underneath the table, as will you, Sister Sally.'

This was a turn-up for the books, thought Rachel. She wondered where all this would end. She got down on her knees and squeezed herself under one table while Sally crawled under the other. Rachel thought that it probably wasn't quite such an ordeal for her friend, being that much smaller, but it was certainly a tight squeeze for her. She put the tray down in the semi-gloom and did her best to make herself comfortable. After a moment or two her eyes had almost completely adjusted to the lack of light. Rachel picked up the cup of coffee and sipped it, then attacked the sandwich. It was ham and tomato. She wolfed it down, took another sip of coffee and waited. A door opened and she realised that more people were coming into the room. Feet approached the table, chairs were pulled back and, rather bewilderingly, several pairs of legs announced the arrival of four Brothers.

She could hear the sound of trays and cups and eating, though most of her attention was now given up to the sight of four well-endowed penises hanging between four pairs of thick muscular thighs. Rachel was still coming to terms with this bizarre turn of events when a pair of legs stretched out and its owner's feet gripped her by the shoulders. At the same time, feet moved in from left and right and began to stroke lightly at her breasts. Rachel pushed the tray to one side, out from under the table, and awaited developments.

The pair of feet around her shoulders drew back, pulling her down between their owner's legs. His penis began to stir, unfurling and becoming erect. Rachel knew an open invitation when she saw one. She lowered her head into the man's lap and closed her lips over his shaft, taking the entire length into her mouth. She felt his body stiffen with anticipation and she knew that she had done the right thing. It was only the fact that her mouth was full that stifled a surprised yelp as something stroked between her buttocks. It took her a few moments to realise that it was yet another foot. At the same time the feet either side of her continued to massage her breasts. It was incredible; these feet were softer and more gentle than the hands of many men she had known. Meanwhile, the foot between her buttocks was beginning to work its own magic, sliding up and around, gently stroking her vulva. She pressed her bottom down, tightening her thighs to extract the maximum benefit. The penis in her mouth began to thrust strongly. Rachel brought her hands up and squeezed its owner's hips, then allowed her palms to slide over his thighs and tickle his balls with the tips of her fingers. She felt his sacs tighten as they filled with seed, and she rolled his penis skilfully around inside her mouth. Then she flicked her tongue across the sensitive eye, drawing the foreskin back as far as she could before plunging her mouth down over the entire shaft several times in quick succession.

The feet either side of her were doing incredible things to her breasts and the one between her buttocks was already soaked with her juices. She felt hands claw through her hair as the man whose penis she was sucking approached the point of no return. The foot between her legs suddenly jerked up hard against the sensitive bud of her clitoris. It was as adept as any fingers might have been. She bore down, squeezing her thighs together one last time and came, her juices flooding from her vulva as she wriggled left and right, moaning over the penis still trapped inside her mouth. She felt the man's body stiffen and his cock began to jerk spasmodically. Semen jetted into the back of her throat and she swallowed it happily, enjoying the taste of male ejaculate as it spat into her mouth. She continued to suck gently as the penis began to soften and wilt, milking the last few drops before it was suddenly plucked away, and she heard the sound of several chairs scraping the floor. The men rose, feet padded across the floor, the door clicked shut and then there was silence. Shortly afterwards, the tablecloth was lifted up and she heard Brother Martin's voice.

'It's time to continue with your duties.'

Rachel crawled out from under the table and stood up with some difficulty. She had now climaxed four times in one morning and found herself wondering if you could have too much of a good thing. Sally crawled out from under the other table and the two girls stood side by side, knowing smiles of pleasure etched across both their faces.

As they were led from the room, Rachel couldn't help wondering if it was Brother Martin, or his friend whom she had fellated. They were taken along a series of short corridors and this time stopped outside a large, mahogany door. Brother Martin opened it and ushered the two girls inside. They found themselves in a large, well-appointed study. It seemed to be in a terrible mess and Rachel wondered if this had been done solely for their benefit.

'This is the Erotica Room,' explained Brother Duncan. Rachel at once saw why. Dotted all around them were statuettes of couples in various stages of sexual intercourse. The walls were hung with suggestive paintings, lithographs and drawings. A large desk in the centre of the room was littered with a vast array of books, the pages of which displayed a mind-boggling array of sexual activities. There was a large ornate mirror covering one side of the room and on the opposite wall was a glass divide, a viewing panel into a second, presently darkened chamber, just like the observation room at The Hall.

'Right,' said Brother Martin. 'While you two tidy up this mess, Brother Duncan and I are going to have a cup of tea.'

He ignored Rachel's perplexed stare and pointed to a camera in the corner of the room. 'No slacking,' was his parting shot. 'We'll be watching you.'

After they had gone, Rachel and Sally quickly set to work. Dusting erotic statues and tidying up books bursting with every manner of licentious behaviour imaginable soon began to have its inevitable effect. Rachel felt her pussy begin to lubricate all over again. At this rate, she reflected, they would have to carry her back to The Hall on a stretcher.

Suddenly a light went on in the adjoining chamber. They saw at once that the room was empty, apart from some sort of pulley apparatus fixed to the ceiling. A young man, naked but reined, entered, accompanied by two Madams. Though the man was not wearing the familiar harness, they guessed that he was a Brother. His skin glistened as he walked and they realised that he was covered in a thin sheen of oil, as was one of the Madams. A voice broke into their thoughts. It was Brother Duncan over the tannoy. 'On with your work, girls, unless you want to receive a punishment,' he barked.

Reluctantly, Rachel and Sally returned to their cleaning duties, dusting statues, closing books and returning them to the shelves. But every now and then they would sneak a quick glimpse at the proceedings being enacted on the far side of the window. It was, Rachel believed, a show being put on for their benefit after all. Within a few minutes, both the Brother and one of the Madams had been secured to a complicated arrangement of ropes and straps so that the man hung suspended from the ceiling and the woman hung just in front, with her back to him. She was now naked, except for a skimpy pair of black panties. Her legs were raised as if she were seated on an invisible chair suspended in mid-air. The man's ankles were cinched into cuffs. From the way he was able to stretch his limbs, however, it seemed clear that the straps to which the cuffs were attached were made of some form of elastic.

'No peeking,' Brother Martin reminded them over the tannoy. Rachel and Sally turned their attention towards a pair of statuettes, conveniently situated either side of the ornate mirror, allowing them to watch the fascinating tableau continue to unfold.

The man raised his legs, bending at the waist. Rachel knew from her own gym work how much strength such a manoeuvre required. His task was made all the more difficult through having to strain against the elastic ropes attached to his feet. Even so, he was able to raise his legs until they were either side of the Madam's waist. With incredible dexterity, he looped his toes under the hem of her panties and began to tug. He was able to pull them down only a fraction, however, before the effort told, and he was forced to lower his legs for a few moments while he recovered his strength. He tried again, this time dragging the woman's panties down to her ankles before his legs fell back.

Rachel finished dusting the statuette and turned her attention to a pile of erotic books. One drawing in particular caught her attention. It seemed to involve one man and six women. The man was lying on his back with a woman astride his face. The woman was bent over, holding on to the man's hands, which were clawing at the air. A second woman was standing on the first woman's buttocks, so that the man must have been struggling to breathe. Two more women were dancing on his chest, while a sixth straddled his midriff and appeared to be in the process of bouncing up and down. Rachel felt her legs go weak at the sight and closed the book carefully, before carrying it to the shelf. She sneaked a glance sideways and saw the young Brother raise his legs again, wrapping his thighs around the Madam's waist. His penis was fully erect and he was clearly attempting to enter her from behind. The angle of his body, the straps and the oil made this a very complicated manoeuvre. Rachel realised why Michael was such an expert lover, if he had gone through this sort of training himself. With a supreme effort, the Brother drove himself forward. His penis entered the woman, but almost immediately slipped out, and he lowered his legs. The effort had proved too much. Rachel felt sorry for him, then saw that her pity was premature. She realised for the first time that his wrists were not held fast by the ropes suspending him to the ceiling. The ropes were looped around his wrists so that if he uncoiled them he could lower himself and alter the angle of his body. This he now did, shifting his stance in mid-air so that he was almost horizontal to the floor. Driving up quickly, his penis entered the woman from below. His face contorted with effort and he pulled hard against the elastic restraints, lifting his thighs and wrapping them around hers, effectively using her to keep his own legs in place. Then he began to thrust, driving himself deep into the woman's vagina. Rachel was so enthralled that she realised it had been several moments since she had last moved. Sally, standing open-mouthed beside her, was clearly equally captivated.

The study door opened and Brothers Martin and Duncan reappeared. Rachel and Sally immediately threw themselves back into their work, but the Brothers were having none of it.

'Well,' said Brother Duncan, addressing Rachel. 'I don't think you've done this job very well, have you?'

'No, Brother Duncan,' replied Rachel, bowing her head. She knew the Brothers were playing a game of their own and was quite happy to join in.

'Your mind seems to be on other things,' he added, glancing towards the window, through which the suspended Brother could still be seen thrusting with happy abandon. Brother Duncan turned to his companion.

'I think these girls need to be punished,' he said. 'Do you have any suggestions, Brother Martin?'

'I think we should first make sure they're not breaking any other rules,' he replied.

'That's a good idea,' agreed Brother Duncan.

Rachel wondered what other rules they had in mind. It didn't take her long to find out.

'Let's make sure they're not wearing any knickers,' said Brother Duncan. He turned to Rachel. 'Have you got any panties on?' he asked.

'No, Brother,' replied Rachel, crossing her hands in front of her legs. 'I've got nothing on under here. And I'd be grateful if you took my word for it.'

Brother Duncan grinned. 'I can't do that,' he replied and moved closer. His eyes never left Rachel's as he slipped his hand beneath the hem of her skirt. She took a deep breath as his fingers smoothed across her bare bottom, fanning out to cup the soft underhang of her left buttock. Then he moved on, stroking both cheeks, and palming her hips. He paused at the top of her rear crack, before pressing one finger into her cleft, pushing down. She knew that she was hot and sticky after all the day's events, but he didn't seem to mind that his progress was slowed by the dampness that glued her cheeks together.

Brother Martin was clearly interfering with Sally, too, judging by the sweet look of contentment on her face. Rachel saw that his hand was circling the front of Sally's skirt, and realised from the misty glaze in her friend's eyes that he was masturbating her. Rachel closed her eyes and sighed as she felt Brother Duncan's other hand cup her vulva, squeezing lightly at her moist flesh. At the same time, she was acutely aware of his finger in her crack, wriggling closer to her sphincter.

Both men's penises were now fully erect, and Rachel felt Brother Duncan's member prod her tummy. His breathing was hard and fast and she knew that despite all his training he was in danger of losing control of himself. Indeed it was obvious that both men were. Still, she had to admit that she didn't much mind. The probing fingers were working their magic and it seemed such a long time since she had had a man between her legs that she didn't much care how he managed it. The events in the next room continued to impinge on her thoughts. The second Madam had now entered the fray. The Brother's head was hanging low, only a couple of feet off the ground; the muscles in his arms standing out like boulders as he fought to maintain his position. The second Madam now stood over him and bent low so that her breasts covered his face. She hugged him to her like a baby at the teat, wickedly cutting off his air supply. Rising above the pleasure that threatened to overwhelm her own body, Rachel realised that this could only hamper the Brother's chances of continuing to fuck the first Madam. Perhaps, she reflected, that was the whole point of the exercise. Anyway, she hardly cared because the feeling engendered by Brother Duncan's fingers was so divine that she felt her breath quickening in anticipation of her release.

His fingers withdrew and he turned to his companion, who appeared to have stopped teasing Sally at the same time. Instead, they pushed the girls down across the desk and moved into position between their parted buttocks.

'I'm afraid you'll have to be punished,' said Brother Duncan. 'You've been very naughty maids and it just won't do.'

'No, Brother,' murmured both Rachel and Sally. Their simultaneous responses mirrored the identical nature of their predicament.

'So, what's it to be?' asked Brother Martin. 'You can lose thirty credits or we can come to some other arrangement.'

'Oh,' giggled Rachel, feeling his penis nudge between her splayed buttocks, 'I think some other arrangement sounds more interesting.'

In the other room, events were fast reaching a crisis. The young Brother was now thrusting harder than ever as he strove to reach his climax before passing out between the second Madam's voluptuous breasts. Rachel was conscious of her sodden pussy and squealed with unashamed delight as she felt Brother Duncan nudge his hardness between her lips.

'What's yours like?' he asked, turning to his friend. Far from upsetting Rachel, Brother Duncan's careless enquiry only served to enhance her pleasure. She closed her eyes and imagined herself as a fresh-faced young maid, being ravished by the master of the house.

'She's very tight,' replied Brother Martin. 'I'm entering her very slowly. It feels as if it's nibbling at my cock.'

'This one's got a huge cunt,' said Brother Duncan. 'I think it could swallow me alive.'

It was suddenly all too much for both Brothers. They must have thrust simultaneously, thought Rachel, judging from Sally's squeal, as Brother Duncan drove fully home, his balls bouncing against her vulva. Rachel opened her eyes and watched the Brother in the other room as he neared his own long-drawn-out release. He was swinging from side to side, his face still trapped between a huge pair of breasts, his penis driving upwards into the first Madam's oil-drenched body. Suddenly, he emitted a strangled moan, almost inaudible in the depths of the breasts smothering his face. He came wildly, thrusting high and hard. So, at that moment, did Rachel and so, apparently, did all the other participants in this strange game. It was, incredibly, the fifth time she had climaxed since breakfast. But this was the best of all, she told herself, for it was with a man inside her, emptying his seed deep into her as her vaginal muscles contracted around his huge shaft and milked him dry.

The rest of the day was spent performing simple cleaning duties. The girls were given a meal in the canteen shortly before 6 o'clock and this time were allowed to sit at the table. There was no more sexual activity and, at 6.30 exactly, Master Stéfan escorted them back to the van. Nothing untoward occurred on their return journey. Unsurprisingly, Rachel nodded off, and was only woken by the sound of the van grinding up the gravel path towards The Hall.

Madam Janet was waiting to meet them. She smiled and said, 'I hope you enjoyed your day out.'

Rachel and Sally lowered their heads and answered positively. Then they were taken back to their room, unclipped and, after a quick shower and a small meal provided on a tray in their room, they climbed wearily into bed. Rachel felt Sally snuggle up close behind her and found that after a day with men she enjoyed the soft feel of Sally's flesh against hers. That was her last thought before, like Sally, she drifted off into a heavy, dream-filled sleep.

Twelve

Rachel awoke with a start. There was a loud commotion in the corridor. Sally sat up beside her, rubbing her eyes and yawning. She looked at the clock by the bedside.

'It's only 5 o'clock,' she moaned. 'What's going on?'

'No idea,' replied Rachel. Whatever was going on, it was getting further away. They could hear the sound of running feet, and then a voice. The words, 'No!' and 'Please!' were all they could make out, but they knew the voice at once. It was Shirley, one of the less extrovert girls, who for some time had given the impression that she was struggling with the course.

Everything went quiet again after that, but neither Rachel nor Sally was able to get back to sleep. They got up and washed, speculating idly and uselessly for the next hour until, at 6.30, the door opened and Madam Janet appeared. They waited for her to say something but, after a brief exchange of pleasantries, she clipped them to her rein and led them outside as usual.

The rest of the day passed much like any other. It was now their thirteenth week at The Hall. In a little over a fortnight's time they would receive their final assessment and learn if they had been judged suitable for membership of the Sisterhood. Whatever the result, reflected Rachel, she knew that a whole new world had opened up to her. She was fitter now than she had ever been, and was proud of her newly acquired talents. It had not been easy but they had all gained something valuable from their time at The Hall. Her knowledge of the arts, of science, of world history, though undoubtedly still basic, had improved staggeringly over the past four months. She felt more confident in her ability to hold her own on almost any topic.

None of which changed the fact that today they were one girl short. At breakfast and lunch, the girls chatted generally about the day's events, but no one mentioned Shirley. It was as if they all knew that it was a subject best left alone. Something had happened to her. Whether or not they would find out what was another matter.

Meanwhile, Rachel's plan to unmask Master Stéfan had run into some difficulty. She had engineered a few minor breaches of the rules during her acting classes over the past few weeks and had been summoned to his office on more than one occasion. He clearly enjoyed chastising her. Sometimes he would simply place her over his knee and spank her, sometimes he would chain her up and allow her to fellate him. She always did her best to leave him under the impression that she would be back for more. The fact that he never asked her why she broke so many minor rules convinced her that he was happy to go along with things.

It was just before dinner that day that Rachel was approached by Madam Janet.

'Master Stéfan wishes to see you in his room,' she said. 'Apparently he was not very pleased with your acting class yesterday.'

Rachel felt her heart skip a beat. With so little time left now, she had decided that it was necessary to force the issue. Ensnaring Master Stéfan had, in retrospect, been the easy part. But it seemed that she was as far away as ever from unmasking him as a traitor. Over the past few days she had given a lot of thought to her next move. It had been almost a week since they had been alone together, and she feared that her influence was waning.

Master Stéfan was speaking into a small hand-held tape recorder as they entered the room. Rachel heard him mention one of the other girls' names and assumed he was preparing an assessment. She expected him to dismiss Madam Janet as he always did. Then they would be alone and she would find out what he had in mind. But this time he did not dismiss Madam. Rachel felt uneasy. She wondered what was going to happen next.

Master Stéfan dropped the recorder on to his desk and stood up. 'You did not perform very well in your acting class yesterday,' he said. 'Now why was that?'

Rachel felt her heart skip a beat. This was not what was supposed to happen. Something had gone wrong. She was in trouble.

'Madam Janet does not believe that you were trying very hard,' he continued.

'I – I was, Master,' replied Rachel. Her mind was racing now, trying to think of some way out of her predicament.

'Madam Janet thinks you may have an ulterior motive.'

Master Stéfan let the words hang in the air, heavy with threat. Rachel fell silent. She felt her stomach churn.

'Well?' enquired Master Stéfan. 'What was the reason? There must be one.'

'If you do not explain yourself,' interjected Madam Janet, speaking for the first time, 'you will be deducted thirty credits. On your recent performance, that will place you perilously close to the punishment zone.'

'There is nothing more I can say,' replied Rachel. She lowered her eyes, afraid to look either of them in the face. This was getting increasingly serious.

'Very well,' said Madam Janet. 'You are deducted thirty credits. I will report this to Mistress Katrina immediately.'

Rachel looked up. She caught Master Stéfan's eye. She put all her concentration into lowering her long lashes that fraction of a second which told a careful watcher that there was indeed more to say, but that it could not be said just yet. She bit her lower lip lightly and swallowed hard. Part of it was acting and part of it was sheer nerves.

Madam Janet turned to Master Stéfan. 'Would you prefer it if I returned Sister Rachel to her room?'

Master Stéfan paused for a moment before replying. 'No,' he said at last. 'She may remain here. I will see if I can get to the bottom of this. It may require a more physical punishment. We shall have to see.'

After the door closed behind her, Rachel wondered what was going to happen next. Master Stéfan came and stood in front of her. She lowered her eyes.

'I will give you one last chance,' he said, then grinned. She suddenly realised that he had orchestrated this whole episode. It was his way of humiliating her, extracting more twisted amusement by making her think she was in worse trouble than she was. The bastard, she thought. Then another thought hit her. If he had chosen to frighten her like this, was it because he was perhaps tiring of their little game? If that were the case, then she would have to act quickly. Rachel took a deep breath. It was now or never.

'I – I'm sorry, Master,' she replied. 'It won't happen again. I – I . . .'

'Well?' he asked, in a clearly annoyed tone.

Rachel suddenly reached out and let her hand brush the side of Master Stéfan's face. He stepped back as if he had received an electric shock.

Rachel reacted as quickly. 'I'm sorry, Master, I'm sorry!'

'What does this mean?' he asked, obviously taken by surprise.

Rachel drew herself up to her full height and pushed

out her breasts as far as she could. His eyes swept over them, as transfixed as ever by her generously rounded flesh. She saw the look in his eyes and knew that she was close to ensnaring him again, if only she could avoid doing anything silly.

'I think you know what it means, Master. I'm sorry. I know this means I must leave the Sisterhood. But I couldn't help myself.'

Rachel was gambling everything. If he bit, she was perhaps one step closer to finding out if he was a traitor to the organisation. If he didn't it might mean the end of her stay at The Hall. It was now a case of all or nothing.

'I am unsuitable to join the Sisterhood. I know that now.'

'Why do you say that?' asked Master Stéfan.

'I thought I was a dominant personality,' said Rachel, 'but since I've been here I haven't been so sure. I was confused. The more I thought about it the more I realised how much I enjoyed being with you. You are very strong and it makes me feel, I don't know – safe, I suppose.'

Rachel paused for breath. Though she had rehearsed mentally the sort of approach she would adopt when this moment came, she was making up a lot of it as she went along and for one awful moment her mind had gone blank. Still, she thought, perhaps it was good to pause for it gave Master Stéfan a chance to digest what she was saying. She was playing mental chess with him, searching for a chink in his armour. She could see him thinking and decided to continue before he could grasp anything. It was important to keep him dangling and, perhaps, ever so slightly confused. If he pondered too long and too well, he might see through her plan and that would be disastrous. He turned away, obviously unsure of himself.

'You must do as you choose,' he said quietly. 'That is always your prerogative.'

'Do you want me to go, Master?' she asked quietly. She knew she was treading on ever-more dangerous ground.

He swung round quickly. 'My views are neither here nor there!' There was something different in the way he now looked at her. It was a look of contempt. That was worrying. Though he had used her in many ways and on many occasions over the past few weeks, he had never looked at her like this before. Something had gone wrong. Before she had a chance to think, he leant forward and pressed a button. The door opened and Madam Janet re-entered.

'Take her away,' he said curtly, then turned his back on the pair of them and reached for a thick tome sitting on the top of his bookshelf.

Rachel struggled through her dinner, pecking at the medallions of pork on her plate and stabbing listlessly at her buttered vegetables. She had no appetite. She was now convinced that she had messed up everything. That look in Master Stéfan's eyes had said it all. He was tiring of her, perhaps had already tired of her. But why? Was it because he believed that she was trying to get too close to him? Was it emotional involvement he feared? Rachel, however, had little time to consider the matter further for Mistress Katrina now entered the room and addressed them. What she said was short and to the point.

'You will all have noticed that Initiate Shirley is not with us today. Unfortunately, after considering her record it has been decided that her progress to date leaves a lot to be desired. It is highly likely that she will be expelled.'

Mistress Katrina paused to allow her news to sink in. No one had fallen by the wayside since day one. Having got this far together the girls were beginning to share a bond, barely definable but it was there nonetheless. To lose one of their number was a blow. It also served as a painful reminder to them all that no one's place on the course was safe. If it could happen to Shirley it could happen to any of them.

'However,' continued Mistress Katrina. 'The Sisterhood wishes to give all miscreants an opportunity to redeem themselves, particularly at this late stage. Having come this far, we believe that Initiate Shirley should be given one last chance. She has spent the day considering her position and it has not wavered, though she has been told of the ordeal she must undergo to remain at The Hall.'

Rachel's ears pricked up. She remembered the punishment that had been meted out to Sally. Was Shirley to undergo something even worse? It was hard to believe that such a thing was possible.

'We will reassemble in the Punishment Room at 8 o'clock tonight,' said Mistress Katrina. 'You will then see Initiate Shirley, possibly for the last time. That is all.'

'What do you think they'll do to her?' asked Sally, after they had been returned to their rooms.

'Heaven knows,' replied Rachel, 'but I imagine it will make what happened to you look like child's play.'

They sat down and decided to get on with some studying but it was hard to keep their minds on anything difficult and the hours dragged by. At last, at five minutes to eight, the door opened and Madam Janet entered. Rachel raised her hand to ask a question. 'Madam, what will happen to Shirley?'

'She will be punished,' replied Madam Janet coldly. 'In a way that will test her resolve.'

'Do you think she'll come through it, Madam?' asked Sally.

Madam Janet thought for a moment or two. 'I very much doubt it,' she replied.

* * *

The Punishment Room was as they had all remembered it, except that now there was a large cage standing in the centre, with an arrangement of thickly linked chains hanging from the ceiling. Shirley was brought in by two of the Madams. She did not resist. To have done so would have entailed instant expulsion. It was clear that even at this late stage she desperately wanted to remain at The Hall.

Shirley was taken into the cage. Her hands and legs were cuffed to the chains which were then raised so that she was suspended slightly, her face towards the ground. Mistress Katrina approached with the duplex. She strapped the instrument around Shirley's waist, taking particular care as she inserted the double-pronged intruder into Shirley's pussy and rectum. Shirley moaned as the dildos entered her, but otherwise she remained silent. Once Mistress Katrina was satisfied that the duplex was correctly attached she left the cage, shut the door and stepped back.

'Initiate Shirley,' she declared, 'you have breached the rules of the Sisterhood. It is the judgment of the Council that you be expelled.'

Shirley's face turned pale and she let out a muted wail.

'However,' continued Mistress Katrina, her voice softening, 'the Council has decided that if you successfully survive trial by duplex you will be allowed to remain here at The Hall. Do you submit to such trial?'

Shirley nodded her head violently. 'Yes, Mistress. I willingly submit.'

Mistress Katrina smiled. 'Very well,' she continued. 'If you survive a period of twelve hours without begging to be released from your torment, you will be afforded an opportunity to mend your ways. Is this agreed?'

Shirley nodded again. 'Yes, Mistress!'

'Then let the trial begin,' replied Mistress Katrina.

She turned to Madam Janet who was holding a small remote control in her hand. She pressed a button on the gadget and immediately Shirley jumped. The duplex began whirring, performing its dreadful work in both her holes.

'Two Madams will remain with you all night,' explained Mistress Katrina, 'in case you wish to end your torment. The rest of us will wait for one hour, as this will add to your humiliation.'

The next hour passed like two or three. Several times, Shirley moaned as the duplex brought her to the edge of orgasm. Defeat would come if she could take no more, in which case everyone knew that she would beg to be allowed to climax and that would be it. She would be given her orgasm and dismissed from the Sisterhood.

Rachel was glad it wasn't her strung up and tormented like this. It must be so humiliating to be suspended in front of your friends, she thought. To be electronically masturbated and weeping like a child each time you were brought close to orgasm and then denied it. More than once she was sure that Shirley was on the point of surrender.

'Oh, Madam! Madam! Please!' she cried out at one point, tears of pleasure and frustration pouring down her cheeks.

'Do you wish to climax?' asked Madam Janet, approaching her.

The word 'yes' seemed to form on Shirley's lips, but at the last minute she shook her head from side to side and fell briefly silent before throwing her head back and wailing loudly. Time after time she was taken to the edge of release, a release cruelly denied to her again and again.

The evidence of her excitement was plain for all to see. Her sap began to leak from between her thighs, hanging in silvery threads from her skin, glistening on her flesh. She swung left and right and up and down as she was repeatedly dragged screaming to the very limits of her endurance. Only the fact that she had been trained and was now strong and fit allowed her to remain suspended, for her body weight was working against her all the time. But whether she could survive all night was another matter. Eventually the first hour passed and Mistress Katrina stood up to address her.

'It is time for the Initiates to retire for the evening. You will now be left alone with the Madams to endure your trial.' She paused for a moment. 'There is a further aspect I had not mentioned. The Madams will be allowed to join you in the cage from time to time. So that the other Initiates can witness what you will undergo and what they will too, should they breach our rules, Madam Saskia will now demonstrate.'

Madam Saskia walked up to the cage, opened the door and stepped inside. The duplex was taking Shirley close again as Madam Saskia reached up with both hands and cupped Shirley's exposed breasts with her fingers. She squeezed the young girl's flesh and pulled at her nipples. Shirley threw her head back and screamed out loud.

'No, Madam, please, Madam! Not this too! It's not fair!'

'You are not to judge what is fair, Shirley,' retorted Madam Saskia. She leant in towards Shirley and kissed her on the mouth while continuing to squeeze her cruelly. The duplex whirred incessantly. A second Madam, Susanna, entered the cage and began to stroke Shirley's legs, running her fingers up the inside of her thighs. The poor girl almost lost control, tossing her head from side to side and weeping out loud.

'No, no, no, no, no!' she repeated over and over again. Mistress Katrina smiled.

'Good night, Shirley. Say good night to Shirley, girls,' she added, turning to the other Initiates. One by one as they left the room they stopped, faced Shirley and wished her a good night. It seemed cruel in the extreme, but then none of them was under any illusion – to be a Sister entailed maximum control over their bodies and this was simply another part of their training.

That night they were instructed to leave their doors open so that they might hear Shirley's almost constant wailing. As a result it was difficult to sleep. Rachel's concerns over Master Stéfan didn't help either. She wished she could have spoken to Sally, or to anyone, but that was out of the question. In the meantime, in the Punishment Room, it was clear that between the duplex and the ministrations of the Madams, poor Shirley was being given no peace. At last, in the early hours of the morning, Rachel finally dropped off to sleep. The following morning, when she and the other Initiates awoke, the first thing they noticed was how quiet it was. It was the last time any of them saw Shirley.

Thirteen

It was a slender chance, but it was all she had left.

With only two weeks of training to go, Rachel was growing increasingly concerned at her lack of progress in unmasking Master Stéfan. She found it difficult to concentrate in many of her classes and was aware that she was losing valuable credits.

It had been several days since she had last seen Master Stéfan. During that time she had spent many agitated hours pondering her next move. She had gone over all that had passed between them, searching for the moment when things had gone wrong. She had examined events from every angle, turned things on their head, seen it from her point of view and from his, but was still no nearer to an answer.

Wednesday had been a miserable night. It had rained heavily. Loud storms had rumbled overhead for hours, making sleep almost impossible. But she had slept, on and off, and she had dreamt. She had dreamt of Master Stéfan and she had dreamt of Michael. But most importantly of all, she had dreamt of Madam Laura. She was lying on the black leather couch and Madam Laura was asking her questions. Rachel was telling her that she was a submissive – but this time Madam was having none of it. She told her she was a liar and that she would have to be punished. She had a huge feather in her hand and was tickling Rachel on her feet. Rachel was screaming at her to stop but she wouldn't. Madam

Laura was calling her a liar and saying that liars must be punished!

An explosion of light filled the room and Rachel sat bolt upright in bed. Sally jumped in her sleep and mumbled but didn't wake. Rachel was relieved because she was too excited to talk. She cursed herself for not paying more attention to Madam Fiona's psychology lessons. She might be wrong, she might be terribly wrong. But now was not the time for a faint heart. She would have to be audacious. She would have to be very audacious.

It was her only hope.

Not for the first time Rachel had been forced to engineer a summons to Master Stéfan's room. She had deliberately fluffed her lines in two of his recent classes. After the first infraction, he had simply called her out and spanked her severely across the bottom. This time, at least, she had made it as far as his office. When she had made the first move he had not resisted, which gave her some hope that her star had not completely waned.

She was kneeling between his legs, holding his penis between her breasts and watching his erection grow. But there was something wrong. He wasn't as excited as he usually was. With a sudden glare of displeasure, he pushed her roughly aside. Rachel looked up at him and could see the look of disappointment in his eyes and knew that he had grown tired of her.

'What's the matter, Master?' she asked. 'Have I disappointed you?'

'I thought you might be different,' he said. 'But I see you are like all the rest.' He turned away. Panic gripped Rachel's insides. Things really were as bad as she had feared.

'You may go,' he said.

Rachel knew she hadn't done anything wrong. She had acted the submissive as he had wanted, and knew that she had played the part well. She took her courage in both her hands and prepared for the last throw of the die.

'I'm sorry, Master,' she said suddenly. 'That really won't do.'

He turned around abruptly. If his face was anything to go by, she had at least caught his attention. Before he could say another word, she reached out and took a firm hold of both his wrists. She knew that he was strong enough to break her grip, though most men would not have been able to. She was gambling that, for a moment at least, he would react like any other man.

'Bow before me,' she said, tugging his hands downwards. She raised her voice as loud as she was able. 'I said bow before me! Kneel, you miserable little worm!'

This was it. It was now or never. She had acted a part since she had arrived at The Hall, masking her true nature, pretending to be what she was not. Her only hope now lay in the belief that Master Stéfan had been playing the same game. She was banking everything on the fact that it was that which had ultimately disappointed him. That he was weakening, she was sure. She had him under her influence, but that was not enough. He craved something else, something that would bring him completely under her control. The only problem was, if she got it wrong it was all over for her. In poker terms she was making one hell of a bluff.

An eternity seemed to pass. Rachel had practically stopped breathing. She knew if she drew breath she would collapse, for the pretence would be too difficult to sustain. Her heart was pounding with terror and excitement. She knew he could break her in two if he chose. She was staking everything on the fact that he would not choose.

She could hardly believe it when he fell to his knees in front of her and bowed his head.

'Yes, Mistress,' he said.

They were words Rachel had never expected to hear. Should she act now or wait? She realised that she needed time to think and she decided to wait. This was all too sudden. Besides, now she had snared him. Now she had discovered his true personality, it was best to bide her time.

'Not now,' she said quietly. 'Later.'

He looked up into her eyes. There was stark disappointment etched across his face, but this time it was the look of a man denied what he most desired, not a man disappointed in her, as it had been a few minutes earlier.

'Don't look me in the face, you piece of dirt!' she cried. Instinctively, she brought her hand first up and then down across the side of his face. It probably hurt her as much as it hurt him, thought Rachel, but it felt good. It was something she had wanted to do for ages. The look of excitement in his eyes was unmistakable. This was turning him on. She looked down, past his freshly bowed head and saw the bulge between his thighs. He was becoming aroused and she knew that she now held him in the palm of her hand. She felt a sudden rush of adrenaline. Her dominant personality was reasserting itself and, having been denied since her arrival at The Hall, it had returned with a vengeance. She realised that she too was becoming very excited. That made up her mind for her. She needed time to reflect, to plan her next move.

'Please summon Madam Janet. I wish to be escorted back to my room.'

Confusion distorted his features. Confusion and despair.

'At once!' she ordered. 'Then I may come back and see you. Or should I say, I may come back and see to you.'

That did it for Master Stéfan. He scrambled to his feet and pressed the intercom switch on his desk. There was a long pause, which was perhaps just as well for it gave him a chance to compose himself. It was incredible, thought Rachel. She had never seen such a change come over a man so quickly.

Back in her room, she found Sally with her nose in a weighty tome. She desperately wished she could confide in someone but knew that was out of the question.

After Madam Janet had gone, Sally moved closer and kissed Rachel lightly on the cheek, then reached out and stroked her left nipple.

'You've got lovely breasts,' said Sally. 'I often wish I had big breasts. Mine are so small you can hardly see them most of the time.'

'Size isn't everything,' replied Rachel and they both laughed.

All the girls were feeling the strain as the course neared its end. They had grown together and, with only two exceptions, it looked as if they would all make it to the end. But they knew also that getting to the end wasn't enough in itself. It was still about how well they had performed throughout. Rachel felt Sally's nimble fingers slip down to her vulva. She lay back on the bed and splayed her legs. It was lovely to be caressed like this. It took her mind off things. She could feel herself growing wetter.

Sally lowered her head into Rachel's lap and Rachel felt the girl's nose graze the inside of her upper thigh. Sally was sniffing near her pussy and Rachel wondered if she were trying to see if Master Stéfan had fucked her. Suddenly the smaller girl's tongue snaked out and ran up and down Rachel's labia. Rachel raised her buttocks and wriggled her hips from side to side. She enjoyed the play of Sally's mouth, circling her opening, her nose rubbing gently against the little hood of her clitoris. Rachel reached out and ran her fingers through Sally's small head of blonde hair, still swaying her hips from side to side. It all felt so divine. She sighed out loud.

'God, I wish I could come,' she moaned.

'Why don't you?' whispered Sally.

'Because we haven't asked permission,' replied Rachel, who was surprised by Sally's reply. She knew the rules as well as her.

'I've asked,' replied Sally. 'I asked Madam Janet while you were out.'

Rachel's eyes opened wide. 'You're not just saying that, are you?' she asked.

Sally looked up for a brief moment. Her eyes were sparkling and her lips glistened with Rachel's juices. 'I'm not joking,' she replied, and lowered her head, attacking Rachel's pussy with renewed fervour.

Rachel opened her legs wide and enjoyed Sally's tongue sliding the length of her vulva. She felt the other woman's lips nuzzle at her labia, and then begin to worry the sensitive bud of her clitoris. Her orgasm came fast and furiously, as if she were emptying herself of all her pent-up worries over Master Stéfan. Afterwards, they lay quietly together and just enjoyed each other's company.

'Have you ever wondered what you'll do once we finish here?' asked Sally.

'I suppose that depends on whether or not I graduate successfully,' replied Rachel.

'I'm sure you will,' said Sally. 'I'm not sure about me, though. That punishment I received must have counted against me.'

'Don't forget the number of times I've been called up in front of Master Stéfan,' said Rachel.

'That's different,' countered Sally. 'That's not really serious.' She paused. 'Just horrible!' She screwed up her face and laughed.

It took Rachel a long time to go to sleep that night. Her mind was turning over several possibilities, forming and dismissing plans. She didn't have long now, but she felt excited. She had turned the tables on Master Stéfan in a way she had not anticipated. But she also knew that she was running out of time in which to unmask him. Of course, as yet, she had discovered nothing to prove that he *was* a traitor. In the early hours, a plan at last began to form in her mind. It was dangerous, but it might just work. One thing she was sure of, however. If it didn't work, she was going to be in a huge amount of trouble.

Two more days passed before she was again called to Master Stéfan's room. Rachel had worked hard in the meantime so, when she received the summons, she knew it could not be for anything she had done wrong. She felt both excited and nervous. She had gambled everything on Master Stéfan wanting to pursue the new path she had offered him. But what if she were wrong? It was not, she decided, something she wanted to dwell on.

There was an awkward silence after Madam Janet had left them. Neither seemed sure of their next move. Rachel knew that if she made a mistake now, that was it. She also realised that hanging back would not advance her cause at all. It was now a case of all or nothing. She drew herself up to her full height, thrust her breasts forward and pointed to the carpet in front of her.

'Kneel!' she ordered, investing the command with as much authority as she was able to.

Master Stéfan appeared to hesitate. For Rachel it was one of the longest moments of her life. Then, as if he were a puppet whose strings had been suddenly cut, his legs buckled and he fell to the floor. His head was bowed. Rachel was glad that he averted his gaze so obediently, because she was sure that if he had looked up at her, her face at that moment would have betrayed her.

'What would you have me do, Mistress?' he asked quietly.

Rachel stepped behind him, and took hold of his hair, tugging his head back sharply. She dropped to her knees and pressed her mouth close to his ear.

'Don't speak unless I give you permission. Is that understood?'

Master Stéfan nodded slightly and with some difficulty.

'Follow me,' said Rachel. 'No!' she added as he began to rise. 'On all fours, like a dog!' She turned her back on him, her heart pounding. She could hardly believe that the tables had been turned so decisively. But now she had to decide what to do next. She had worked out a vague scheme, but putting it into practice was something else. Entering the dungeon, she took hold of the various chains that hung from the ceiling, casting about for the other props she would need. She felt like a chef, making sure that all the necessary ingredients were in place. It was time to make a meal out of Master Stéfan.

Rachel stood back and admired her handiwork. If the other Initiates could see him now, thought Rachel, they wouldn't be so afraid of Master Stéfan. He was suspended from the ceiling, his arms and legs securely bound and his head forced back at what must surely have been a most uncomfortable angle. Only one final touch was needed now. She reached for a black latex mask, hanging from a hook on the wall.

'No,' protested Master Stéfan, his eyes widening dramatically.

Rachel knew she didn't have much time. She pulled the mask down over his face.

'If I say you wear a mask, you wear a mask,' she shouted, ignoring his protests. It was a tight fit. There were small holes for the nose and mouth but the eyes were covered as were the ears. It was important that he couldn't see or hear properly. She wandered around and admired her handiwork afresh. Picking up the whip she curled it back.

'Can you hear me?' she asked. Master Stéfan's body jiggled in mid-air. He could. That was all right up to a point. But she didn't want him to hear too much. She lowered her voice a little.

'Move if you can hear this,' she said. He remained motionless. She moved closer and raised her voice.

'You've been a bad boy, Master Stéfan. I'm going to have to punish you.' His body jiggled again.

'Mummy is going to have to spank her bad boy,' she whispered into his ear. 'I hope little Stéfan won't cry too much. Mummy doesn't like to see her naughty boy cry.'

His body jiggled violently. Rachel brought her hand down and cracked the whip across his leather-trousered backside. She knew how important it was not to mark him. Well, not at least where it could be seen. His body jumped. She put the whip to one side and took hold of his trousers, tugging them down. His body jiggled even more. She tugged until the top half of his arse was exposed. She looked down and admired his muscular cheeks, smoothing her palm across his tight flesh. She pressed her mouth against his skin and felt him wave languorously. She bared her teeth and bit into his flesh, happy to hear him moan. She bit long and hard but was careful not to mark him. Then, kneeling down beside him, she raised one side of his mask exposing his ear.

'I'm going to hurt you, Master Stéfan. I'm going to really hurt you. For all the girls you've frightened. This is their revenge. Imagine them all climbing over you, trampling on you, sitting on your face, smothering you between their breasts. Imagine all that while I hurt you.' Then she let the mask slip back into place. Between his legs, his penis bulged free of his pants, and jutted up hard against his belly. He was very excited now, despite his protests. It was amazing to think that Master Stéfan who so terrorised the girls was really a submissive at heart. Still, this wasn't why she was here. She didn't have long, but she had a plan and must put it into action fast. If she failed to make her presence felt, he might suspect something. She lashed out with the whip to remind him she was there, then stepped quickly back into his office. She crossed to the desk, picked up the small Dictaphone, ejected the cassette and opened a drawer. She hit lucky first time, finding an open pack of fresh tapes. She picked one up, slipped it into the machine and stepped back into the dungeon. She moved to the far side and raised her voice, so that he would know where she was standing. Switching on the Dictaphone, she began talking loudly, swearing at Master Stéfan, abusing him verbally. She didn't know if he could hear precisely what she was saying, and indeed she hoped he couldn't. Her plan would only work if her language, however obscene, was indistinct. Occasionally, she switched the machine off and whipped him across his bare arse. Once she knelt beside him and fingered his penis. Squeezing beneath him, she wrapped her breasts around his shaft and was rewarded with a particularly energetic roll of his hips.

After several minutes of this, Rachel rewound the tape, walking back and forth and occasionally whipping Master Stéfan's legs. She knelt down and took his cheeks in her hands squeezing them very hard, then pressed her breasts tightly to his masked face, making it difficult for him to breathe. After a while, she decided to give him something else to think about. Pressing one hand between her thighs she allowed her wetness to soak into her fingers. She pulled his mask up and pressed her fingers over his nostrils, smearing her smell on to his flesh. Then she pulled the mask back into place, sealing her smell inside. Master Stéfan rolled his head from side to side and Rachel heard his breath come in short sharp bursts of pleasure. She smacked him several times across his tight buttocks. It stung her hand, but he seemed to enjoy it. Kneeling down, she held his penis in her hand, rolling it from side to side. His balls were heavy and full of seed. She squeezed, then let him go then squeezed again. She was surprised at how wet she was becoming, increasingly aware of the pleasure to be gained from wielding power over a helpless man. She knew now where her true nature lay.

It was time to put the next phase of her plan into action. Placing the Dictaphone on the floor by the dungeon door, she switched it on at full volume. Her voice rang out loud and clear. Though to the naked ear it was obviously a recording, she was now gambling everything on the fact that to Master Stéfan's masked ears it sounded like her muffled voice continuing to abuse him. Rachel darted back into the office, crossed to his desk and began rifling through the drawers. The first one yielded nothing but a lot of uninteresting papers and a small book of erotic sketches which she had to force herself not to examine further. She didn't have the time. After a minute or two she crossed back to the door. Her voice had been playing for a while without interruption and she was worried that Master Stéfan might become suspicious. She switched the Dictaphone off, crossed to his side and ran her hands over his bare back. Lowering her head, she sank her teeth into one buttock, moved her hands beneath his midriff and took hold of his penis. Sinking her teeth as deep as she dared she squeezed him hard, pulling back the foreskin and feathering his testicles with the tips of her fingers.

An idea occurred to her. She took hold of the whip handle and pressed it into his crack. He clenched his buttocks tight as if he feared or suspected what she was about to do. She brought the whip down hard on his bared flesh and his cheeks parted. She pushed the handle up against his anus, and again he tightened his buttocks, wriggling furiously. She crossed back to his head and knelt beside him, her mouth close to his ear so that he could hear her clearly this time.

'Mummy wants her boy to be big and brave. I'm going to push this naughty little whip into your bottom. You must relax. Do you understand?'

Master Stéfan shook his head from side to side and grunted uselessly into the gag stopping up his mouth. It was clear that he understood only too well and wanted none of it. Or did he? It was so difficult to be sure. Rachel decided to try a different tack.

'Very well, then,' she said. 'No more games today. Mummy will untie her bad, bad boy and go away.'

Rachel knew she was taking a big chance. At this moment Master Stéfan was helpless. She suspected that it was not a position he had ever been in before and she doubted whether the opportunity to restrain him like this would present itself again. He went suddenly quiet, his breathing laboured; his body trembling with effort not resistance. Rachel stroked his buttocks gently and felt them soften in her hands.

'That's a very good boy,' she whispered. 'Now try to relax, this won't hurt and it will make mummy so very happy.'

She began to ease the whip handle forward, impressed by Master Stéfan's ability to control his rectal muscles, for they gave only the slightest resistance as she fed an inch or two of leather into his backside. Once the hilt was firmly in place, she took hold of his penis and began to pump it gently. His balls were hanging down between his legs. They looked huge and heavy, and Rachel had to resist the urge to masturbate him to climax there and then, just to remind herself how much seed this monstrous man was capable of discharging.

She reached up and wiggled the whip handle in his backside as she played with his penis. His body went into some sort of spasm and it was obvious that he was dangerously close to orgasm. That wouldn't do at all. Once he had climaxed, her power over him would end. She released his penis, stood up and slapped him hard on the backside. 'Such a bad, bad boy!" she cajoled, moving back towards the office door. By now she was sure that she had searched the room thoroughly, and yet she had found nothing. Something was nagging at the back of her mind. There was something she had seen and yet not seen. Of course! She restarted the tape, ran across to the desk and examined the three open drawers carefully.

She was right! The bottom drawer was deeper on the outside than it was on the inside. She emptied the contents neatly on to the floor, reached inside and felt around. There must be a secret catch. Suddenly the drawer bottom clicked upwards. Beneath it was a hidden compartment stuffed with papers. She knew at once that these were the documents she had been looking for. There were copies of financial accounts, photographs and personal details: entertainment figures, businessmen, Cabinet ministers, the list seemed endless. She was stunned to discover how many well-known people were members of the Fellowship. But there was something else, too, something she had not expected, and it threw her. This complicated matters and she needed time to think. She tidied up the documents, closed the secret compartment and replaced the drawers.

Retrieving the Dictaphone, she ejected the tape, and put the original cassette back into the machine. Now the only problem was how to dispose of her own tape. Back in the dungeon, Master Stéfan was wriggling like a stuck pig. Rachel had half a mind to leave him there. She had discovered all she needed now. Well, no, not quite all. If she had, then she would have left him there and called Mistress Katrina. But there was something else that now troubled her. She would have to think again.

She put the cassette down on the floor, out of Master Stéfan's line of sight, then reached forward and stroked his penis. It was time to end this charade. She ripped off his mask and he blinked several times. The room was quite dull so it didn't take him long to readjust his eyes to the low light. Rachel positioned herself beneath him, locked her hands around the back of his neck, then lifted her legs and wrapped them around his waist.

'How strong is mummy's boy, I wonder?' she murmured as his muscles struggled to cope with the extra weight. His eyes widened like saucers as she began to move her hips, manoeuvring her pussy over the top of his penis. His muscles bulged and sweat broke out across his forehead. He was having to support both their weights now and it was obvious that the effort was taking its toll. Rachel remembered the young man at Brotherhood Manor, suspended in the dungeon, fucking his Madam. She had little doubt that Master Stéfan's own strength was more than equal to the task.

She made contact, suddenly and effectively, her labia opening to admit the huge glans twitching between her legs. She had been wanting to do this since her first day at The Hall. Her feelings towards Master Stéfan himself were largely irrelevant but he had the biggest penis she had ever seen and she knew that she had to have him. Rachel felt her pussy stretching around his shaft and was thankful that her own excitement had made her so wet. She sighed with delight as she engulfed him fully and was rewarded with a grunt of pleasure from Master Stéfan as he rolled his eyes backwards for one moment. As she held on tight and began to rock gently, he did his best to push forward, though his freedom of movement was severely limited. Rachel came quickly and furiously, her climax breaking out from her groin and across her belly. She hugged Master Stéfan tight and felt his seed erupt into her. She had intended releasing him at the last moment and watching his penis empty itself on to the cold dungeon floor. But she was enjoying herself too much. She didn't care if the opportunity did not present itself again. She wanted to feel him climax inside her, and continued to swing, hugging him tight until the last eddies of pleasure had fled her body.

When it was all over, Rachel eased herself off his penis, dropped to the floor and stepped to one side, out of his line of vision. She bent down, retrieved the tiny cassette tape and tucked it into the rear of her harness, between her buttocks. Finally, she untied Master Stéfan, lowering him gently to the floor. He appeared genuinely exhausted and suddenly vulnerable. It was not a sight she had ever expected to see.

On an impulse, she leant forward and kissed him softly on the side of the face. It was not meant as a show of affection, just another attempt to reel him in. He reached up and touched her lightly on the cheek, his usually clear blue eyes hooded with fatigue. Rachel covered his hand with hers for a moment and smiled. Back in the main office, neither of them spoke for a while. Rachel toyed with the idea of continuing her role as the mistress, but for the moment she felt that her ploy had run its natural course. Now she wanted him to think of her differently, in a way that would draw them closer together so that, having solved one mystery, she might be able to solve another.

Master Stéfan looked up at her from the relative safety of his desk. 'You told me recently that you felt you were not Sisterhood material. Do you still believe this?'

Rachel's heart skipped a beat. Was this the moment of no return for Master Stéfan? 'I haven't changed my mind, Master. I want out. I'm sorry. I don't want to lose what we've got, but I want something that not even the Sisterhood can give me.' She pushed her chest forward and watched with quiet satisfaction as Master Stéfan's eyes lingered lovingly on her large breasts. His fascination with her bosom was quite touching really, she thought. He seemed to be on the point of saying something, but struggled with his feelings, afraid to commit himself. In the end he remained silent, but Rachel could sense that he was troubled. She said nothing more, not even when Madam Janet arrived, clipped Rachel to the rein and led her back to her room. She still had a lot of thinking to do.

'I hope you've learnt your lines,' said Madam Janet, when she had returned Rachel to her room. 'Tomorrow's client is one of our most important. He doesn't like to be let down. A lot will depend on it.'

Rachel dragged herself back to the present. In all her excitement she had completely forgotten tomorrow's punishing schedule. It was their final acting assessment. This latest script had proved to be far more complex than the playlet she and Sally had performed for Darren. This next client must indeed be a powerful man, she reflected, for his fantasy, unlike Darren's, seemed to involve just about everyone at The Hall.

Lying in bed that night, however, there was only one thing on Rachel's mind. It concerned what she had discovered in Master Stéfan's desk drawer. Not just evidence of his being a traitor, but something else, maybe something even worse. There were two airline tickets in the secret compartment, tickets to South America, both dated for the day after tomorrow. Master Stéfan was obviously on the point of fleeing The Hall, which was bad enough bearing in mind his plans to expose the Sisterhood. But why two tickets? It could mean only one thing. Master Stéfan must have an accomplice. Someone else at The Hall who was a traitor to the organisation, someone Rachel hadn't reckoned on. But who was it? That was the question now.

Fourteen

From their vantage point in the observation chamber, Rachel and Sally had an unrestricted view of the proceedings. The sitting room in which they had fulfilled Darren's fantasy had gone, and had been replaced by the rich wooden panels of an Old Bailey-style courtroom. Madam Janet leant forward and adjusted the volume button on one of her camera monitors.

'The client has been kept in one of Master Stéfan's mock-up cells for the past 48 hours,' she explained. 'It's all part of the build-up he requires for his fantasy.'

'Has he been punished?' asked Sally.

'It depends what you mean by "punished",' replied Madam Janet. 'He's been chained throughout, allowed to relieve himself in a pot, fed and occasionally cleaned.'

'He hasn't been whipped or anything, then?' enquired Rachel.

'Strangely, no. This particular client holds extreme views on the ways in which criminals should be punished, but he's not into personal pain. Well, not that sort anyway.'

Rachel smiled. Though she dare not ask, it sounded to her as if the so-called 'client' was a judge. This entire set-up seemed to point to it.

'So apart from being chained,' she asked, 'has he been prepared in any other way?'

'He's been masturbated every three hours,' replied Madam Janet. 'Helga and Candie have been taking it in turns, along with a team of Madams. The walls of his cell are covered with nude pin-ups and, during waking hours, there's been a series of soft-porn movies playing constantly. Our client likes to look at his women.'

'Has he been allowed to orgasm?' asked Sally.

'Of course not,' replied Madam Janet. 'That would ruin everything. No, at this moment, I should think he'd do almost anything to relieve himself. Not that he'll be allowed to, of course. Not until we're ready.'

On the screen there was a movement. A door opened and six women filed into the courtroom: Madam Della, Madam Anita, Helga, Candie, Ruth and Kimberley. They were out of their normal basques and harnesses and dressed to kill: heavily made up, in a variety of provocative outfits, from catsuits to miniskirts, low-cut tops and see-through blouses. They resembled not so much a panel of jurors as an outing of high-class hookers. A second door opened, below the well of the courtroom, and the client appeared – his wrists and ankles chained together – escorted by two familiar guards: Evie and Tina. He was, at a guess, in his mid to late fifties. He was stocky and rather ordinary looking, with grey, thinning hair. The two women were dressed alike: black PVC bustiers with tie fronts, black thongs, suspender belts, fishnet stockings and short black boots. The client himself was naked, his penis limp but swollen between his legs. Madam Janet pressed a button on the remote control and the camera zoomed in on his genitalia.

'Look at his balls,' she remarked. The result of two days of unrelieved masturbation was immediately evident. His testicles were large, still and rounded, and from the way he moved it was clear that he was in some discomfort, even pain.

'One touch and he'll flood the dock,' Madam Janet added with a wry grin.

The Madam pressed the zoom-out button and the camera withdrew to a wider angle.

Another door opened, and a voice cried, 'Pray silence for her Honour Judge Rowena!' The tall, wide-hipped brunette strode towards the bench. Though she wore the familiar wig, collar and gown of office, it was clear that beneath her long, flowing robes she was naked. The jurors rose, allowing the man in the dock to cast his greedy eyes over their scantily clad bodies. His hands tried to edge towards his penis, but the chains prevented him from touching himself.

A section had been cut from the front of the bench so that as Rowena sat down, her long legs deliberately splayed, the client had an unrestricted view of her vagina.

Madam Janet pressed the zoom-in button and the camera focused on Rowena's hairless pussy. Her labia were glistening and slightly parted. It was obvious that she was already aroused. Rachel wondered if Rowena had been masturbating herself so as to add to the client's visual excitement.

'We are now convened,' declared Rowena, hammering her gavel twice in quick succession.

As the jurors reseated themselves, one of them, Helga, caught the prisoner's eye. She began to fondle her left breast, squeezing herself through the thin fabric of her blouse. Rachel knew from her script that this was all part of an elaborate game being acted out for the client's benefit. It was his fantasy and one, she reflected, for which he must surely have been paying a small fortune. Here was practical evidence of the rich and powerful forces that lay behind the Fellowship. As Helga continued to tease him, the client leant forward so that his penis made brief contact with the front of the dock. Evie grabbed him by the shoulder and dragged him back sharply. Thwarted, he turned his head once more towards the bench, feasting his gaze on the bare V of Rowena's pussy.

The usher spoke. 'The Supreme Court of Amazonia is

now in session. Thomas Hamilton, you are charged with two counts of treason: one, that you did plot the overthrow of the Amazonian state, and the merciful rule of the Amazonian women; and two, that in the presence of your mistress, Lady Varda, you succumbed to an unauthorised erection, suggesting feelings of arousal for which permission had not been granted. How do you plead?'

'Not guilty,' declared Hamilton in a quiet voice. It was obvious he was already becoming aroused. His penis had begun to visibly thicken and was no longer hanging limply between his legs.

On the other side of the glass partition, Rachel flipped through the pages of the script. She was pleased that the client now had a name, though she doubted it was his real one. Darren's fantasy had been ridiculously mild by comparison with today's proceedings. Hamilton, or whatever his real name was, had taken matters several stages further. 'Over the top' was an understatement, she reflected. Still, it was not her place to question the client's wishes. This was their final acting assessment. All their futures might well depend on how well they performed. Rachel felt nervous. She and Sally had been selected to bring the curtain down. She hoped they were up to it.

'Call the first witness,' declared the usher, and Maria, the last of the Initiates, entered the courtroom. She was wearing a tight red miniskirt, with a halter-neck top that emphasised her large bosom. The blouse was so low cut that Rachel wondered how she managed to keep her breasts from spilling out.

The usher was speaking again. 'Is your name Lady Maria?'

'It is,' replied Maria.

'Will you tell the court what happened on the night of Friday, the twenty-second of July, please.'

'Yes,' replied Maria. 'I was visiting my friend, Lady

Varda. I was feeling rather horny and asked Lady Varda if I might have sexual intercourse with one of her male servants.'

Rowena intervened. 'A perfectly legitimate request,' she announced. 'I know Lady Varda well and have often enjoyed sexual relations with her staff.'

'I chose the footman, Charles, because he's barely eighteen and can sustain himself for many hours if necessary. He's also an expert at cunnilingus, which I had a particular fancy for at that moment.'

'Please describe what happened next, if it's not too distressing,' said Rowena.

'Yes, my Lady,' replied Maria. 'The accused, Thomas Hamilton, was also in the room, serving tea to Lady Varda's other guests, when Charles was ordered to be brought to me.'

'The accused was presumably naked also?'

'Certainly,' replied Maria. 'Lady Varda's male servants are permanently naked in case her Ladyship has a sudden wish to use them. It's also a way of checking for unauthorised erections.'

'So what happened next?'

'Charles arrived and asked how he might serve me. I told him that I was hot and sticky from my journey and that he might begin by licking me clean. I turned round, bent over and presented my bumhole, telling him that he could begin there. I hasten to add that I had of course taken a shower on my arrival but, as Lady Varda knows, talking dirty is one of my favourite pastimes.'

'I rarely wash my privates before instructing a servant to clean me,' said Rowena, 'but I suppose you know your own business.'

'As I bent over, the accused glanced across in my direction. Lady Varda was naturally furious. She said, "Thomas, are you feasting your eyes on Lady Maria's bottom?"'

'And what was his response?'

'He denied it. But I knew he was lying because his penis had grown larger.'

'Disgusting behaviour!' observed Rowena. 'What happened next?'

'Lady Varda said that as a punishment he would be forced to watch the rest of the proceedings, which began with Charles kneeling behind me and paying homage to my behind.'

'He kissed you on the anus?'

'Yes, my Lady. Such a kiss signifies obedience and is customary before using a servant in Lady Varda's household.'

'An excellent practice which immediately puts a man in his place and one which I recommend to all right-thinking persons. Lady Varda is to be congratulated. Did the servant perform to your satisfaction?'

'He did, my Lady.'

'And how did the accused react?'

'He was seen to experience the beginnings of a state of arousal.'

'And this was when he looked at your bottom?'

'It was, my Lady.'

'It will be necessary for the court to see what prompted this outrageous reaction on the prisoner's part. Will you lift up your skirt and show us what you showed the accused, please?'

Maria stepped down from the witness box and turned to face Rowena, her back to the jurors. Bending over, she hoisted up her skirt to reveal a tiny string, barely visible in the depths of her crack.

'Usher, will you please show the jurors exhibit number one?' instructed Rowena.

From her observation point, Rachel found it hard to believe her eyes. This whole scenario was both exciting and a little mad all at the same time. The client clearly had the most convoluted fantasy life, and again she wondered how much he was paying to have it acted out.

The usher stood behind Maria, reached forward, and hooked her thumbs beneath the elastic of her knickers then eased them over her hips. Pressing her fingers into the crack of her buttocks, she spread Maria's big, fleshy mounds. In the observation room, Madam Janet pressed the zoom-in button and Rachel and Sally were treated to a close-up of Maria's crudely exposed anus. The opening was dark and partially distended, the wrinkled knot fanning outwards like a tiny starfish. The usher allowed her finger to stray into the well of Maria's anus and the woman uttered an audible moan of delight, squirming back against the intruder. Behind her, the jurors leant forward for a closer look.

'I see no reason why a man should think himself permitted to reach a state of arousal simply because a woman's backside is presented to him in such a manner,' declared Rowena. 'And I hope no thought of kissing this lady's hole or even – heaven forfend – inserting a tongue or finger into the well has crossed the accused's mind, for the court would view that very seriously indeed.'

In the dock, Hamilton leant over, craning his head to get a better look. His sudden surge forward took Evie and Tina by surprise and for another brief moment his penis touched the edge of the dock. He jiggled his cock from side to side and a low, guttural moan escaped his lips. Madam Janet swivelled the camera and zoomed in on his shaft.

'He's going to come . . .' she murmured. 'Stop him girl, stop him!'

Tina shot forward, her fingers circling the top of Hamilton's engorged penis. She took him between forefinger and thumb and squeezed hard, while Evie tugged fiercely on the chains, pulling him back and away from the contact he so desperately craved. She brought up the tawse and whipped him sharply across the buttocks.

Hamilton threw back his head and screamed in pain, at the suddenness of the blow and in frustration at his thwarted release. His head lolled forward on to his chest and his legs bent weakly at the knees.

Rowena slammed her gavel hard on to the desktop. 'Enough!' she cried. 'The accused has condemned himself through his own actions. Look at the size of his cock. It's clear that his balls are filling with seed even as we speak. I have never seen such a shameless exhibition. If you repeat your behaviour I will halt the trial and have you taken back to the cells where you will be masturbated without relief for 24 hours. Is that understood?'

Hamilton bowed his head. There were tears in his eyes. 'Yes,' he murmured. Evie struck him a fierce blow across his buttocks.

'The judge cannot hear you, prisoner!' she barked. 'Louder!'

Hamilton raised his head. 'Yes, my Lady,' he repeated, his voice noticeably shaking. Tears were running down his face, though whether they were tears of pain or of pleasure it was hard to tell.

'I had a taste for doggy style,' continued Maria, 'so I got on to my hands and knees and presented Charles with my rear end. I then invited him to enter me slowly but firmly in order to maximise my pleasure. I also asked Charles to describe what he was doing.'

'And did he?'

'Yes. Lady Varda's other guests became quite excited. Lady Joel confessed that she was growing wet simply watching what was going on between my legs, and listening to Charles describing it.'

'I have myself found that on these occasions other guests often wish to join in the proceedings,' observed Rowena. 'Is that what happened here?'

'It is, my Lady,' replied Maria. 'Lady Joel asked if she might fondle Charles's balls while he penetrated me. I informed her that she must feel free to use him as she wished, as long as she did not interfere with my own pleasure. Charles was thrusting quite furiously now and I was very close to relieving myself.'

'And while all this was going on, what was the accused doing?'

'He was still casting furtive glances in my direction,' replied Maria. 'His penis continued to grow bigger, though he attempted to hide it with his hands. Lady Varda told him that she would not warn him again and that he should know that an unauthorised erection was a serious offence.'

'Sound advice,' observed the judge. 'A pity for him that he paid no heed.'

'Lady Joel came round behind us and knelt between Charles's legs. She began to stroke him quite slowly at first, rubbing his balls around in the palm of her hand. I could hear his breath catching and knew that together we were in danger of taking him over the edge.'

'But he continued to thrust vigorously?'

'Oh yes, my Lady. I had no complaints. Indeed, if anything the ferocity of his penetration increased. It was so enjoyable that I had become quite noisy. That was when Lady Varda was kind enough to ask me if I would like a second servant to stop up my mouth. Indeed, she suggested two if I was in the mood for a little extra fun.'

'Lady Varda's largesse knows no limits,' observed Rowena. 'I take it you agreed?'

'It was hard to resist,' confessed Maria. 'However, because I have a small mouth Lady Varda suggested two of her younger stablehands.'

'An excellent suggestion,' observed Rowena. 'I myself once enjoyed the cocks of two young men in my vagina while a third tested the limits of my back passage, and all with Lady Varda's generous approval.'

'The two youths were brought in and made to kneel before me, side by side. I think they were a little nervous at having to share my mouth, but it only excited me the more to think about it.'

'I believe it was then that the accused was asked to assist, is that right?' asked Rowena.

'Yes,' replied Maria. 'The young men were not fully erect. Apparently they had been used quite vigorously the day before by half a dozen guests and, despite their youth, had not yet made a full recovery. Lady Varda asked Hamilton to fetch some warm, scented oil and rub it on to their shafts.'

'And did he obey?'

'Yes. He seemed to enjoy the task more than he should, rubbing quite furiously until they were both standing to attention.'

'And by the time he had finished, was he also now fully erect?'

'Almost, but not quite, which allowed Lady Varda to issue him with a final warning.'

'Lady Varda's patience is inexhaustible,' observed Rowena. 'I myself would have had the fellow arrested by the Bondage Police there and then.'

'In order to punish the accused for his insolence, Lady Varda instructed him to insert the young men's erections into my mouth. I remember that his hands were trembling as he fed the two lengths past my lips, and it was a tight squeeze. The two boys began to thrust and I to groan, enjoying two penises in my mouth while a third pleasured me from behind. Every now and then Lady Joel's fingers would stray towards my clitoris and give it a naughty little rub.'

'Did you come soon after?'

'I did, my Lady. It was the most incredible climax. And of course the three men timed theirs so that they filled me to overflowing at both ends. The two young stablehands had clearly not recovered from their previous day's handling, but Charles's seed spilled out of me all over Lady Joel's hands as she squeezed his balls and helped his own orgasm along.'

'It sounds like a wonderful time was had by all,' observed Rowena, widening her thighs so that Hamilton was afforded a clear view of her pussy. Madam Janet pressed the zoom-in button. It showed that Rowena's vagina was now dribbling sap, her lubrication running in tiny rivulets along the insides of both her thighs.

'But it was now that we saw that Hamilton had a full erection, one for which he had not been given permission,' continued Maria.

'So what happened next?'

'Lady Varda told him that she had no choice other than to report him to the Bondage Police who would deal with him according to the law, which in this case was a capital offence.'

Rowena turned to face Hamilton. His penis was stiff, hard against his belly, and his balls looked larger than ever. Evie and Tina pulled on the chains and forced his legs apart so that he could gain no relief by rubbing himself against his own thighs.

'But this was not the worst of it,' remarked Rowena. 'Under questioning, the accused admitted to lustful thoughts about his employer and her guests and to wishing to have intercourse with them against their will. Such behaviour is tantamount to an attempted overthrow of the state, for wishing to subdue women is to wish to subdue the state.'

Hamilton leant forward in the dock. 'Please, your Ladyship,' he whispered. 'I beg the court's permission to be allowed an opportunity to defend myself.'

'Your request is denied,' retorted Rowena. During her short speech, she had been deliberately fingering her pussy, opening her lips so that Hamilton could see the shiny pink interior. She had reached such a pitch of personal excitement that only her long training had saved her from losing complete control and climaxing on the spot.

Hamilton looked anxiously towards the jurors. One

pulled down the top of her blouse, releasing her breasts so that they spilled on to the jury table. Another leant back in her chair and began to play with herself. A third pulled her skirt up to reveal a hairy, knickerless crotch, while the juror next to her lowered her face into her neighbour's lap and began to lick gently.

Watching from the observation room, Rachel felt herself growing damp between her thighs and crossed her legs to increase the pleasure. She felt Sally's hand stray across her thigh, stroking her gently, and enjoyed the warm glow that spread upwards from her groin to her belly.

'You may play with each other,' said Madam Janet, looking across to the two girls. 'But remember, no orgasms. Leave those for later on, when you punish the client.'

Rachel reached across and felt for Sally's small hairless pussy, so different from her own heavily matted one. Sally reached up and stroked Rachel's bare breasts, pulling at the nipples, squeezing the teats between forefinger and thumb, stretching her friend's skin while she enjoyed the play of fingers against her clitoris. Both girls were now sopping, their juices leaving wet patches on the leather chairs they were seated on.

Madam Janet pressed a button and the camera zoomed out.

'It will soon be time for the judgment,' she said. 'Make Rachel nice and wet, Sally. The client likes his women nice and wet.'

Sally removed her fingers from Rachel's breasts and pressed them into the dark V of her friend's pussy. Rachel was already as wet as she had ever been, but still, it was too good an opportunity to miss. Sally began tweaking Rachel's clitoris, running her fingers up and down her upturned labia, smearing her hand with her friend's copious juices.

Down in the courtroom, matters were heading towards a conclusion. Rowena hammered the gavel twice and called the court to order. The jurors stopped playing with themselves and with each other. Maria stood up, smoothed her short skirt back into place and returned to her chair.

'I see no reason to prolong these proceedings further,' declared Rowena. 'Thomas Hamilton, you stand accused of two counts of treason, in that you did permit yourself an unauthorised erection, and entertained lustful thoughts towards women – actions calculated to overthrow the rule of women. These charges are, by your behaviour in this court today, proved beyond a shadow of a doubt. Ladies of the jury, have you come to a unanimous decision, or do you need further time to consider your verdict?'

Helga stood up and spoke. 'My Lady,' she said. 'We have come to a verdict.'

'And is it the verdict of you all?' asked Rowena.

'It is, my Lady,' replied Helga.

'Do you find the prisoner guilty or not guilty?'

Helga's voice was loud and clear. 'We find him guilty.'

Hamilton staggered and fell forward. He would have collapsed completely if Evie and Tina had not held on tight to his arms. In the observation room, Rachel smiled at how well the client had entered into the spirit of his own fantasy. She began to wonder if this was the first time he had indulged himself, and came to the conclusion that it probably wasn't. Still, if he had the money, it was his own business.

Rowena reached to one side, picked up a square of black silk, and placed it on top of her judge's wig.

'Thomas Malcolm Hamilton,' she intoned in a low, sombre voice. 'You have been found guilty of crimes against womanhood and against the merciful state of Amazonia. The law allows of but one penalty. It is therefore the sentence of this court that you be taken from this place to a place of execution –'

In the dock, Hamilton's jaw dropped open and he lurched forward again. 'No!' he cried. 'I am not guilty! I have not been given a fair trial! This is a travesty!'

'You are a man in a woman's world,' said Rowena. 'And it is women who stand over you in judgment today, as it is women who will carry out the sentence of this court. You will be taken from this court to the Arena of Ultimate Ecstasy where you will suffer the penalty decreed by our law!'

'No!' Hamilton screamed. 'No! Please, I beg you. Have mercy on me. Have mercy, oh please!'

Rowena stood up. Her gown fell back from her shoulders and her shaven vulva glistened beneath the courtroom lights.

'Bring the prisoner forward!' she ordered. Evie and Tina took hold of Hamilton, and dragged him, stumbling, from the dock. Rowena moved to the front of the judge's bench and drew herself up to her full height, her legs proudly parted. Hamilton was forced to his knees and made to bow before her.

'Worthless wretch!' declared Rowena, staring down at him. She reached out with both hands and took a firm grip on his head, pulling her towards him.

'You may kiss my vulva and plead for leniency!' she declared. Hamilton raised his face and allowed himself to be pulled against Rowena's vagina.

'Worship us,' cried Rowena, 'and we may show you mercy!'

Hamilton began to slobber like a baby at the teat, lapping his tongue up and down. Rowena swivelled her hips, gyrating from side to side. Back in the observation room, Rachel had to resist an urge to reach down between her own legs and masturbate herself. Sally, too, was breathing hard and fighting to control her own arousal.

'Yes! Ah, yes!' moaned Rowena, bucking to and fro. 'That's it, push deeper, use your tongue, put it into me, yes, as far as it will go. Oh, you bastard! You bastard! I'm coming! I'm coming! I'm coming!' She threw her head back and emitted a banshee-like wail. At the same time, she drove her hips forward, tugging at Hamilton's hair, pulling him tight against her cunt, using his mouth to milk herself freely. Between his legs, his cock was stiffer than ever and his balls were now so full that it must have been excruciating. Rowena's juices ran down her thighs, coating his face as she emptied herself into his open and receptive mouth.

Recovering herself, she pulled away, stepping back. Her breasts bounced gently as she steadied herself with deep lungfuls of air. Hamilton raised his head and stared up at her, his eyes wide and pleading, her juices dribbling down his chin. Even Rowena was shocked to see how heavily she had come.

'Mercy, your Ladyship,' he murmured. 'I beg mercy from the court, please.'

Rowena drew herself up to her full height. 'No mercy,' she replied curtly. 'Take him away. Let justice be done!'

Evie and Tina seized Hamilton by the arms and hoisted him to his feet.

'No!' he screamed, and tried to break away. Evie locked her arms around his neck, pushing his head down. Tina drew her tawse and struck him viciously across the buttocks.

Up in the observation chamber, Rachel winced. Madam Janet had said that the client was not into pain, but the blow had appeared harsh to her. She watched silently as Hamilton was dragged away, weeping and continuing to protest his innocence. Beside her, Madam Janet leant across and switched off the courtroom camera.

'Right,' she said, 'it's your turn now. You'd better make a good job of it.'

'How long do we have?' asked Rachel.

'One hour,' replied Madam Janet.

'What will happen to the client in the meantime?' asked Sally.

'Oh, he likes to string out his fantasy for as long as possible. He'll be taken back to his cell and masturbated for half an hour. Then he'll be given a last meal, followed by a final few minutes' slow wanking. Then he'll be brought to the Arena of Ultimate Ecstasy where you two will complete his fantasy for him.'

'So what do we do in the meantime?' asked Rachel.

'First, I'll show you your outfits,' said Madam Janet, ignoring her question for now. She crossed to one of the vast wardrobes, opened the door and took out two hangers. On one was a large, black outfit, and on the other a smaller, white one. She handed the first to Rachel and the second to Sally.

Sally's outfit consisted of a white bra, G-string, stockings and suspenders. There was also a small white mask and a pair of white stiletto heels. The uniform was finished off with a floor-length white cape. Rachel's outfit consisted of a black cape and mask, but no bra. Instead of a G-string, she had a pair of black French knickers, which laced up at the back. She had never seen anything quite like them before.

Under Madam Janet's watchful eye, the two girls removed their leather harnesses. Rachel was glad to be free of the thing. Even though she was more used to it now, the harness still chafed from time to time. She much preferred being naked, an experience which she had rarely enjoyed since arriving at The Hall.

Madam Janet inspected the two girls as they dressed and, when they had put on their outfits, she made them twirl around as if they were models on a catwalk. Rachel liked the way the cape flowed. It made her feel like something out of a Gothic novel and lent her an aura of powerful authority.

Madam Janet smiled approvingly. 'Yes,' she said, 'I

think the client will be delighted when he sees the pair of you.' She looked at the clock on the wall. 'We have about forty minutes before we begin. How would you like to spend the time?'

Both girls were silent. They weren't sure how to respond.

'I think you should get yourselves in the mood,' suggested Madam Janet. 'The client likes his women warm and wet.' She crossed to the wardrobe and reached into a small compartment. When she turned back, Rachel saw that she was holding a rubber dildo with a series of straps attached. She handed it to Sally. 'Take your panties down and put this on,' she instructed.

Sally removed her G-string and placed it on the table, then strapped the dildo to her waist so that it hung between her thighs. Rachel felt her stomach flutter.

Madam Janet turned now to Rachel. 'Take off your gown and bend across the table, please,' she said.

As Rachel leant forward, Madam Janet came up behind her and unlaced the lower half of her panties. Rachel jumped as something warm and wet was applied to her crack, then realised that Madam Janet was lubricating her anus with some gel. She hadn't expected this. Madam Janet stood to one side and said, 'Sally, please insert the dildo into Rachel's bottom.'

Sally was taken by surprise and instinctively hesitated. But when Madam Janet's hand moved towards her tawse, she hurriedly reconsidered, pointing the dildo in the direction of its delectable target. Settling herself between Rachel's legs, she leant forward so that the head of the phallus nudged into Rachel's crack. Madam Janet stepped forward and placed her hands on Rachel's buttocks, easing them apart, exposing Rachel's darkened anus. Sally placed the head of the dildo at the mouth of the vulnerable little opening.

'That's right,' said Madam Janet. 'Now push slowly. Let's see how flexible Rachel is.'

Rachel didn't know what to say. She could refuse to be used like this, of course, but assumed that it would count against her. Besides, she was curious to know what it would feel like. Sally pushed gently forward and Rachel's ring flexed around the intruder. She heard Sally sigh gently and realised from the way her friend was moving that the dildo must be double headed and was rubbing against her clitoris, stimulating her in the process. Madam Janet moved in front of Rachel and stood by her face. She reached down and took hold of Rachel's head, tilting it upwards.

'Kiss me,' she said, 'through my panties.'

In for a penny, in for a pound, thought Rachel as she leant forward and pressed her lips to the thin leather of Madam Janet's thong. She could feel the swell of Madam's labia beneath the thin material and, as her nose pressed into the thong, she could smell her excitement, too. Behind her, Sally continued to push, and Rachel winced as her backside tried to accommodate several inches of hard rubber. She felt her rectum contract around the invader in a way that wasn't unpleasant. In fact, sandwiched between Madam Janet and Sally, both of whom were clearly moving towards individual release, she felt her own juices begin to flow freely.

'Madam,' moaned Sally, 'may I have permission to climax, please?'

'Not yet,' replied Madam Janet. Her own breath was now escaping in short sharp blasts as Rachel's tongue pushed through the thin gossamer of her thong and found her clitoris. Rachel began to squirm her tongue round and round. Her long hours of oral practice were certainly paying off.

'Put your hands on my bottom,' ordered Madam Janet. Rachel wrapped her arms around Madam's broad hips and pressed her fingers into the other woman's fleshy buttocks.

'Hold me closer!' she ordered. Obediently, Rachel hugged Madam's backside as tightly as she could, almost cutting off her own air supply as she continued to probe Madam's pussy with her tongue, stretching the thin fabric of her panties and tasting Madam's juices as they oozed from inside her.

Rachel's nose was now pressing hard against Madam Janet's clitoris, while she lapped at her concealed labia. She was suddenly aware that Madam had dropped her hands to her own waist and was struggling with the bows that held her panties in place. Madam tugged left and right. Rachel, with her face pressed suffocatingly tight to Madam's crotch, felt the material slip away. One last tug and Madam's wetness swamped her face, her juices dribbling across Rachel's chin as her tongue pressed into the warm, fragrant folds of flesh. Above her came the partly muffled sounds of Madam reaching the very limits of her self-control. Rachel realised that Madam Janet had also been turned on by the client's fantasy and was in as much need of release as she and Sally were.

Madam Janet's hands clawed the back of Rachel's head, her fingers tearing through her hair as she ground her crotch into Rachel's face. Rachel felt the labia swell and unfold inside her mouth, engorged with excitement. Suddenly, Madam was thrusting with her hips, driving herself as far into Rachel's mouth as she could. Behind her Sally began to pump more furiously than ever, penetrating Rachel's bottom as far as the phallus would reach.

'Now, Sally, now!' screamed Madam Janet before yelling, 'Yes! Yes! Yes!' in quick succession as Rachel's tongue brought her off with expert ease. Rachel felt Madam's juices flood her throat, and was aware of Sally bucking wildly behind her. She tried to close off her mind to what was happening because, once again, Madam had denied her her release and she felt as if she would explode with frustration.

Madam Janet pulled away, picked up her panties and quickly retied the bows. Behind her, Sally withdrew, exhausted by her efforts. Madam Janet crossed to Sally and told her to remove the dildo, which Madam quickly returned to the cabinet. Rachel wanted to say something but knew it was pointless. Madam Janet smiled cruelly.

'I know you don't think it's fair,' she said, then suddenly added, 'bend over!'

Rachel did as she was told, wondering what fresh torments Madam Janet was about to inflict on her.

'Part your legs,' instructed Madam Janet. 'Wider than that. Yes, that's it!' She reached forward and pressed her hand between Rachel's thighs, cupping her vulva in her hand. 'You're very wet,' she observed. Rachel winced as two fingers suddenly pierced her. How she wanted to wriggle on them and bring herself off. Involuntarily, her vaginal walls closed and unclosed around the exquisitely probing digits.

'Naughty, naughty!' laughed Madam Janet, removing her fingers at once. 'I know you're excited, but you're supposed to be,' she continued. 'That's how the client wants you. And remember you get the chance to climax this time. Just think about it. You can really let yourself go with this one.'

Rachel felt her legs weaken at the thought. She wondered how far off that moment was. Ten minutes, twenty, an hour? And all that time she would remain on edge. Though she knew she could hold back her climax, frustration still gnawed at her belly. But Madam Janet was right. When she did climax, it would be a big one. What worried her now was that she might not be able to hold back.

Madam Janet glanced at the clock on the wall. 'It's almost time,' she announced. 'Back into your uniforms, girls. We have an execution to attend.'

The Arena of Ultimate Ecstasy was a large, dimly lit circular chamber, directly below the mock courtroom.

By the time Rachel and Sally arrived, the other Initiates and the various Madams involved were already sitting in a semicircle around a raised central platform. The client clearly liked an audience.

Hamilton was escorted into the chamber, his arms and legs shackled. Evie and Tina walked either side of him. They forced him to mount three small steps up to the main platform, which itself supported a further, Y-shaped structure. Thick, leather straps were fitted at close intervals along the entire length of the construction. The top end was raised and padded, and a large dark square of silk, edged with thin cords, was draped over it. Hamilton was made to lie on his back, with his arms by his sides. His legs were forced apart and thick cuffs snapped around his wrists and ankles. The remaining straps were tightened around his calves, thighs, waist, arms and chest.

'That hurts,' complained Hamilton as Evie pulled hard on the final strap.

'Tough luck!' she retorted.

'Don't talk back to a woman!' shouted Tina and smacked him across the face.

Evie moved out of sight behind Hamilton's head, then bent forward so that her breasts covered his face. With deliberate nonchalance, she pulled lightly at the straps around his chest. 'Everything seems secure,' she confirmed, ignoring the lips that closed around her nipples as Hamilton licked at her flesh. She returned to Tina's side as Rachel and Sally entered through an arched doorway. In the observation room, Madam Janet pressed a blue button and an ominous drum-roll swept around the chamber. Rachel strode towards the platform, her black cape flowing behind her. The dark hood covered her face. Sally followed behind, dressed in her virginal white outfit. They stopped in front of Hamilton, studying him silently. His eyes widened like saucers and he strained hard against the leather straps that held him down. His penis was now fully erect, bobbing against his lower belly.

Rachel spoke calmly, in measured tones designed to extract the most from an already highly charged situation.

'Thomas Malcolm Hamilton,' she intoned. 'You have been found guilty of crimes against the state. You have been sentenced to death. I have been chosen to carry out that sentence!'

She brought her fingers up to her neck and pulled lightly at a thin cord around her throat. The long cape slipped past her shoulders and fell in a dark pool at her feet. Hamilton's eyes locked on to the black silk knickers that covered Rachel's midriff, then swept over her wide hips, up to her large, rounded breasts. A weak gurgle escaped from the back of his throat.

In the observation chamber, where she was keeping careful watch on the proceedings, Madam Janet smiled.

'He thinks he's died and gone to heaven,' she murmured in the quiet of her sanctuary. She had seen this look on his face before. But never had it been quite so intense. Looking at Rachel she could understand why.

Back in the Arena, Sally stepped forward, reached for the tie at her neck and divested herself of her own cape. Beads of sweat broke out on Hamilton's forehead as his eyes feasted on her small, curved figure. Her breasts and vulva were concealed by the three tiny white triangles. The white mask around her eyes only increased his sense of excitement. She looked both menacing and delectable at the same time.

Rachel was speaking again. 'Do you wish to be blindfolded?'

'Blindfolded?' asked Hamilton, managing to inject a curiously believable note of surprise into his voice for someone who had scripted the entire fantasy. If she had required any further convincing that he had acted out this role before, Rachel now had it.

'Some men have refused,' she continued, 'then wept like babies when the moment of truth has arrived. The choice is yours.'

He paused for a moment, considering his decision. Rachel recalled that the script was open at this point. She had no idea what choice Hamilton would make. He'd probably done this several times before, varying his decision each time.

'No blindfold,' he replied quietly.

'Very well,' she whispered, investing her voice with sombre gravity.

Sally knelt between Hamilton's outstretched legs, raised her head and smiled. He stared back in silent anticipation, as Sally licked her lips, slowly running her tongue from one corner of her mouth to the other. Rachel stepped forward and swung one meaty thigh across his body, her bottom towards his face, her legs either side of him. She took a few moments to settle herself, allowing her juices to dribble from under the crotch of her panties and smear his chest. In the observation room, Madam Janet pressed a button and a second, more ominous drum-roll echoed around the Arena. Rachel could feel Hamilton's heart pounding beneath her hands which were resting on his chest. She realised that she was growing wetter still. The dominant in her was now uppermost. She would enjoy this little piece of play-acting, she decided, especially as this time she had been given permission to reach orgasm.

Sally leant forward and took Hamilton's penis into her mouth. He groaned at the sudden force of her assault and his body shook violently despite the large number of straps that held him down. Rachel glanced towards his hands to make sure they were within easy reach of the two red panic buttons, set into each side of the structure. It was essential that he was able to signal when the proceedings were to be brought to an end. Once they began, it was the only way he was going to be able to alert anyone if he got into trouble.

Having confirmed that the safety procedures were in place, Rachel looked at Sally and nodded. Sally immediately raised her fingers and pressed the tender flesh near the top of Hamilton's penis to prevent any possibility of premature ejaculation. She felt his balls roll heavily against her chin as she squeezed. Rachel, meanwhile, manoeuvred herself back over Hamilton's head. Evie and Tina approached from either side and took hold of the laces in her knickers. Quickly and efficiently they undid them, pulling back the material and exposing her backside. Rachel heard Hamilton's sharp intake of breath as she reached back and parted her cheeks, allowing him to see right into her crack. At the same time, the two girls lifted the edges of the silk square behind Hamilton's head and began feeding the cords into the holes in Rachel's knickers.

Hamilton strained every muscle in his body. 'Oh, no!' he screamed. 'No, please, not this! Not this! Please, no!'

'Women of Amazonia!' cried Rachel, turning her attention to the assembled Sisters and Madams. 'Shall I show him mercy?'

'No mercy!' they shouted back, clapping their hands and stamping on the floor. 'Death to the traitor! Death to the traitor!'

'Thomas Malcolm Hamilton,' intoned Rachel, ignoring his continued protests. 'Those who hold your life in their hands have spoken. There is no escape for you now. I hereby carry out the sentence of this court!'

Wild applause broke from the audience and they leapt up, punching the air and cheering enthusiastically. A cacophony of screams filled the Arena.

'Sit on his face!' screamed one woman.

'If you don't smother him, I will!' yelled another, ripping off her panties and throwing them to one side, her skirt pulled up around her waist.

In the observation chamber, Madam Janet pressed a familiar button and the camera zoomed in on the woman's vulva. Her labia were pink, wet and ever so slightly parted. The client could see nothing now, only Rachel's backside poised over his head. But afterwards she knew that this was a sight he would enjoy very much.

Back in the Arena, the noise from the audience had become deafening. The atmosphere was mildly intoxicating, and everything was vaguely unreal. Football supporters had nothing on this lot, reflected Rachel, gathering herself for the moment of truth.

'No!' pleaded a distraught Hamilton one last time. 'Please! Have mercy! Noooo!'

'No mercy!' yelled Rachel, dropping her hips over his face, trapping his nose and mouth between her buttocks. Immediately, Evie and Tina pulled hard on the cords either side of him, joining them in a large bow, so that Hamilton's head was effectively sealed inside Rachel's panties. She watched as his hands clawed the empty air, and was surprised to see how gnarled and twisted they were. Here was a man used to wielding power over others. Rachel wondered what he was thinking now that he knew that another human being wielded ultimate power over him. That was what this was all about, of course. He wanted to know what it felt like to taste fear, to be dominated by a woman who held his very life in her hands. And the wonderful thing was that it was all so perfectly safe. All he had to do was press either of the red buttons within easy reach of his fingers, and the fantasy would end. Of course, for Rachel and Sally, the real skill lay in timing everything to perfection. It was important that Hamilton should extract the maximum pleasure from his ordeal, because then they would be awarded higher credits. Sally had to fellate him to the point of orgasm but no further. Rachel for her part had to pretend to be smothering him with her bottom, but in such a way that every now and then she would swivel her hips just a little too far, enabling him to snatch a breath of air. If she didn't, he would be unlikely to last more than a few minutes before either stabbing at the buttons or passing out.

Rachel could feel herself growing wetter and wetter as Hamilton shuddered beneath her. His nose was wedged up against her anus, and it thrilled her to know that each time he inhaled he was breathing in the bitter-sweet scent of that secret place. Her pussy was lubricating freely, her juices running down over his mouth. She was aware of his lips squashed flat against her labia as she swung from side to side. She was so wet now that he was almost drinking from her cunt. In front of her, Sally was sucking him slowly, like a baby at the teat, tickling his balls from time to time and pressing hard with her forefinger and thumb whenever it seemed that he was straying too close to orgasm.

Rachel threw her head from side to side, and the audience began a slow, sensual handclap in time to her movements. Beneath her, her victim suddenly stiffened. Rachel heard a muted groan, then realised it was Hamilton. His squeals of pleasure were muffled by the sheer weight of her buttocks, squeezing his nose and mouth so tightly shut that he could barely breathe. It was obvious that he was reaching his peak; the moment of no return. Rachel gathered her thoughts and raised herself ever so slightly one last time, allowing him to snatch a final breath of air. She knew that for a second or two he could hear her speak.

'I've never known a prisoner struggle this much before! But there's no escape for you, Hamilton! Say your prayers! This time you're going out!' And with that she slammed her backside down over his face for the last time, holding her hips and grunting loudly.

Up in the observation room, Madam Janet zoomed in on Rachel's hooded face, then down across her sweat-soaked breasts. The muscles in her arms were tight with effort as she pushed down with all her strength. The client would be very happy when he played this back.

Hamilton's body began to thresh as wildly as he was able, given how tightly he was secured. His hands clawed at the empty air. Rachel was sitting bolt upright, her full weight now centred over his nose and mouth. She unbent her legs, and stretched them straight out so that her feet rested on his thighs. The effect was to concentrate her entire upper body weight over her victim's face. Hamilton had stipulated that at the end there should be no respite. He wanted to enjoy the feeling of total domination, of Rachel's backside smothering him fully. Suddenly his body tensed, and his every muscle stiffened. Between his legs, Sally pulled her mouth back for one, agonisingly brief moment, before plunging forward, sucking furiously. Hamilton's hips jerked up and down several times in quick succession, his penis dancing between Sally's lips as he finally came, emptying his semen into the warm haven of her mouth. Rachel, too, surrendered blissfully, bouncing her hips up and down. Her juices seemed to pour from her pussy, drenching the man beneath her, filling his mouth. Her sense of release was overwhelming. At that moment she felt she could happily die.

A loud buzz rent the air as Hamilton's fingers closed on both panic buttons. Evie and Tina stepped forward and pulled at the cords, releasing him from his dark prison as Rachel rose from his face and reluctantly dismounted. Her pussy was still quivering and she was only able to stand with some difficulty. Hamilton was sucking in huge draughts of air, his lungs gasping like an asthmatic, and Rachel suddenly realised how close she had taken him to the point of collapse. She was relieved that Evie and Tina were there, but knew also that Hamilton was no ordinary man. From start to finish, and for Hamilton it had been a long 48 hours, no ordinary man could have held out the way he had. She now had little doubt that he, too, was a Brother.

* * *

In the observation room, Rachel and Sally had just changed back into their harnesses when the door opened and Master Stéfan entered. Madam Janet looked surprised at the unexpected intrusion. Master Stéfan was smiling.

'I hope I am not being premature, Madam Janet,' he began. She shrugged her shoulders as if to say she didn't know what he was talking about.

'I was very pleased with everyone's performance,' he announced. 'Tomorrow,' he added, glancing at Rachel, 'will be your last day at The Hall.' He turned to Sally. 'We will not meet again.'

Rachel felt her heart sink. Wouldn't meet again? What was he saying?

'I am aware that students do not always think kindly of me,' he said, his attention still focused on Sally. 'But that is no reason for leaving them in suspense. Everyone has done very well. I shall be recommending complete passes for acting. How you do in your other classes is, of course, not my concern.' He stretched out both arms to Sally and shook her warmly by the hand. 'Congratulations, Sister Sally.' He turned away and shook Rachel's hand, too, though with noticeably less interest. Then he addressed Madam Janet. 'I apologise if I have disturbed your routine.'

'Not at all,' she replied. Master Stéfan bowed sharply and turned on his heel. Rachel coughed loudly as the door closed behind him.

'I hope you're not catching a chill,' said Madam Janet. She suddenly reached out and took hold of Rachel's wrists, twisting them so that she opened her hands in pain. She smiled. 'It's lucky I don't punish you for coughing without permission, but then I wouldn't want you to think I was entirely without feeling.'

Rachel went cold. There were times when Madam Janet seemed quite human, and other times when she thought she was as bad as Master Stéfan. Thank goodness that, after tomorrow, she would never have to worry about either of them again. In the meantime, she was glad she had had her wits about her. If she had not, Madam Janet would have seen the note that Master Stéfan had passed to her when he shook her hand; the tiny square of paper she had quickly put in her mouth and which was now pressed up against the inside of her right cheek.

Back in their room, she slipped it beneath her pillow so that Sally wouldn't see it. She stole a quick look at it in the few seconds before lights went out, turning her back briefly on Sally as if trying to find a more comfortable sleeping position. The note was typed, presumably to hide its author's identity, slightly smudged and totally meaningless. It simply read: *3.30 a.m.*

It took Rachel until one in the morning before she finally realised what it meant.

Fifteen

Rachel did not sleep that night. Whatever it took, she knew that she must stay awake – not that it was easy with Sally curled up quietly beside her, breathing so gently. She remembered how Master Stéfan had looked at Sally and told her they would not meet again. He had been at pains to address Sally, not Rachel, almost as if he were trying to tell Rachel that they *would* meet again.

She wondered if Madam Janet had suspected anything. Was that why she had suddenly grabbed at Rachel's hands, suspecting perhaps that a note had passed between her and Master Stéfan? Another crazy thought hit her. What if Madam Janet were Master Stéfan's co-conspirator? What if she had guessed that Master Stéfan was becoming involved with Rachel? If she were right about the note, and she was sure she was, it was going to be a long night. Tomorrow was her last day at The Hall. 3.30 a.m. had to mean this very morning, or it made no sense at all. But what else did it mean? Clearly, something would happen at 3.30 a.m. Would Master Stéfan come for her? Or was she to go to him? She decided that it must be the latter. Master Stéfan's room was on the ground floor. It would be easier to leave from there, so it must be *his* room they were to meet in. That meant she would have to remain awake and go to him at 3.30 exactly. He had obviously decided that it was time to make a break for it and wanted her to escape with him. But what about his accomplice? Who was he running out on?

It was the longest night of Rachel's life. It was, she reflected, like being a child again, trying to remain awake because Father Christmas will be arriving with all the presents and you don't want to miss him. The hours ticked slowly by. But at last it was 3.20. She got up. Her bladder was bursting but she didn't dare wake Sally. She mustn't involve her friend in case anything went wrong. Sally was sleeping quietly, her breasts rising and falling in that gentle way they always did. Rachel wanted to lean over and kiss one of her nipples but thought better of it. Instead, she reached for the clip around her neck, pushed hard and it came undone. It seemed like a deliberate act of rebellion, and her adrenaline began to pump. Everything was coming to a head now; the end of the game fast approaching. Rachel sat up and slipped out of bed, crossed to the door and, without a backward glance, crept quietly into the corridor. There were many things jostling for attention in her mind, but uppermost at this defining moment was the urgent desire for an early morning pee.

Master Stéfan handed her a long dark coat.

'Is this all?' she asked.

'It's all I could find,' he replied. 'Besides, I didn't know if you would come.'

'I almost didn't,' she lied. 'But I know it's what I want to do.'

Master Stéfan crossed to his desk. 'You won't regret this,' he said. He picked up a heavy briefcase and glanced at his watch. 'We haven't got long. There's a car meeting us in fifteen minutes. There'll be a full set of clothes waiting for you. You won't freeze. It's a warm night.'

'But where are we going?' asked Rachel. 'And why are we going like this?'

'It would take too long to explain.' He shook the briefcase lightly. 'But what I have in here will make us rich. And blow this place sky-high.'

'You're betraying the Sisterhood?' asked Rachel. She knew that he was, but she wanted verbal confirmation, just to be absolutely certain.

'I'm just getting what's rightfully mine.' He looked around him and there was a sad, bitter edge to his voice. 'I've given my life to this place but they don't think I'm good enough to run a Hall of my own.' He took a deep breath. 'Whatever we do now will serve them right. We can sell the secrets of this place to the highest bidder.'

'But where will we go?' asked Rachel. She was playing for time now. She hoped that the longer she kept him there the greater the chance of being caught. She certainly didn't fancy trying to deal with Master Stéfan on her own.

He waved the airline tickets in his hand. 'Somewhere far away and very warm,' he grinned.

Rachel suddenly realised what a mistake she had made. She had assumed that the two tickets indicated a co-conspirator and in a sense, of course, she was right. She hadn't realised that the co-conspirator was her.

'When did you decide?' she asked quietly.

'I think it was your first day at The Hall,' he replied. 'I could sense then that there was something special about you.' He looked at her for a long, quiet moment. 'Are you sure you want to go through with this?'

For one awful moment, Rachel felt her resolve weaken. Master Stéfan was a traitor, but he trusted her, even cared for her in his own, twisted way. She was going to betray him just as he was betraying the Sisterhood, and it made her feel uncomfortable. No, she reminded herself, it wasn't the same thing at all. She was helping to defend the Sisterhood. That had meant taking in Master Stéfan, but it was for a greater good, unlike the selfish motives that spurred him on. Rachel pushed her doubts to one side. She had a mission to complete and was determined to do so to the best of her ability.

'I haven't come this far to back out now,' she said.

Master Stéfan smiled. 'That's my girl.' He leant forward and squeezed her cheek. He did it too hard and it hurt. He turned away for a moment, checking that he had left nothing undone and Rachel rubbed her face. She pondered her next move. Surely her actions had been monitored? The Hall bristled with cameras and she assumed, from the time Sally had been punished, that their rooms were also bugged. Why had nothing happened yet? She wondered if she should grab hold of Master Stéfan there and then and just scream. Then she remembered that a car was waiting for them. That meant another party, perhaps another traitor to the Sisterhood. If she raised the alarm now that other person might get away.

Master Stéfan crossed to the door. 'Right,' he said. 'Put your coat on and let's get out of here.'

Rachel was convinced that something had gone wrong. She needed reinforcements. She could hardly be expected to tackle Master Stéfan on her own. She decided to play for time again.

'I need a pee,' she said, dancing from one foot to the other.

'There's no time,' he replied.

'But I'm bursting!' she complained.

'Then you can go in the bushes or out of the car, anything, but not yet.'

Rachel decided to try another tack. 'Are you sure it's safe? What if they're on to us? They could be waiting for us in the corridor.'

Master Stéfan glanced at his watch. 'Not if I've planned everything correctly,' he said.

At that moment there came a loud wailing noise somewhere in the distance.

'What's that?' asked Rachel.

Master Stéfan smiled with quiet satisfaction. 'It's the north-west perimeter alarm. The Sisters are clever. It's possible we've been watched. I triggered the alarm to go off to divert attention, just in case.'

'Very clever,' conceded Rachel, her heart sinking. 'You've thought of everything.'

'I like to think so,' he replied. 'Now come on, let's get out of here.'

It was a warm, cloudless night. A full moon lit up huge tracts of open space, and Rachel realised that if she were really trying to escape, she wouldn't have rated her chances very highly. There were several security cameras set up around the walls, and others hidden in the trees and bushes. She had never been aware of them before, and had to admire Master Stéfan's cunning as they hurried across the first stretch of clear ground. He was obviously gambling everything on attention being diverted to the far side of The Hall.

Rachel realised that she would have to play along and await an opportunity – if one presented itself – to foil Master Stéfan's plans. It crossed her mind to fall and pretend to twist her ankle. But he would probably either leave her there or pick her up and carry her. He was a powerful man and she doubted it would slow him down very much. Besides, though she was a good actress, it would be disastrous if he realised that she was faking. She couldn't afford to take any chances at this stage. Lady Frances wasn't stupid. Surely she would know by now that Rachel was not in her room, that the alarm was a ruse, and that Master Stéfan must be escaping via the south-east perimeter?

They reached the bushes and welcome cover. Master Stéfan took Rachel firmly by the hand, pointing towards a swathe of sparsely covered ground, and into the darkness beyond.

'There must be no mistakes now,' he said. 'This is very dangerous. The main perimeter wall is half a mile away. If they catch us we'll be dead meat.'

It took them eight minutes to reach the bank of trees that skirted the wall, ducking and diving to avoid the sensors that lined the way. More than once Rachel considered accidentally passing in front of one, but it was too risky. Master Stéfan had a high opinion of her. He might not believe she could make such a mistake. She had to keep her head and wait her chance. But she knew that time was running out. The ground felt suddenly wet and soft beneath her feet. Rachel looked down and saw her ankles disappear into the mud. It had been raining heavily the night before and this part of the grounds had clearly soaked up some of the worst of it.

Suddenly, a cry went up from the front of The Hall. Master Stéfan froze. 'They're on to us!' he exclaimed. 'Come on, we have to move fast.' He dropped the briefcase and bent down behind a tree. Scrabbling at the leaves, he pulled out a folded-up rope ladder, hooked at the base.

'Stand back!' he barked, uncoiling the contraption, and launching one end towards the top of the wall.

The hooks caught first time and the ladder unrolled. He gave it a hard tug and it held. He hunted around for the briefcase, then looked up to see Rachel standing a few feet away, holding it in her hands. She had thrown off the coat, and was naked now apart from her harness. The moonlight caught her breasts and they juddered brightly in the shadows. The sound of voices grew louder in the background, though they seemed as far away as ever.

'What are you doing?' he cried.

Rachel's voice was firm, though her insides felt as if they had turned to jelly. 'I'm sorry, Master Stéfan, but this is as far as you go.'

'Don't be a fool!' he hissed. 'I could break you with

one hand. And don't think of running. I'll catch you before you've gone twenty yards.'

'Better come and get it, then,' taunted Rachel, waving the briefcase in one hand.

'I will,' he replied, stepping towards her.

She waited until he was almost on top of her before throwing the briefcase high above his head. Instinctively, he turned to catch it, raising his arms and for a moment taking his eyes off Rachel. It was all she needed. She hurled herself at him, arms flailing around his calves, wrestling him to the ground.

They pitched forward into the mud, rolling awkwardly. Master Stéfan kicked out and caught her a sidelong blow, which sent her spinning and the briefcase flying. Dragging herself to her knees, Rachel saw Master Stéfan trying to scramble away through the mire. She launched herself at him a second time, her arms around his neck, her thighs around his waist. They fell together and rolled down a steep embankment into a ditch. Master Stéfan brought his elbows back, winding Rachel in the stomach, but she held on grimly. He tried to struggle to his feet but could get no further than his hands and knees. Rachel clung limpet-like to his back. He fell on top of her and rolled over, breaking her grip. She threw herself forward, her hands around his neck, then he spun round, his face contorted with anger. Rachel saw her chance, wrapped her arms around his shoulders and pulled him down between her breasts, securing him in a reverse headlock, a hold Madam Kyra had used on her countless times. She held on for dear life, hugging him as tight as she could, aware of his confusion. He adored her breasts, but now she was using them to subdue him. She heard him groan as his mouth brushed against one of her nipples. He began to sink into the soft earth, unable to move freely, slipping and sliding in the mud. And still Rachel held on. Suddenly, Master Stéfan tugged at her wrists, breaking her grip for an instant, pushing her away. He rolled on to his side, slithered to his knees, then fell again. Rachel struggled to her feet, stumbled, and flung herself awkwardly forward. She straddled his back, striking out with her legs, one either side of his head. One of her hands gripped at his waist, the other scrabbling into the mud, beneath his body, pushing up and linking with the fingers of her first hand, holding him tight. His hands came up to her thighs, his nails digging into her flesh. She screamed with pain as he tore at her skin, but held on, her face pressed tight against his right buttock as they wriggled in the mud. With his back towards her, his freedom of movement was severely restricted.

'Let me go, you bitch!' he yelled. 'Let me go!'

'Never!' she retorted, tightening the muscles in her thighs, emptying her mind of the pain as he clawed at her hips. Master Stéfan was thrashing about helplessly, unable to use his legs for purchase or attack. But he was a strong man. Rachel knew he would break her grip, given time. If she were to restrain him until help arrived, she would have to weaken him first, and there was only one sure way to do that. She unlocked her fingers and snatched at the zip of his trousers, tearing at his waistband, tugging the top of his pants down.

'No!' he screamed as she freed his penis, taking hold of it with her upper hand, circling his shaft. She was surprised to discover that he was already erect. The filthy devil, this was turning him on! He clawed at her calves, swearing obscenely and kicking out with his feet. Rachel dragged her other mud-spattered hand out from beneath his body, pressing it between his buttocks. She pushed down with her index finger, probing for his bumhole. He could hold back his orgasm for ever if she simply pumped him, but not if she entered his back passage. Master Devlin's classes had taught her that much. She had only one chance, and she must get it right first time.

His hips bucked fearfully as Rachel wriggled her forefinger into his anus, up to the top knuckle. Buried in his bowels, she felt something small and hard. Master Stéfan drove his hands between her calves, in a last desperate attempt to scissor them apart and free himself. Rachel felt her legs weakening and knew she could not hold on much longer. Grunting with effort, she scratched her finger back and forth and heard Master Stéfan wail in distress. His cock stiffened for one long, tentative moment. Rachel twisted her finger inside him, still squeezing with her other hand as the first jets of spunk pumped from his penis and splashed across his belly. His whole body shook convulsively, his white seed merging with the mud. His rectum went into some sort of spasm. Rachel felt his sphincter contract, squeezing beneath her top knuckle, a rapid pulse running up and down the finger lodged in his backside. Master Stéfan jiggled his hips, his seed running over his belly, less and less of it spurting from his penis now, until it stopped altogether, though his shaft continued to bob haphazardly. His fingers still clawed viciously at her thighs, but Rachel held on, determined not to give an inch, to hold on to him until help arrived.

'Submit!' she cried. 'Submit to the Sisterhood!'

He groaned and swore and kicked, but he was growing weaker now, she could tell – all the fight was gone from him. She was subduing him, slowly but surely, when suddenly and unexpectedly, a pair of strong arms took her by the shoulders and she was hoisted up into the air. Her bladder no longer felt tight and she realised with some embarrassment that in her excitement she had peed all over the back of his head. But there was no time to think about that now. Opening her eyes, she found herself looking into three familiar faces: Madam Janet, Mistress Katrina and Lady Frances De La Vie.

* * *

They were back at The Hall. Rachel had been allowed to clean herself up, take a hot bath and put on fresh clothes. Proper clothes this time. Master Stéfan had been taken away by Madam Janet and Mistress Katrina. She had no idea where to, or indeed whether she would see him again. She was sitting in Lady Frances's private office, wearing a black miniskirt and a black top that showed off her breasts to perfection. The material clung to her skin and made her feel good. Her outfit was finished off with stockings, suspenders and high heels. She had been allowed to put on lipstick and make-up and, for the first time since her arrival at The Hall, she felt sexy in a perfectly normal way.

'Congratulations,' said Lady Frances. 'You are by far the most promising Initiate we have had for some time.'

Rachel blushed. It was nice to receive such fulsome praise, yet a little embarrassing, too. She tended to clam up whenever people told her she had done well at something. But there was another matter to be dealt with now. Four months ago, Rachel would have kept quiet. Indeed, four weeks ago she would probably have held her tongue. But that was then and this was now. She had had time to think and she knew she was right.

'It was a set-up, wasn't it?' she said quietly.

Lady Frances lowered her eyes for a moment, then raised her head and smiled. 'How did you guess?'

'It wasn't that difficult,' replied Rachel. 'Well, no, that's not true. If it was, I would have guessed straightaway.'

'So when did you guess?'

'I don't know really,' said Rachel. 'Back in the woods, I suppose. There's been something not quite right about this from the beginning. I didn't guess before now, because I trusted you.'

Lady Frances leant back in her chair, pressed her hands together and looked at Rachel over the tips of her fingers. 'And do you trust me still?'

There was a long pause before Rachel replied. 'Yes,' she said. 'Though I don't know why.'

Lady Frances smiled. 'There is always one Initiate who possesses, shall we say, that extra something. That's why we devised the test you have just undergone. We wanted to see how you would react under pressure, how adaptable you were to changing circumstances, how resourceful you could be.'

'So Master Stéfan isn't a traitor, then?'

Lady Frances shook her head. 'Far from it. He is a consummate actor, though he will be very disappointed to learn that you saw through him in the end.'

'I wouldn't say that, exactly,' admitted Rachel. 'It just seemed too easy, that's all. No organisation as powerful as the Sisterhood is going to trust its security to a novice like me. It wouldn't make sense.'

'You do yourself an injustice. I can think of few other people I'd be happy to entrust our security to at this moment.'

'I enjoyed wrestling with Master Stéfan,' said Rachel, 'but I'm not stupid enough to think I could beat him unless he wanted me to. And having an erection was a bit of a give-away. It made me think he was enjoying himself, not trying to escape.'

'You'll go far in our organisation,' said Lady Frances. 'Indeed, if you're amenable, I already have a posting in mind for you.'

Rachel smiled. 'You know I want that more than anything,' she said.

Michael lay on his back. The hooded Amazon sat astride his face muffling his tortured response as she flicked idly at his engorged penis. It kicked in the air once or twice, little specks of pre-come issuing from the tip. A second woman stood nearby, smaller than the first. She too wielded a whip and flicked gently at the man's penis while the first woman sat heavily on his head to contain his furious complaints. At last the first woman rose from his face.

'Well?' Rachel asked, pulling off her mask and smiling at him.

Michael smiled back. 'Very well,' he replied.

Sally took off her mask and sat down beside them. Lowering her head, she took Michael's cock between her lips and sucked until he was once more fully erect. As she let him slip from her mouth, Rachel slid forward, sinking on to his stiffened shaft. Sally moved to the front and straddled Michael's face. He parted her labia with his tongue and gently speared her, savouring the honey-sweet taste of her pussy. Sally leant forward and began to lick at the base of his shaft as Rachel rode him silently and happily. Michael was in seventh heaven. So were the girls.

Rachel remembered the words he had spoken not so long ago. *This is only the first step.* And he was right. She had taken the first step. Now she was taking the second. Soon she would be running. And she couldn't wait to get to wherever it was she was running to. She was glad that all the other girls had graduated successfully, especially Sally, for whom she knew she would always have a very special soft spot.

Rachel allowed herself to enjoy the moment as Sally's tongue caught her clitoris and the three of them began their long, luxurious descent into bliss.

NEW BOOKS

Coming up from Nexus and Black Lace

There are three Nexus titles published in March

The Black Widow by Lisette Ashton
March 1999   Price £5.99   ISBN: 0 352 33338 3
Spurned by her husband, and cheated of her heritage, the Black Widow feels justified in seeking revenge. Determined to lay claim to Elysian Fields, a health farm with a unique doctrine of sensual pleasure and erotic stimulation, the Black Widow wants what is rightfully hers. Indulging a new-found passion for sexual domination, she is only too pleased to deal with those that get in her way. Punishments are cruel and explicit as she forces subordinates to do her bidding. Caught in the middle of the hostile takeover, Jo Valentine finds herself entangled in the Black Widow's web. By the author of *The Black Room* and *Amazon Slave*.

The Reluctant Virgin by Kendal Grahame
March 1999   Price £5.99   ISBN: 0 352 33339 1
The beautiful Karina Devonside is due to inherit a fortune on her twenty-first birthday, but she is far from happy. Unlike her naughty best friend Sandy, she is still a virgin, and circumstances are conspiring to keep her that way. But Sandy's tales of sluttish behaviour have been driving Karina wild for too long now – who will she choose to help her sate her lust? By the author of *The Training of Fallen Angels* and *The Warrior Queen*.

Choosing Lovers for Justine by Aran Ashe
March 1999   Price £5.99   ISBN: 0 352 33351 0
Chosen to live a life according to discipline and subservience, the young Justine is introduced to a succession of lovers. Each one has favoured methods of taking pleasure from her willing body – pleasure which is often found through the demands of pain and submission. Presided over by her strict guardian Julia, we follow Justine's initiation into a world of obedience, dominated by the less than genteel ladies and gentlemen of the Edwardian well-to-do. This novel, by the

author of *The Handmaidens* and *Citadel of Servitude*, is the second in a series of Nexus Classics – dedicated to putting the finest works of erotic fiction back in print.

There are three Nexus titles published in April

Displays of Innocents by Lucy Golden
April 1999   Price £5.99   ISBN: 0 352 33342 1
The twelve stories in this collection reveal the experiences of those who dare to step outside the familiar bounds of everyday life. Irene is called for an interview, but has never been examined as thoroughly as this; Gemma cannot believe the demands made by her new clients, a respectable middle-aged couple; Helen learns that the boss's wife has an intimate way of demonstrating her authority. For some, it widens their horizons; for others it is an agony never to be repeated. For all twelve, it is a tale of intense erotic power.

Disciples of Shame by Stephanie Calvin
April 1999   Price £5.99   ISBN: 0 352 33343 X
Inspired by her grandfather's memoirs, the young and beautiful Amelia decides to begin her own erotic adventures. She soon draws all around her into her schemes as they help her to act out her most lewd fantasies – among others her best friend, Alice, who loves to be told what to do, and her shy aunt, Susan, who needs to be persuaded. All her friends take part in her increasingly bizarre games, before the final, most perverse drama unfolds.

The Institute by Maria del Rey
April 1999   Price £5.99   ISBN: 0 352 33352 9
Set in a strange institute for the treatment of delinquent girls between the ages of eighteen and twenty-one, this is the story of Lucy, a naughty young woman who is sentenced to be rehabilitated. Their disciplinary methods are not what she has been led to expect, however – they are, in fact, decidedly strange. This is the third in a series of Nexus Classics – dedicated to bringing the finest works of erotic fiction to a new audience.

The Top of Her Game by Emma Holly
March 1999   Price £5.99   ISBN: 0 352 33337 5
Successful dominatrix Julia Mueller has been searching all her life for a man who is too tough to be tamed. But when she locks horns with a no-nonsense Montana rancher, will she discover the perfect balance between domination and surrender, or will her dark side win out?

Raw Silk by Lisabet Sarai
March 1999   Price £5.99   ISBN: 0 352 33336 7
When software engineer Kate O'Neil leaves her lover David to take a job in Bangkok, she becomes sexually involved with two very different men: a kinky member of the Thai aristocracy and the charismatic proprietor of a sex bar. When David arrives in Thailand, Kate realises she must choose between three very different men. She invites all three to join her in a sexual adventure that finally makes clear to her what she really wants and needs.

Stand and Deliver by Helena Ravenscroft
April 1999   Price £5.99   ISBN: 0 352 33340 5
It's the 18th century. Lydia Fitzgerald finds herself helplessly drawn to Drummond, a handsome highwayman. This occurs despite the fact that she is the ward of his brother, Valerian, who controls the Hawkesworth estate. There, Valerian and his beautiful mistress initiate Lydia's seduction and, though she is in love with Drummond, Lydia is unable to resist the experimentation they offer.

Haunted by Laura Thornton
April 1999   Price £5.99   ISBN: 0 352 33341 3
A modern-day Gothic story set in both England and New York. Sasha Hayward is an American woman whose erotic obsession with a long-dead pair of lovers leads her on a steamy and evocative search. Seeking out descendants of the enigmatic pair, Sasha consummates her obsession in a series of stangely perverse encounters related to this haunting mystery.

NEXUS BACKLIST

All books are priced £5.99 unless another price is given. If a date is supplied, the book in question will not be available until that month in 1999.

CONTEMPORARY EROTICA

AMAZON SLAVE	Lisette Ashton		
BAD PENNY	Penny Birch		Feb
THE BLACK GARTER	Lisette Ashton		
THE BLACK WIDOW	Lisette Ashton		Mar
BOUND TO OBEY	Amanda Ware		
BRAT	Penny Birch		May
CHAINS OF SHAME	Brigitte Markham		
DARK DELIGHTS	Maria del Rey		
DARLINE DOMINANT	Tania d'Alanis		
A DEGREE OF DISCIPLINE	Zoe Templeton	£4.99	
DISCIPLES OF SHAME	Stephanie Calvin		Apr
THE DISCIPLINE OF NURSE RIDING	Yolanda Celbridge		
DISPLAYS OF INNOCENTS	Lucy Golden		Apr
EDUCATING ELLA	Stephen Ferris	£4.99	
EMMA'S SECRET DOMINATION	Hilary James	£4.99	
EXPOSING LOUISA	Jean Aveline		Jan
FAIRGROUND ATTRACTIONS	Lisette Ashton		
JULIE AT THE REFORMATORY	Angela Elgar	£4.99	
LINGERING LESSONS	Sarah Veitch		Jan
A MASTER OF DISCIPLINE	Zoe Templeton		
THE MISTRESS OF STERNWOOD GRANGE	Arabella Knight		

ONE WEEK IN THE PRIVATE HOUSE	Esme Ombreux	£4.99	
PENNY IN HARNESS	Penny Birch		
THE RELUCTANT VIRGIN	Kendal Grahame		Mar
THE REWARD OF FAITH	Elizabeth Bruce	£4.99	
RITES OF OBEDIENCE	Lindsay Gordon		
RUE MARQUIS DE SADE	Morgana Baron		
'S' – A STORY OF SUBMISSION	Philippa Masters	£4.99	
'S' – A JOURNEY INTO SERVITUDE	Philippa Masters		
THE SCHOOLING OF STELLA	Yolanda Celbridge	£4.99	
THE SUBMISSION OF STELLA	Yolanda Celbridge		Feb
SECRETS OF THE WHIPCORD	Michaela Wallace	£4.99	
THE SUBMISSION GALLERY	Lindsay Gordon		Jun
SUSIE IN SERVITUDE	Arabella Knight		
TAKING PAINS TO PLEASE	Arabella Knight		Jun
A TASTE OF AMBER	Penny Birch		
THE TEST	Nadine Somers		Jan
THE TRAINING OF FALLEN ANGELS	Kendal Grahame	£4.99	
VIRGINIA'S QUEST	Katrina Young	£4.99	

ANCIENT & FANTASY SETTINGS

THE CASTLE OF MALDONA	Yolanda Celbridge	£4.99	
NYMPHS OF DIONYSUS	Susan Tinoff	£4.99	
THE WARRIOR QUEEN	Kendal Grahame		

EDWARDIAN, VICTORIAN & OLDER EROTICA

ANNIE AND THE COUNTESS	Evelyn Culber		
THE CORRECTION OF AN ESSEX MAID	Yolanda Celbridge		
MISS RATTAN'S LESSON	Yolanda Celbridge		
PRIVATE MEMOIRS OF A KENTISH HEADMISTRESS	Yolanda Celbridge	£4.99	
THE TRAINING OF AN ENGLISH GENTLEMAN	Yolanda Celbridge		May
SISTERS OF SEVERCY	Jean Aveline	£4.99	

SAMPLERS & COLLECTIONS

EROTICON 4	Various		
THE FIESTA LETTERS	ed. Chris Lloyd	£4.99	
NEW EROTICA 4			

NEXUS CLASSICS
A new imprint dedicated to putting the finest works of erotic fiction back in print

THE IMAGE	Jean de Berg	Feb
CHOOSING LOVERS FOR JUSTINE	Aran Ashe	Mar
THE INSTITUTE	Maria del Rey	Apr
AGONY AUNT	G. C. Scott	May
THE HANDMAIDENS	Aran Ashe	Jun

Please send me the books I have ticked above.

Name ....

Address ....

....

....

.... Post code........................

Send to: **Cash Sales, Nexus Books, Thames Wharf Studios, Rainville Road, London W6 9HT**

Please enclose a cheque or postal order, made payable to **Nexus Books**, to the value of the books you have ordered plus postage and packing costs as follows:

UK and BFPO – £1.00 for the first book, 50p for the second book and 30p for each subsequent book to a maximum of £3.00;

Overseas (including Republic of Ireland) – £2.00 for the first book, £1.00 for the second book and 50p for each subsequent book.

If you would prefer to pay by VISA or ACCESS/MASTERCARD, please write your card number and expiry date here:

....

Please allow up to 28 days for delivery.

Signature ....
